DAY OF THE FASTLE

Richard Dalglish

DAY OF THE FASTLE

DOUBLE DRAGON

Chapter 1 - Stone

The most surprising thing about waking up with no memory was how long it took him to realize it. At least ten seconds—maybe fifteen—passed between opening his eyes and the sudden realization that he didn't know who he was. In those seconds, as he lay on his back on a carpet of cool grass, something like a fever dream scuttled through his half-awake, half-asleep mind, but when he wakened fully, the visions were gone.

He scrambled to his feet and looked around, peering at his surroundings—rolling green grassland sprinkled with red and white wildflowers, a range of low hills looming in the distance, a nearby forest to his right, a road between the forest and himself. None of it looked familiar, and he felt the cold, sharp edge of panic begin to bite. He spoke aloud, if only to hear his own voice—"This is not possible"—but even his own voice was unfamiliar.

"This is madness," he murmured, frowning and shaking his head. He turned all the way around, peering at the forest, the road, the distant hills. "Hello," he called out. There was no answer.

A clear blue sky above gave him some slight comfort, and the sun felt warm on his face, but panic tugged at him again. He shook it off, closed his eyes, and searched his memories. A fleeting image from his dream tried to surface, but it slipped away before he could grasp it.

"This is madness," he muttered again, still straining to find a memory.

A sudden thought seized him, and he felt his heart freeze in his chest. Perhaps a sorcerer had robbed him of his memory, a sorcerer who might be lurking nearby to observe the results of his dark magic. But no, he was quite alone. He considered what to do. He looked at the wide meadow, wondering which way he had come, but the grassland gave away none of the secrets of his passage through it. It occurred to him that his manner of dress or something on his person might provide a clue to his identity. He glanced down at a pair of finely worked black leather boots, which came nearly to his knees, and the plain gray trousers tucked into them. His dark blue tunic was unadorned and equally devoid of clues. His felt his chin and discovered a close-cropped beard. Then he saw the sword, a fine one-handed weapon hanging from his waist in a plain leather scabbard.

He drew the sword and gripped it tightly, savoring the feel of it in his hand. He hefted the weapon and felt its perfectly balanced weight, listened to it whip the air as he flicked the point with snaps of his wrist. When he sheathed the sword, he noticed a small quatrefoil insignia etched on it just above the hilt, with a small faceted blue gemstone in the center of the insignia. At the same moment, he saw a ring on the third finger of his right hand. The ring bore the same quatrefoil emblem and also had a faceted blue gemstone in the center. He stared at the jewel and the symbol, searching his mind for scraps of memory. Once again, he found none. He slipped off the ring and peered closely at the inside of the band, but it was smooth and unmarked. He put the ring back on and headed for the road. When he reached it, he stopped and looked one way and then the other, but he saw nothing to suggest which way he should go. After a moment, he turned north and began walking.

He had been walking for nearly an hour when he heard the sound of cantering hoofbeats behind him. He turned around and saw in the distance a horseman heading his way. For some reason that he couldn't have explained even to himself, he fled the road and ran toward the forest, running in a low crouch, hoping he might conceal himself in the tall grass between the road and the woods. As the sound of hoofbeats became louder, he dropped down and lay as still possible. The hoofbeats stopped.

"You there, skulking in the grass." The voice was gruff and unpleasant.

He stood up, brushed himself off with as much dignity as he could muster, and faced the horseman. "Good day to you, sir," he said as evenly as he could.

"Identify yourself," the man growled. He was massive, with a torso the size and shape of a cask of ale and a dark red beard that fanned out from his jaw like an old straw broom. He wore a black mantle over a chainmail tunic, along with black leggings, black boots, and a plumed black helmet. The front of the mantle bore an insignia, a triangle inside a circle. The triangle was subdivided into four smaller triangles of equal size, and another triangle, smaller yet, was set in the middle. The man was clearly a soldier or a knight of some kind. "I said identify yourself," he repeated.

"I'm only a poor traveler."

"Do you have a name, traveler?"

"Who is it asks for it?"

"I don't want your impudence, I want your name."

He glanced up and saw in the distance a pair of falcons spiraling against the blue sky. "Falconer," he said without hesitation. "My name is Falconer. Who is it wants to know?"

"And your given name?"

"Stone," he replied quickly.

The knight frowned. "Stone Falconer, is it? The name has a whiff of guile about it."

"With whom am I speaking, if you please?" the newly named Stone Falconer asked.

"You are speaking with Sir Borus Renovar, special courier of His Excellency the Ordseer."

Stone Falconer wanted only to be gone, but he stood his ground, waiting and watching.

"Where are you bound?" Sir Borus asked.

"The next village."

"Tallindin?"

"Aye, Tallindin."

"What's your business there?"

"To collect on a small debt. A man there owes me a few silver coins. For some work I did."

"What work?"

"I'm a … a stone mason."

"Stone the stone mason, is it?" Sir Borus said, shaking his head as if he doubted it.

"Aye," Stone replied.

"Have you come from Klell, then?" Sir Borus asked, nodding in the direction from which he'd ridden.

"That's right, from Klell."

"And why do you find it necessary to hide from an honest knight?"

Stone allowed himself a crooked smile. "Ah, well, sir, in truth I was daydreaming as I walked, and when I realized a horseman was approaching, I foolishly imagined you might be a brigand."

Sir Borus frowned. "Is that why a stone mason carries a sword? To defend against brigands?"

"Indeed. Even a poor stone mason must be ready to protect himself."

"You'll find no brigands on this road," Sir Borus said. "You won't need your weapon."

"I'm relieved to hear it. I'll just be on my way then."

"Not so fast. I'd like to have a look at your fine sword."

Stone unsheathed his sword and held it up for the man to view.

"Give it to me. I would have a closer look."

Stone put the sword back in its scabbard. "I think not."

Sir Borus frowned. "Do you not trust me?"

"I don't know you."

Sir Borus's frown deepened. "I've told you who I am. Have you signed the Ordseer's fastle pledge?"

"Fastle pledge?"

"Yes, you lackwit fool, have you signed?"

Stone shook his head.

9

"I'll have your sword now, and I won't tell you again. Hand it over."

Sir Borus spurred his horse forward. Just then, a slight rustling sound in the tall grass caught Stone's attention, and he peered into the meadow and spotted its source.

"Perhaps you'll let me keep the scabbard," Stone said as Sir Borus stopped barely a yard away from him.

"Perhaps I'll let you keep your head. Now draw the blade out slowly and hand it to me hilt first."

As Stone slowly drew the sword, he saw movement in the tall grass. He dropped the point of the sword to the ground and flipped it back up, flinging the snake he had spotted toward the horse's head. The beast bellowed and reared, and Stone took off toward the forest, Sir Borus's curses following him as he ran.

The horse had failed to throw its rider, however, and within seconds the ground was shaking beneath the charger's pounding hoofbeats. Stone looked back just in time to duck a savage swipe of Sir Borus's blade as the knight thundered past him.

Sir Borus wheeled around and dismounted and strode toward Stone, holding his sword out in front of him as he approached. He snarled and unleashed a barbaric yell and hurled himself forward, swinging his blade with two hands. Lighter and more agile than the massive knight, Stone sidestepped the blow, the force of which spun Sir Borus halfway around. The big knight charged again, and again Stone leaped away from his whirling blade. Sir Borus's failure to separate Stone's head from his body had enraged him, and he redoubled his attack, slashing and swinging as Stone danced madly out of the way, jumping back, darting sideways, spinning and whirling as the soldier's frenzied blade flashed in the sunlight.

The knight's ragged breaths were coming faster. His relentless attack slackened and soon deteriorated into a flailing, half-stumbling parody of single combat. He bent over, leaning on his sword as if it were a cane as Stone looked on, staying just out of his range.

"Stop dancing and fight, you craven wretch," Sir Borus bellowed between ragged breaths.

Stone felt his blood rise at the challenge. He knew he should flee while he had the chance, but he knew just as surely that he would not. He circled Sir Borus and made two or three feints with his sword, feeling sudden confidence in his ability to use the weapon. It was as if the sinews in his arms and legs remembered what his mind did not. Sir Borus raised his sword and stepped forward. Stone held his ground, and their weapons clashed. The knight lunged, and Stone parried and took the offensive, thrusting and slashing and surging forward with a lightning thrust of his blade. As he did, a small whirlwind began to spin nearby, picking up dust and leaves and bits of grass.

Sir Borus sneered. "Stone mason, eh? A mummer's apprentice is more like it, but your paltry illusions fool no one. Fight or yield, but don't try your petty tricks on me." He swung his sword violently but clumsily and Stone easily dodged it.

He made ready to counter Sir Borus's next blow, but it never came. The exhausted knight was walking backward, away from Stone and toward his horse.

Stone whipped the air in front of him with his blade, as if he were testing it. As he did, a sharp breeze began to blow, and another little whirlwind rose up.

"Petty illusions," Sir Borus muttered, still backing away. "When I return with a company of my men, we'll see how your tricks fare then."

Then he was gone, riding back the way he had come.

Stone knew Sir Borus would report the encounter to his superiors, perhaps even to the Ordseer, whoever that was. The knight would come looking for him with a squadron of armed men, which meant that the road and whatever towns and villages lay upon it were now lost to him. His only choice was the forest. He entered it and began to pick his way through the trees.

After a half hour of slow progress, Stone discovered a narrow path. He followed the trail's winding course through the forest in what he guessed was a northerly direction, and after what seemed like a couple of hours of steady hiking he thought he heard the soft murmur of flowing water. He quickened his pace and followed the path to the banks of a gently flowing stream. He walked to the edge, knelt down, and drank. When he had drunk his fill, he peered down at his reflection.

Dark eyes stared back at him from a face that had seen perhaps thirty summers. It was a lean sort of face, with a strong chin and wide-set blue eyes. A thatch of short dark hair and a trimmed black beard completed the picture. He stood up, and the reflection revealed a tall, spare figure with long legs, a fit-looking man who might be a soldier or a miner or a shipwright. He wasn't entirely displeased with what he saw, but the reflection revealed nothing about who he might be. He drew his sword and peered at the quatrefoil insignia, searching his mind again for a memory. No memory surfaced.

Chapter 2 - Brook

She woke up in a forest. She heard a stream gurgling, a sound pleasant to her ears. She was lying on a grassy bank, on her side, her knees drawn partway up. She was comfortable and enjoyed listening to the sound of the flowing water. She smiled. She didn't want to open her eyes. A shaft of sunlight beaming through the trees felt warm on her face, and she felt happy and contented.

Something was wrong. She opened her eyes and saw the tops of trees looming overhead. She sprang to her feet and looked around. She didn't know where she was or how had she had come to be there.

Panic threatened to take hold of her. She heard the babbling stream and turned to it, gazing at the flowing water until the feeling of dread subsided. She calmed herself and cleared her thoughts. Her gaze followed the course of the stream, which meandered through a dense wood. Sunlight filtered through the trees, and when she looked up she could see ragged patches of blue sky. That's when she realized she didn't know who she was.

She squeezed her eyes shut and sought her memories. She found none. "What?" she said aloud, simply to hear the sound of her own voice, but even that was strange to her ears. "Think," she ordered herself. So she thought. She thought of the words for "tree" and "sky" and "river" and "stream," relieved that she knew the names of things, that her mind still functioned. She closed her eyes again and tried once more to find a memory, but none came. She wondered what could have happened to her. She felt her head, but there was no blood, no bumps, no pain anywhere. Had she gone mad? Or …?

"Sorcery?" she said aloud, making it a question. She frowned. "But why?"

She began walking along the stream. She had taken only a few steps when she saw something lying in the grass, glinting in the sunlight. It was a dagger, sticking halfway out of its sheath. She stopped and picked it up, examining it before tucking it through her belt. Having the knife made her feel better, despite her lack of memory.

She followed the stream, crossing it from time to time on large rocks, drinking from it, soothing her brow with its cool water. Just past midday, she heard voices. The voices were coming from somewhere ahead of her, around the next bend of the stream. She hesitated a moment and then continued until she came within sight of two scruffy men holding fishing poles over a part of the stream that had widened into a pond.

"Gentlemen," she said as she approached them. She wasn't afraid, but she was glad they were on the opposite side of the stream. She spotted a large earthenware jug on the ground between the two men and detected a faint scent of strong spirits.

The older-looking of the two men grinned at her. He was lean and not as tall as his companion, with small dark eyes and a sneering sort of smile. "Well, well, well," he said in a loud voice. "What have we here?" He pulled his line out of the stream and dropped his fishing pole.

"I seem to have become lost," she said. "Would you be so kind as to direct me to the nearest village?"

"Lost are we?" the older man said, leering and looking at her the way one might examine a side of mutton.

The younger man giggled. He had a round head and bulging eyes that made him look like a toad. He was soft-looking, with a bulging stomach, sloping shoulders and a pudgy neck that jiggled when he laughed.

"If you'll just point me in the right direction, I'll be on my way," she said.

The older man pointed at his chest. "Right here. Here is the right direction." His toady companion snorted and licked his lips.

"Never mind," she said. "I'll find my own way."

"What's your hurry, mistress?" the lean one said. "What's your name, anyway?"

She wasn't about to tell them she didn't know her name, so she said nothing.

"I'm Foskit, and this here's my brother, Little Demmie," the older man said.

She ignored him and walked on, glad to have the dagger she had found, but the two men picked up their gear and walked in the same direction on the other side of the stream.

Little Demmie finally spoke. "What did you say your name was, Mistress Pretty?"

"You can call me Brook," she said without looking at them and without stopping.

"Forsook by Brook," Demmie said, and he began snorting like a pig.

"Me brother's a poet," Foskit said, and the two men laughed. Then Foskit ran ahead and disappeared around a bend.

The woods were thicker there, and not as much sunlight filtered through the trees. She picked up her pace and looked around. There was no trail to be seen, no clear path by which she might escape, so she kept walking along the stream. When she rounded the bend, Foskit was on her side of the river, smiling and holding a large knife. She spied a couple of large rocks in the middle of the stream, which he had apparently used to cross. He was twenty feet away, still grinning.

She drew her dagger and Foskit made to look surprised. "What's this then, Mistress Brook?" he said. "Are you a warrior woman?"

She said nothing, but she kept her eyes on him, wondering where his brother had gone.

"You must be more friendly to Foskit," he said. "Why don't you put down that knife and come here?"

"Put down your own knife and stand aside," she said. "I have no intention of being friendly."

"A pity," he said and moved toward her. Just then she heard a sound behind her. She spun around to see Demmie nearly upon her, about to swing a heavy tree branch at her head. She ducked and sidestepped, but he grabbed at her shoulder with his other hand. She twisted away, and Demmie dropped the branch, but now Foskit was on her, grabbing her hair and laying the flat of his knife against her neck while Demmie tried to wrest her dagger away from her. She kicked as hard as she could and caught Foskit in the groin.

He howled and swore and backed off. He went down on one knee and gave Brook a look of such hatred that she nearly dropped the dagger. Demmie had one arm around her waist, trying to topple her, and he was still grabbing for the dagger with his other hand. She went down, but as she fell, she twisted her body toward the stream. She hit the ground and rolled, but Demmie had hung on and was rolling with her, trying to stop her momentum. She could smell his foul breath, and she used all her strength to keep rolling. They rolled into the water together, their momentum carrying them away from the bank.

The stream was deeper than she had expected and perfectly clear, clearer, it seemed to her, than the air. They touched bottom, still entwined, and she kicked off from it, finally dislodging herself from Demmie's grasp. She was still holding the dagger.

Pushing off from the bottom stirred up some silt, but she could see through it. Demmie was flailing and trying to swim to the surface, and she thrust the knife at him, stabbing him in the leg. He kicked violently and made for the surface, his blood clouding the water. Yet she could still see. She dived and touched bottom again.

She looked up and saw the sun shining down. She saw ripples where the commotion had been. It occurred to her that she had been without air long enough to need another breath, but for some reason she didn't. She sheathed her blade and swam underwater with the current, only a foot above the river bottom. She swam quickly, not stopping, not going up for air, for what seemed like an hour, until she figured she was far away from the two brutes. Then she swam to the surface and breathed in the cool air. She looked around to make sure her two attackers weren't nearby and spotted a lone man on the riverbank staring at her and holding a sword.

Stone was still contemplating the insignia on his sword when he heard what sounded like a splash from the stream. He looked toward the sound and saw a woman in the middle of the stream staring at him. She turned and quickly swam to the other side of the stream and got out. She had long dark hair, bright green eyes, and a dagger in her right hand.

They stood there for a moment, each considering the other, until Stone finally broke the silence. "You need not fear me."

"I don't," the woman replied in a voice pitched lower than he expected but not unpleasantly so.

"You can put away your weapon then," he said, sheathing his sword. "Unless you mean to skewer me."

She sheathed her blade without taking her eyes off him. He glanced around, wondering if there was anyone else nearby.

"Did you fall in, milady?" he asked.

"Not exactly," she replied.

"I see," he said, not seeing at all. "It's a nice day for a swim, I suppose."

She gave a brief laugh and looked down at her dripping white dress.

"It should dry quickly under this warm sun," he said. "Do you live near here?"

"Who wants to know?"

"My name is Stone Falconer."

She nodded but remained silent.

"And you are …?"

"You can call me Brook."

"I'm pleased to meet you, Brook. Did you say you lived near here?"

She remained silent.

"I ask only because I seem to have lost my way. Perhaps you could direct me to the nearest village."

She laughed again and shook her head slowly.

"You find that amusing?"

"No," she said.

"This is a most frustrating conversation," Stone said.

"It's been a frustrating day," she replied.

"Perhaps we should begin anew," he said. "As for me, I'm lost in these woods, hoping to find my way out, when suddenly I espy a young woman emerging from this stream like a river nymph." He narrowed his eyes at her. "You're not a river nymph, are you?"

"Perhaps I am," she said.

"I'll be quite happy to leave you to your river if you could just direct me to the nearest village."

"What would a river nymph know about villages?"

They stared in silence at one another for a long moment.

"I have a feeling you're lost, too," Stone said, breaking the silence.

She nodded.

"Perhaps we should ally ourselves, temporarily, and attempt to become unlost."

She nodded again.

They set out, following the stream, until they reached a section spanned by a narrow wooden footbridge. Stone crossed to the other side and they continued on their way. As they walked, a troubling thought occurred to him. If some dark sorcery had stolen his memory, it might be that Brook was the very sorceress responsible. He gave her a sidelong glance. "Do you know anything of sorcery?" he asked, watching her face closely, hoping to detect any change in her demeanor.

She stopped and stared at him. "Why do you ask?"

He hesitated a moment before replying. "I have reason to believe I may have been a victim of dark magic."

She frowned at him. "What reason?"

"Perhaps I shouldn't say."

"I sense another frustrating conversation coming."

He shrugged but said nothing, and they started walking again.

After a few minutes, she said, "I may also have been the victim of dark magic."

"How so?" he asked.

"If I tell you my tale, will you tell me yours?"

He thought for a moment and then nodded. "Fair enough."

She told him her story.

"Extraordinary," he murmured when she was finished. That she also had suffered the loss of her memory convinced him that some sorcery was indeed at work. Unless, of course, she was lying and merely toying with him.

"It's your turn," she said.

Despite his misgivings, Stone nodded and began. "I was making my way north along a road that runs near this forest when I was accosted by an armed soldier on horseback, a man who called himself Sir Borus Renovar. He claimed to be a special courier of the Ordseer."

Brook frowned. "Who is the Ordseer?"

"I don't know," Stone admitted. "But Sir Borus tried to disarm me. I refused, and we dueled."

She looked surprised. "You engaged an armed knight in a sword fight?"

"I did."

She frowned and squinted at him, as if sizing up his potential prowess as a fighting man. "Why did he want to disarm you?"

"I don't know. He mentioned something about signing some kind of pledge to this Ordseer fellow. He called it a fastle pledge. We fought to a draw, and he rode off. I headed for the forest."

"He'll try to find you again," Brook said.

"I know. That's why I headed for the forest."

"He'll bring more knights with him. And if they find you, they'll find me. They won't take kindly to someone found in the company of a criminal."

"I'm no criminal," he protested, hoping it was so.

"In Sir Borus's eyes you are."

"True enough," he said.

"You should have killed him."

He felt a slight shiver at her bloodthirsty reproach, but he had to admit that she had a fair point. "Perhaps I should have," he said. Just then, an idea occurred to him. "Your dagger, perhaps it has some identifying mark that might provide a clue to your identity."

"I thought of that, and, indeed, it does bear an emblem, but it means nothing to me."

"What sort of emblem?"

Brook drew her dagger and handed it to Stone. He took it and stared. The handle bore the same quatrefoil insignia that was etched on his sword.

Chapter 3 - Bennald

"Why has your mouth fallen open?" Brook asked.

Stone handed the dagger back to her and then drew his sword and pointed at the insignia on the hilt. As she stared at it, she spotted his ring and drew in a quick breath. She looked into his eyes and raised her right hand to show him the ring she wore. A faceted green jewel, the same size and shape as his blue one, was set within the quatrefoil insignia. They stared at one another.

"Who are you really?" she asked.

"I don't know," he said. "I woke up in a meadow this morning with no memory of myself."

Brook glared at him. "Why didn't you tell me? What else haven't you told me?"

Stone told her about the whirlwind that had suddenly risen as he wielded his sword.

"Are you a sorcerer?" she asked.

"I don't know. Are you?"

"I don't know."

They began walking again. The winding path eventually led back to the stream, and they decided to follow it, hoping it would lead them out of the woods and eventually to a town or village or farm. Without horses, the prospect of a long march seemed likely. The presence of a ready supply of water they counted as a blessing, but before long it began to remind Stone of their lack of a ready supply of food. He tried to put it out of his mind, and they spoke of other things.

The woods came to an end, but the stream, which had widened into a proper river by then, went on. They continued following it, through rolling fields of grassland not unlike the meadow in which Stone had first found himself. The sun was two hours from setting when they spied a thin streamer of smoke, gauzy white against the blue sky. They left the river and headed toward it. Less than an hour later, they crested a shallow rise and saw a small but busy encampment spread out below. A dozen heavy wagons and a score of carts and other small vehicles were parked in a rough circle, their teams browsing on the lush grass of a meadow. Sixty or so people, men and women and a smattering of children, were scattered around a campfire, waiting their turn at a large cooking pot suspended above glowing red embers.

Stone and Brook looked at one another, shrugged, and made their way down the shallow slope, trying their best to look harmless. Before they'd gone halfway, Stone saw the mass of the people gather themselves closer as they noticed the two strangers. A group of five men set down their bowls, picked up stout walking sticks, and approached. Stone and Brook stopped when the men came within ten feet.

"Hello," Stone said, sweeping his gaze across the five, as if to include them all in his greeting.

One of the men nodded.

"We saw the smoke from your fire," Stone continued. "We're traveling by ourselves, just the two of us, without benefit of horses or a wagon or companions, so we thought we might pass part of the evening in the company of fellow sojourners. With your permission, of course."

The man who seemed to be the leader nodded again, and Stone thought he detected a slight squinting frown on his craggy face.

Stone looked quickly from one to the other of the men down the line, but each face remained impassive. He cleared his throat. "I am Stone Falconer, and this is Brook." He gestured toward his companion, who nodded and smiled.

"I am Pemquist," the craggy-faced man said.

"Happy to know you," Stone said.

"Where ye come from?" Pemquist asked.

"Klell."

"Where bound?"

"Tallindin."

Pemquist frowned. "You ain't on the road from Klell to Tallindin."

"Quite right, sir. Unfortunately, we were accosted by two villains, brothers they were, who meant to kill me and ravish poor Brook. We escaped from them and retreated to the woods so they wouldn't find us again."

Pemquist nodded at Stone's sword. "How is it that your blade hasn't been confiscated?"

"Family heirloom. More ceremonial than soldierly."

"You've not signed the pledge, then?"

"No," Stone said, hoping it was the right answer this time. "Neither of us has."

"Come along, then," Pemquist said, abruptly turning on his heel. "You may join us for supper. We've more than enough."

The other members of the camp gave the two strangers quick but thorough glances, and then studiously ignored them. The twenty or so children, however, made no attempt to hide their curiosity, and Stone rewarded them with a steady stream of chatter, most of which, out of necessity, he invented on the spot. He felt more at ease with the children than with their parents, and he surprised himself with his ability to respond to them with so much inspired nonsense. The children peppered him with questions as he related tales of taming a fierce red dragon, living in a magic house at the top of a tree tall enough to pierce the clouds, and fighting off a band of highwaymen. The children devoured his stories as eagerly as they devoured their suppers.

Stone kept up his running dialogue with the children until Pemquist served him and Brook bowls of steaming lamb and vegetable stew and thick crusts of dark bread. The children reluctantly dispersed to their wagons or tents to bed down for the night or find other mischief to occupy them.

Pemquist introduced his wife, Sova, a short, solid woman with ginger hair, a round face, and a ready smile, who gestured for Stone and Brook to sit near the fire with her and Pemquist. They ate their meals with gusto and did not object when Sova refilled their bowls. The setting sun turned a flaming pink above the western horizon, and a light breeze fanned the embers of the campfire. Someone put another log on the fire, and the people wordlessly gathered themselves closer around it, settling into the approaching night. Flagons of a coarse but tasty red wine appeared and were passed around. Some of the men lit pipes, and the sweet aroma of pipe tobacco mingled with the lingering scent of stew and the sharp smell of burning logs.

Stone felt drowsy. He glanced at Brook and saw that her eyelids were drooping. He put his empty bowl on the ground beside him and leaned back on his elbows, staring up at the dim stars that were beginning to appear. He closed his eyes for a moment and sighed contentedly.

***

When he opened his eyes again he was lying on the ground, staring up at a dark sky sprinkled with stars. His muscles were stiff, and he realized he must have been asleep for hours. He raised his head, and it began to throb. He lay back down.

"You're awake," said Brook, who was sitting cross-legged a few yards away.

Stone raised his head again, despite the pain, and squinted at her. "I'm awake. What's happened?"

"They're gone," she replied. "They must have put something in the food to knock us out."

"Savages," Stone muttered. "They might have killed us."

"I don't think they meant us any harm."

"Then why slip us a potion to knock us out?"

"I think they're afraid of something."

"We're no threat to them. What could they be afraid of?"

Brook gazed at him. "What are you afraid of?"

Stone thought about it. After a moment he gave her a grudging nod. "Spell-making. Dark sorcery. Evil wizards."

She nodded back. "And strangers who suddenly appear, carrying weapons."

Stone jumped to his feet, despite the pain in his head, and looked around frantically.

"Don't worry, they didn't take your sword or my dagger," Brook said. She pointed to a nearby tree. Stone's sword, inside its scabbard, was leaning against it.

Stone went to the tree and retrieved his weapon. He drew the sword from its scabbard and flicked it through the air, listening to it whistle. He sheathed it and strapped on his sword belt. "Seems all right," he said. "Your dagger?"

She pulled her blade from the scabbard at her waist, drew back her arm, and threw. The point of the dagger hit the tree and stuck. Stone pulled it free and handed it to her.

"You threw that knife as if you were born to it," Stone said.

She nodded. "Perhaps I was. The skill seems to be part of me, as if my arm remembers what my mind doesn't."

"That's how it is with my sword. I'm surprised those people didn't make off with both weapons."

"They probably think they're endowed with dark magic," Brook replied.

Stone nodded. "Perhaps they are."

"We should be off," Brook said.

"Give me another minute or two," said Stone. "My head is still throbbing."

She walked over to him and began to rub his scalp, gently kneading. After a few minutes, she stopped. "Better?" she asked.

"Aye. I think your fingers may be endowed with magic. Perhaps another minute or two."

"We should go," she said.

They decided to follow the trail of the caravan, reasoning that Pemquist and his people would eventually head to a town or village to purchase fresh supplies. They hoped such a town or village lay within a day's walk, preferably a half day's walk. They were thankful for the hearty meal they'd consumed the night before, but they knew it wouldn't sustain them for more than a few days.

They set off just before sunrise, as the eastern sky turned pink, heading west across a vast field of tall grass. As they walked, Stone imagined a neat little town with a bustling marketplace and a crowded square, busy streets leading to inns and taverns with buxom serving maids carrying platters piled high with roasted meat and warm bread and hearty ale and wine. Perhaps he'd cross paths with someone who knew him, someone who could tell him who he was. A brother or cousin or close friend, perhaps—someone so happy to see him again that he or she would invite him and his beautiful raven-haired companion to be guests at a sumptuous meal. He tried to ignore his growling stomach and think of something else.

Brook finally broke the silence. "That Pemquist fellow asked you if you'd signed a pledge. Didn't your Sir Borus ask you the same question?"

"Yes. He called it a fastle pledge. When I told him I hadn't signed, I got the feeling that was the wrong answer."

"When you told Pemquist we hadn't signed, he seemed relieved," Brook said.

"Which didn't stop him from putting a sleeping potion in our stew," Stone replied.

They walked all morning over the rolling grassland without spying any sign of farm or village or homestead. Around noon they came to a vast forest through which a road wide enough for a wagon had been cut. They rested a while and then plunged into the woods, hunger plucking at their bellies.

The trees of the great forest soared above them, blotting out the sky. Sunbeams slanted through the high green canopy, picking out swirling dust motes suspended in the cool air like morning mist. A blanket of leaves covered the road, softening their footfalls.

As they walked through the deep quiet of the forest, Stone pondered the mystery of the quatrefoil insignia that appeared on both his sword and Brook's dagger. Was it a sign of the sorcery that had robbed them of their memories? Or had his and Brook's lives been intertwined before the memory spells had been cast? Were they from the same family, perhaps brother and sister? Cousins? Husband and wife? Stone looked at his companion, searching for some resemblance to himself. He detected none.

By midafternoon, their mouths felt like cotton and their stomachs were protesting loudly. As they crossed a wide clearing, the sky darkened and a shower broke. Stone took off his tunic and let the rain soak it. Brook tore a strip from the bottom of her dress and did the same. They wrung the water into their mouths until the rain stopped, as suddenly as it had begun.

"At least we won't die of thirst," Brook said, wiping raindrops from her brow.

Stone was about to remark that they had probably been saved from thirst so that they might die of starvation when he noticed a pair of bright eyes peering out from the trees on the other side of the clearing. His expression froze, and the words died on his tongue.

"What is it?" Brook asked.

"Something looking at us," he whispered, pointing. "That way."

As they watched, a four-legged creature slinked out of the woods and into the clearing, its eyes dead on them. Stone felt the blood drain from his face, heard Brook's sharp intake of breath. The creature resembled a cat, but one that stood at least three feet high at the shoulders.

"Start walking away from it, slow and easy," Stone said. His knees felt like water, but he was determined not to appear craven in front of his companion. "Don't turn around, and don't make any sudden movements. I'll walk backwards and keep an eye on it."

Brook nodded and began to walk. Stone drew his sword and followed her, walking backwards, his eyes on the beast. The animal followed, keeping pace.

"What's happening?" Brook whispered.

"He's following."

Brook unsheathed her dagger. The creature kept coming.

"When we get to other side of the clearing, you keep going," Stone said, trying to keep his voice from vibrating. He could practically hear his heart pounding in his chest, and he took a slow breath to calm himself. "I'll try to keep his attention on me."

A moment later, he bumped into her. "No, keep going," he hissed.

"There's another one," she whispered.

Stone looked over his shoulder. Another of the catlike beasts had entered the clearing, followed by a third. When he looked back at the first one, he saw that it, too, had been joined by a companion. The four creatures spread out and surrounded the two humans.

"Stay back to back," Stone said. "If I turn, you turn with me."

The creatures began to pace back and forth, gradually closing the circle. As they came closer, Stone heard a low growl that sent a chill down his spine. He clutched his sword in a death grip and prepared to fight.

The creatures stopped suddenly and turned toward the woods on the far side of the clearing, angling their ears forward. One of them hissed, sending another chill skittering down Stone's spine. The cats broke their circle and formed a rough line between Stone and Brook and the tree line on the other side of the clearing. They crouched low, like barn cats ready to pounce on a mouse, their long tails quivering, their eyes gleaming.

"Now's our chance," Stone said, and he and Brook took off running. As they bolted from the clearing and entered the woods, Stone heard the sound of hoofbeats and clanking armor behind him.

Brook veered off the road and onto a narrow footpath, and Stone followed, ducking to avoid low-lying branches. He heard something running behind him, and nearly froze when one of the cat beasts brushed past. All four of the cats sprinted by him and then surged past Brook, and he was struck by the fine absurdity that he and Brook were now following the animals, possibly to their lair. But there would be no turning back, not with a squadron of knights, most likely led by Sir Borus, eager to hunt him down.

Stone and Brook ran fast, leaping over downed tree trunks, exposed roots, and half-buried rocks. The cats had vanished ahead of them, and Stone felt a brief moment of horror when he realized the beasts could be lying in wait. He shook off his fear and quickened his pace, taking in huge draughts of air as he sprinted along the path. Brook was more agile and pulled ahead, and soon all Stone could see of his accidental companion were glimpses of her white dress through the trees. He nearly called after her, but she disappeared into the gloom of the dense forest.

The path eventually led upward to a ridge, and Stone had to climb the last ten feet up a steep and craggy rock face. When he reached the top, Brook was standing there, breathing heavily, her face flushed and her green eyes flashing. Directly opposite her, no more than ten paces away, stood a man in a brown tunic and brown leggings holding a walking stick. The four cat creatures sat next to him, two on either side. The man was stroking the head of the nearest beast, which purred and rubbed its head against the man's leg. Somewhere below, the sound of hoofbeats faded away into the deep woods.

"Greetings," the stranger said evenly. "Who might you two be?" His hair was sand-colored and his face ruddy, with a roughhewn look about it. He was not quite as tall as Stone, who stood over six feet, but he had broader shoulders, a sturdy neck, and thick wrists.

Stone raised his left hand, palm outward, and said, "I am Stone Falconer, and this is my friend Brook." As he spoke, he kept his eyes on the nearest cat creature and his right hand near his sword.

"Who are you?" Brook asked the stranger.

"I call myself Bennald. Why have you left the road?"

"To get away from those riders," Brook replied.

"You're not with them, then?"

"No," said Stone. "We're with each other."

"Have you no horses?"

"No. We were with a caravan, but we got left behind."

Bennald raised an eyebrow.

"Are those beasts your pets?" Stone asked to change the subject.

"No, not pets. Friends."

Stone and Brook shared a quick glance. "Have you any other such friends?" Brook asked.

35

"I don't know," Bennald replied. "I've lost my memory and know nothing about myself."

Stone and Brook looked at one another again and then turned to Bennald.

"Others have lost their memories as well," Brook said. "We believe there may be some sorcery or enchantment at work around here."

"I know nothing about sorcery or enchantment," Bennald said. "All I know is that I woke up here in the forest yesterday morning with these creatures licking my face and this staff lying next to me."

"But if you have no memory of yourself, how do you know your name?" Stone asked.

Bennald shrugged. "One of these cat-a-mountains told me."

Stone gaped at him. "You speak the beasts' language?"

Bennald furrowed his brow, as if deep in thought. "It wasn't a language, exactly. It was as if I heard him inside my head."

Stone looked at the cat Bennald was stroking. The beast seemed to be grinning at him. He felt another chill run down his spine and looked away.

"What have you done since you discovered yourself here?" Brook asked.

"I've been gathering roots and berries and nuts to eat, getting to know the creatures of the woods."

"Perhaps you'd consider sharing some of your roots and berries," Stone said. "We haven't eaten since last night."

"Of course," Bennald said, and without another word he disappeared into the woods with two of the cats, leaving the other two to keep Stone and Brook company. He returned a half hour later with a pile of nuts and berries in his tunic, the hem of which he held up to form a makeshift basket.

After they'd eaten, Stone and Brook told Bennald their own tales. Stone concluded by telling him about the quatrefoil insignias on his sword and Brook's dagger. Bennald looked thoughtful for a moment, and then he handed his walking stick to Stone. Its handle was carved into the shape of a stylized cat-a-mountain, the body of the beast serving as the grip, the head facing forward. Burned into the top of the handle was the same quatrefoil insignia that Stone and Brook had discovered on their weapons, a small orange jewel in the center of it. Bennald held up his right hand to show them a ring with an orange gem set inside the familiar insignia.

The three were silent for a moment. The four cats yawned and stretched and then got up and padded away. Bennald looked at the creatures, and one of them stopped and turned and looked back at him. "All right," Bennald said softly. The big cat purred and then continued on its way with his companions.

The three wanderers stared at one another. Finally, Stone said, "Let's think. All three of us woke up yesterday with no memory of ourselves. All three of us have in our possession an object with a four-sided insignia, and each of us has a ring with the same insignia surrounding a jewel. One of us has a seemingly magic sword and can possibly call up whirlwinds, another can stay underwater for an hour without drowning, and the third can communicate with wild animals."

"And the three of us have somehow found one another," Brook said.

Stone nodded. "What are we to make of all that?"

His question was greeted with silence.

Stone heaved a great sigh and looked at Brook. "We must continue on, try to find a town, try to find someone who knows one of us."

Brook looked at Bennald. "Will you join us?"

"I prefer to remain here," Bennald said.

"And do what?" Stone asked.

"Get to know more of the animals of the forest."

"Don't you want to get to know more of your own kind?" Brook asked.

"I've seen soldiers passing by along the road. If that's my own kind, then no, perhaps I don't."

"Surely you can't stay here," Stone said.

"Why not?" said Bennald. "I like it here. I don't know if I'd like it as well anywhere else."

In the end, Stone and Brook were unable to persuade Bennald to join them, but he agreed to help them. He suggested they stay off the road, and the next day the three wanderers and the four cat-a-mountains made their way through the deep forest, foraging for wild nuts and berries and edible shoots and leaves, enough to eat and also store in baskets that Bennald wove from vines and slender branches. Near evening, they came to the end of the woods. They found a clearing and bedded down for the night on piles of leaves and pine needles. Three of the cat-a-mountains curled up near Bennald, but the fourth stayed awake, keeping watch.

The next day they came to another stream, and Bennald helped Stone and Brook construct a rude log raft to carry them down it. They also wove more rough baskets to carry nuts and berries and other forage. When all was ready, Stone and Brook took their leave of Bennald. It had been four days since the three had awakened with no memory of themselves.

Chapter 4 - Drumkin

The stream flowed west, meandering through wide loops and sometimes quick turns as it went. They saw their first farm two days after setting out and soon were passing farms and mills and small wooden docks every few miles or so. Two days later, they spied a wide river into which the stream emptied. A bustling town had grown up on the west side of the river where it met the stream. They entered the river and beached their raft not far from the town. They dragged it up the embankment and into the woods, where they hid it under a pile of brush. They took what was left of their supplies and walked along the stream to the town, a mile away. For now, Stone placed his sword in a long basket that Bennald had woven for it and put the basket on his shoulder, the way someone might carry a length of timber. Brook concealed her dagger under her dress.

After a twenty-minute walk, the two travelers entered the town and began strolling down a street that ran alongside the river. The town was called Drumkin and was the second-largest in Misheroon, one of the four provinces that made up the Kingdom of Ruxland. It was a prosperous river port, with weathered but sturdy-looking docks, a dozen mills, and fertile farms all around. Dozens of fishing boats and other vessels were tied up to the docks, and other boats were plying the quarter-mile-wide river. The town boasted a sizable marketplace, cobblestone streets, inns and taverns, and various shops. As they strolled past the docks, Stone saw workers building what appeared to be small castle-like structures at the bow and stern of three merchant cogs.

"That's odd," he murmured.

"What's odd?" Brook asked.

He pointed to one of the cogs. "Those extra little decks they're building fore and aft. The sides are crenellated, like the walls of a castle."

"What does it mean?" she asked.

Stone shrugged. "It's as if they're turning them into warships."

"Perhaps they are."

They entered a reputable-looking inn called the Bell's Knell and asked the innkeeper, a short, gnome-like man named Sidge, about the possibility of employment. Sidge told them he needed no help but that his cousin Heggott, innkeeper of the Pilot's Wheel, might be looking for a serving maid.

They made their way to the Pilot's Wheel to see Heggott, who took one look at Brook and hired her on the spot. "A room comes with the job," Heggott explained. "It's a small one, in the attic, but it's comfortable enough."

Brook was to begin learning her job immediately, so she and Stone parted company with a promise to meet later that night at the Pilot's Wheel.

Stone made the rounds in the village, inquiring about work at various inns and taverns and shops, eventually finding a job as a stable hand at the Stream's End Inn, five blocks from the Pilot's Wheel. The innkeeper, a large, garrulous man

41

named Gart Daver, told him his first assignment was to muck out any stalls that were empty. "You'll find a wheelbarrow and a pitchfork outside, and some gloves that the last stable boy left behind. There are fresh burlap sacks and lengths of rope as well," Gart said. "You're welcome to them."

"What are the burlap sacks for?" Stone asked.

"To tie around those fine boots of yours so you don't ruin them."

"Oh."

"When you're finished, come in the back, wash yourself down, and we'll see about feeding you," Gart said. "After I check your work."

The man left, and Stone set about his task. He put on the gloves, tied the sacks around his boots, and hauled a water bucket and feeding tub out of the first stall. He put the wheelbarrow at the stall's entrance and used the pitchfork to lift straw and horse droppings into the barrow. When that was finished, he pushed the wheelbarrow to the manure pile and emptied it. Then he took a hay bale and spread clean straw over the floor of the stall. He fluffed it up with the fork and then paused to admire his work. His face was covered with sweat, and he was breathing hard, but he felt unexpectedly content. He filled the water bucket from the well behind the inn, and then returned it and the feed tub to the stall before moving to the next empty one.

When he finished cleaning out the rest of the empty stalls, he found a broom and swept up loose bits of straw from around the stall entrances and then used it to knock down the cobwebs that festooned the corners of the ceiling. Then he went to fetch Gart.

The innkeeper looked around at the stable and nodded appreciatively. "You've got a natural talent for mucking out," he told Stone, who was oddly pleased at the compliment. "No doubt you've experience in the work, eh?"

Stone nodded, reasoning that although he didn't really know if he had any such experience, he didn't know for sure that he didn't. "You mentioned something about feeding me."

"Come along, then," Gart said. "Wash yourself first, and then you'll eat."

Stone washed himself outside, in a small enclosed area behind the inn that had a barrel of water and a small bucket, and shook as much of the dust off his clothing as he could. He went into the kitchen and took a meal of rabbit stew and warm bread prepared by a woman named Maryl Faygaard, the inn's cook, and accompanied by a tankard of dark ale. Afterwards, Gart showed Stone his quarters, located in a storage area at the back of the stable's tack room. The space was modest, and the work would be hard, but the meal had been delicious, and Stone counted himself lucky to have found work and a place to sleep. His newfound situation would also allow him to save most of the coppers he earned.

***

After Stone's first week at the Stream's End Inn, he took on the additional task of driving a horse-drawn cart filled with manure to some of the surrounding farms, exchanging the muck for a small portion of each farmer's produce or freshly baked pies for serving in the inn's dining room.

Stone quickly befriended the farmers he visited—and their wives and daughters—who sometimes offered him a plate of sliced fruit or a tankard of cool cider on a hot day. Since he knew little about Misheroon or the provinces that bordered it, at first he listened more than he spoke, eager for any news or gossip that the farmers wanted to share. Soon he was passing along stories and rumors to others, retelling tales in a dramatic fashion, using his voice, hand gestures, and frequent embellishment to add a dash of spice to his narration. His audiences appreciated his storytelling skills, and he began to wonder if he might have been a player or a street performer before he lost his memory.

Three weeks after arriving in Drumkin, Stone delivered a load of manure to a sturdy but amiable farmer named Cregg, whose farm was five miles south of the town. Before he even halted the cart, Cregg's dog Ezzie, a three-legged mongrel with a long ratty tail that seemed never to stop wagging, ran up to him for a petting. Stone stroked the dog's head and let him lick his hands. "There's a good dog, Ezzie," Stone said, and then he headed for the farmhouse.

Cregg's wife, Moll, had made a couple of pinkberry pies for Stone to take back to the Stream's End Inn in exchange for the manure, and she and Cregg insisted that he come inside to sample a slice before heading back to Drumkin. Stone readily agreed and followed Cregg into the stone kitchen that was attached to the large wooden farmhouse. The two men sat down at a huge oak table in the middle of the kitchen, and Stone wasn't surprised when Cregg's daughter Bellanna, a pretty nineteen-year-old, appeared with two tankards of cool cider. Moll cut some generous wedges from a pie, and Bellanna served her father and Stone at the table, smiling and blushing and looking mostly at the floor.

"Thank you, Bellanna," Stone said, flashing a bright smile. "Did you bake this wonderful-smelling pie with your own pretty hands?"

Before she could respond, Cregg said, "Aye, she and Moll baked 'em up. Bellanna is becoming one of the finest cooks in the province, if not in all of Ruxland. She'll make some lucky man a fine wife one day."

"That she will," Stone agreed before taking a long pull of his cider. He had no doubt that Bellanna would indeed make someone a fine wife, but whoever her future husband might be, it wasn't going to be him.

Moll and Bellanna left the men to their pie and cider, and Stone asked Cregg what news he had to report.

"A man at the market yesterday told me about some strange doings in Redmond Province," Cregg said.

Stone raised an eyebrow. Reports of strange doings always drew his attention. "What sorts of strange doings?"

45

"This fellow said King Harrin had dismissed his chief counselor and taken on a new one, some oddkin from across the sea."

"Perhaps the chief counselor got caught with his hand in the royal coffers," Stone offered.

Cregg shook his head. "Not likely. The man is a wizard from the old virrling clan."

Whenever there was talk of wizards, Stone listened closely. "Perhaps King Harrin found a better wizard."

"None better than Jole Arrick, or so I've always been told."

"Have you been to Redmond Province?" Stone asked. All he knew of that neighboring area was that it bordered the Eastern Sea, was said to be prosperous, and that its capital, the Red City, was also the capital of the whole Kingdom of Ruxland.

"I have not. But Moll's sister, Temma Smotts, lives there with her husband, Santosh, though we ain't heard from them in a while." Cregg looked thoughtful. "A longer while than usual, come to think on it."

Stone watched as Cregg gazed out through a window, almost as if he expected to see his wife's sister and her husband strolling toward the door. "You seem worried, Cregg. Why don't you send a message to your Redmond kin?"

"We have done," Cregg said. "We got no reply."

"Of course, messages can be notoriously unreliable, especially in the hinterlands," Stone said in his most reasonable tone, wondering if it was really so but wanting to keep the conversation going. "They may not have received it. Or they may be too busy. Do they live on a farm?"

Cregg shook his head. "They live in the Red City, the capital. Santosh is a chandler. They always get our messages. And they always reply. Moll says maybe the wandremes took 'em."

"Wandremes?" Stone said before he could stop himself. It was a word he hadn't heard before.

Cregg snorted. "Aye, lost enchanters who roam the land looking for their memories and causing mischief when they're not slaying dragons or rescuing damsels. A pack of old maid's tales. Faerie stories for the young ones."

"Wandremes," Stone murmured, forcing himself to smile. "It's been a long time since I've heard any faerie stories."

"Any road, Moll won't leave off talking about them. Sometimes I think the woman is daft."

"She's just worried," Stone said. He finished his pie and cider and gladly accepted another tankard of cider. Cregg seemed eager to talk some more, and Stone was eager to listen.

"One man at the market said he heard that a lot of Redmonders were leaving Redmond Province," Cregg said. "Some were heading our way, others were going north or taking to the sea."

"And you're thinking this flight from Redmond might have something to do with the strange doings you mentioned?"

"Aye. The man told me some of the travelers had organized into caravans, for their own protection."

Stone felt a chill run up his spine. The people in the caravan he and Brook encountered had obviously been afraid of something. "Protection from what?" he asked.

"I don't know," Cregg said. "Perhaps it's all rumor and tripe."

"Yes," Stone said. "Perhaps it is." He stood up. "Thank you for the pie and cider, Cregg, but now I must be going. I hope you hear from your people."

Stone met with Brook that night, as he did most nights, after she finished her serving duties at the Pilot's Wheel. As usual, they met in her small garret in the inn's attic to exchange their news and gossip, his from farmers and field hands, hers from the travelers, merchants, and sailors who patronized the Pilot's Wheel. Stone had brought a small bouquet of wildflowers he'd picked earlier that day along with a flask of sweet mead to share. Brook put the flowers in a small vase and found two pewter cups for the mead.

Brook took her cup of mead and sat on the edge of the bed. "Have you any news to share?"

Stone sat on the floor and pulled off his boots.

"Make yourself comfortable," Brook said.

"Thank you, I will."

"News?"

Stone told her what Cregg had said about strange doings in neighboring Redmond Province. "What do you make of it?" he asked when he was finished.

"It makes me wonder if the answer to our own mystery might not lie in Redmond Province," Brook said.

Stone nodded. "I'm thinking the same."

"If we decide to go there, we should find Bennald and tell him."

Stone thought about the four cat-o-mountains that were Bennald's closest companions. "Let's hope those cat-beasts haven't made a meal of him."

"They're his friends," Brook said. "They won't hurt him."

"So you say," Stone replied. "Meanwhile, we need to learn more about the situation in Redmond. Keep your eyes and ears open."

"I always do," said Brook.

"One more thing," Stone said, and he told Brook what Cregg had said about the wandremes. "Ever hear the word?"

"No."

"What do you reckon it means?"

Brook shrugged. "Faerie stories, just as your farmer said. Like the witches that people say live in the northern wasteland or the giants who are supposed to occupy the Southern Islands."

"But there really are giants," Stone protested. "I've met one, a field hand at Farmer Skeema's. He stands more than seven feet."

Brook waved a hand dismissively. "Tall, perhaps, but hardly giantish."

"But that's the nub of it—in his land he's a dwarf and so his people exiled him."

She narrowed her eyes at him and then began laughing. "Sometimes I don't know whether to believe anything you say. I suppose you've met a few witches on your travels as well."

Stone gazed at her but made no reply.

"Why are you looking at me like that?" she asked.

"Never mind," Stone said. "I suppose I should be going. Pleasant dreams."

He put on his boots and stood up. A light rain had begun, and they could hear the drops softly pattering on the steeply pitched roof above Brook's garret. Stone took his leave and walked through the soft rain back to the Stream's End Inn and his bed.

The next evening, Brook served a pair of merchants named Mank Hemple and Stubbard Kordru, frequent guests of the Pilot's Wheel who had recently returned from Redmond Province. She paid them particular attention, offering friendly smiles, making sure their bread was warm from the oven, and diligently refilling their wineglasses before they were empty. As she carried a full pitcher of strong red wine to their table, she heard one of them mention King Harrin. She took her time filling their glasses, focusing her eyes on her task, but her ears were tuned in to the conversation.

"King Harrin is too young to rule a kingdom without help," said Mank, a gray-bearded gentleman with a fringe of pewter-colored hair surrounding a bald pate. "Too young and too weak. He's lucky this stranger came from across the sea and offered his service."

"For an old-timer, you're awfully gullible, Mank," said Stubbard, a clean-shaven man with short brown hair. "No one offers his service unless he expects something in return."

"Of course he expects something in return, Stub," Mank replied. "That doesn't mean he won't give good advice."

"It doesn't mean he will," said Stubbard. "I was talking to a tobacco factor outside the Red City who claims this Ordseer fellow has beguiled the king and his counselors into giving him all of Redmond's gold and silver."

Mank waved his hand dismissively. "Hog's breath. I heard just the opposite. A wine merchant told me the Ordseer is a learned and benevolent sage who's helping the Redmonders become rich beyond imagining. Besides, how would he beguile a king?"

"My tobacco factor thinks the Ordseer might be a sorcerer of some kind, that's how."

"If he's conjuring riches for the Redmonders, I hope he comes here to Misheroon Province to do the same for us."

"If he's conjuring riches for the Redmonders, why are so many leaving?"

Mank frowned at his companion. "Who told you that? Your tobacco factor?"

"I heard it from more than one Redmonder. Didn't you?"

"I heard a few such rumors. But sensible folk are staying put and enjoying their newfound wealth."

The door opened, and Brook looked up as two men attired all in black stepped into the dining room. They took a table next to the one she was serving and sat down.

"You there, serving wench, what's on offer tonight?" one of the newcomers demanded.

"River trout cooked in milk or boar roasted with onions and peppers," Brook replied with a smile and a curtsy.

"Bring us wine and boar, and be quick about it," the man said. He had a slight accent, one that Brook had not heard before.

"Yes, your worthiness," Brook said before retreating to the kitchen to tell the Pilot's Wheel's young cook, Ronsin Leach, to prepare two plates of the roast boar. "No hurry," she told Ronsin as she left the hot kitchen and returned to the dining room with a pitcher of strong red for the newcomers.

Mank and Stubbard had already engaged the strangers in conversation. As she strained to listen, she was startled to discover that her hearing seemed to be more acute than before.

"I don't believe I've seen you gentlemen before," Mank was saying. "I'm Mank Hemple, and my friend here is Stubbard Kordru."

"Dace Orter and Arvil Prayne," replied the man who had spoken to Brook. "It's our first time in Drumkin, or anywhere in Misheroon for that matter."

"Welcome," Mank said. "What brings you to Drumkin?"

The man who called himself Dace Orter smiled. To Brook, who was pouring wine for the newcomers, there was more chill than warmth in it. "The Ordseer sent us here from Redmond on business for King Harrin."

Mank and Stubbard exchanged a quick glance. "What sort of business, if you don't mind my asking?" Stubbard asked.

"Business that could be of mutual benefit to both provinces," Dace replied.

"Tell us more," Mank urged.

Dace took a long pull of his wine, keeping his eyes on Mank, as if sizing him up to determine what information he might be entrusted with. Brook moved off, but her heightened sense of hearing allowed her to listen in on the conversation as if she were still standing next to the table.

"There are untapped riches to be had for those smart enough to deserve them," Dace said.

"What riches?" Stubbard asked.

Brook wanted to continue listening, but she worried that someone might notice her lingering. Reluctantly, she went back to the kitchen. By the time she returned to the dining room, more guests had arrived, and they kept her bustling. Nevertheless, she managed to glean a few scraps of the conversation between Mank and Stubbard and the strangers in black, and she learned of a tentative plan to send a delegation of merchants from Misheroon to Redmond to discuss the two provinces' common interests. The last comment she heard before the strangers left was that "the Ordseer would be more than glad to grant an audience to such a delegation."

Stone showed up later that night, and she told him about the conversations she'd overheard.

"The Ordseer again," Stone muttered as he took off his boots and wiggled his toes. He had brought some sweet wine and a couple of leftover redberry tarts that Maryl Faygaard at the Stream's End Inn had given him.

"Yes," said Brook, taking one of the tarts. "And if his men are here in Drumkin, then your friend Sir Borus may show up as well."

Stone heaved a long sigh. "And I was beginning to like it here."

"I as well," Brook said.

"Have I ever told you about Farmer Cregg's dog?"

Brook nodded. "Ezzie the three-legged marvel."

"Happiest dog I've ever seen," Stone said. "It's as if he doesn't know he's missing a leg. Or doesn't care, and refuses to let it ruin his enjoyment. Shows you can get used to anything."

"Even not knowing who you are?" Brook asked.

Stone shrugged. "We seem to be getting used to it. We have lives here, Brook."

She gave a little laugh. "Aye, lives. I'm a serving wench and you're a stable hand. Who knows but I might really be a princess and you a wealthy landowner or the master of a fleet of ships."

"True enough. But if we never discover who we are …"

"Perhaps you'll marry pretty Bellanna after all."

He shook his head. "No. I may already be married. You, too."

She nodded. "I know."

"So then, we must keep trying to discover who we are," Stone said. "And what connection we have to one another, and to Bennald."

"Yes, we must," she said. "I'll try to learn more from those Black Cloaks."

"And keep an eye and an ear out for Sir Borus. I have a feeling he isn't yet finished with me yet."

Chapter 5 - Kaemon

Two nights later, Brook served three men she hadn't seen before, who were conversing quietly among themselves at a corner table. The three were youthful, a few years younger than Stone, she guessed, but well past boyhood. They had a noble bearing and an air of culture and learning, as if they might be well-born knights or the sons of wealthy landowners. Though they were dressed plainly, their clothing was well made, and their boots were wrought of fine leather, excellently worked and clearly purchased at some expense. The man she took to be the leader had short hair of a dark gold color, a short beard of the same color, broad shoulders, pale blue eyes, and fine features.

The three had finished their evening meal and called for tankards of mead. As Brook served the man she assumed was the chief among them, he gave a little start and his eyes went wide. He was staring at her signet ring. She quickly set down the tankard and clasped her hands behind her back. He recovered himself and looked to his friends, but as she turned to leave, she saw him give her a curious glance.

That night in her room, she told Stone about the incident.

"He recognized the emblem on the ring," she said. "I'm sure of it."

"Who were these three strangers?" Stone asked.

"I don't know. I hadn't seen them before, and I wasn't about to engage them in conversation. But they were well-mannered and appeared to be respectable."

"Appearances can be deceiving," he said.

"Nevertheless, we should talk to them. Before they leave Drumkin."

"That could be dangerous. What if they're allied with Sir Borus or this Ordseer fellow?"

"I thought of that, but what if they're honorable and they know what these symbols mean? What if they can help us discover who we are?"

Stone looked thoughtful. "Perhaps we could press them for information without revealing too much about ourselves."

"They don't know about you. I should meet with them alone."

"Perhaps, but we need to plan this carefully."

"I already have. I plan to ask them to meet me at Jerd's Tavern, on the far eastern edge of the town."

Stone frowned. "Jerd's is in The Lags. It's no place for a lady."

Brook flashed a smile at the mention of the word *lady*. "Thanks, but I chose Jerd's because it's away from prying eyes. I thought you could come to the tavern a little while after I get there, but act as if you don't know me. Just stay close and be ready."

***

Brook arranged to take the next evening off, and early that morning she slipped a note under the door of the room occupied by the three men from the night before. She addressed it to "the golden-haired gentleman," asking him to meet her that evening at Jerd's Tavern to discuss a matter of "some importance." She signed it *Serving Maid With the Pretty Ring*.

Moments after leaving the note, she began to have doubts. Had he really noticed her ring or had she allowed a too-lively imagination to delude her? And if he had noticed her ring, what matter? Perhaps he was just admiring its beauty and workmanship. Now that she'd invited him to meet her at night in a disreputable part of town, would he think she was a flirtatious tart or, worse yet, a brazen woman of the night?

A half hour after leaving the note, she received a message in reply, slipped under her own door.

To the Pretty Serving Maid with the Pretty Ring. I will meet you at Jerd's after the supper hour to discuss your matter.

He had signed his note *Kaemon K.*

As soon as she read the note, she slipped out the back of the Pilot's Wheel and hurried to the Stream's End Inn to inform Stone of the meeting.

***

After Brook told Stone about the meeting, he could think of little else for the rest of the day. He worked feverishly, as if trying to distract himself from his thoughts, finishing his duties an hour early and using the time to prepare himself for the possibility that he and Brook might finally get a clue to their identities—or have to deal with a dangerous confrontation.

The lamb stew at the Stream's End Inn was especially delicious that evening, and Stone ate his fill, washing it down with a tankard of dark ale. He would have liked a second tankard, but he didn't want to take advantage of his position as a worker at the Stream's End Inn. He was glad for the job and grateful that his meals and quarters came with it. The quarters were modest, but the fine and filling meals more than made up for the lodgings' lack of space.

He was sitting at a tiny table in a corner of the kitchen, keeping an eye on the cook, Maryl Faygaard, a thin woman of late middle age who was as shy as a maiden. She liked Stone, who made it a point always to praise her cookery after every meal he took. When the inn was especially busy, he even helped her peel potatoes, chop onions, or dress fish, maintaining a constant friendly banter with her, banter that often included promises to steal her away from Drumkin and take her to a secret, enchanted castle in the Northern Wilderness, where he lived among a clan of witches.

Maryl's gray hair was tied back and covered with a kerchief, and she was stirring a big pot of the lamb stew with a long wooden spoon, keeping an eye on the bread oven and occasionally tapping on the casks of ale and wine to gauge the amounts left in them. Her face was flushed from the heat of the cook fire, and her outsized knuckles looked like gnarled peaks looming over the brown-spotted landscape of her strong right hand.

Stone drained his tankard, pushed away from the table, and stood up. He belched appreciatively and shot Maryl a big smile. "You've outdone yourself tonight, Milady Maryl," he said. "That's the best lamb stew I've ever tasted. You should be cooking for kings and princes, not for a modest establishment in an isolated river town."

Maryl smiled shyly and said, "Hush, Master Stone, don't let Gart hear you nattering on like that."

Stone waved away her concerns. "He knows I'm right. He knows he's lucky to have you. I've no doubt the Stream's End Inn of Drumkin is known far and wide for the excellence of its cookery."

"You're a charming pretender, you are," Maryl said.

Stone feigned a look of shock. "Every word I said is true, my dear Maryl. You're the queen of cookery. The sovereign of stew. The monarch of meals."

"Yes, yes, do go on."

Stone furrowed his brow and then brightened and said, "You're the princess of potatoes."

She snorted and flipped a potato peel at him. He caught it, dropped it into the pile of peelings, and then bowed, exited the kitchen, and headed back to the stable to rest and think until it was time to head to Jerd's Tavern. He had already decided to take his sword. No sensible man ventured into The Lags without a weapon.

***

As the sun neared the western horizon, Stone strapped on his sword and exchanged his short tunic for a long gray one. He pulled the garment over the weapon to partially cover it. In Misheroon Province, it was permissible for common folk to be armed, but he didn't want to draw attention to himself. When he was ready, he left the stable, crossed the yard to the back door of the inn, and stepped into the kitchen. He intended to tell Gart that he would be gone for a few hours but would check with him when he returned, in case Maryl needed his help in the kitchen.

She was ladling steaming fish stew into big white bowls when he entered, but she looked up and smiled at him, and he gave her a wave as he continued toward the door that opened to the common room. He entered and glanced around, looking for Gart. As he did, a man sitting at a table near a front window looked up and caught his eye. Stone felt the blood drain from his face. The man staring at him was Sir Borus Renovar, the knight who had accosted him five weeks before.

Stone saw Sir Borus's eyes go wide in recognition. He spun around and flung open the door to the kitchen, hearing a clamor of scraping chairs and angry voices rising up behind him. He ran through the kitchen and out the back door and sprinted toward the alley behind the Stream's End Inn. He fled down the alley and then tore down another street, heading in the general direction of The Lags. He thanked the gods that he had brought his sword with him.

He ran like a man possessed, faster than he would have thought possible. He heard the air rushing past his ears, saw dirt and dust and bits of chaff swirling in tiny whirlwinds on either side of him. He pumped his legs faster and felt as if he had broken some invisible bonds restraining him, almost as if he had taken flight. The buildings he swept past were a blur of brick and stone and painted wood. He listened hard but heard no evidence of pursuit.

Stone didn't slow down until he arrived at The Lags, a small and surprisingly tidy precinct that bulged from the northern end of the town like a toad's eye. The area was only two blocks long and two wide, comprising the tail ends of Longboat Lane and Cog Street where Longboat curved around in parallel with the river and ended at the bottom of Cog. The Lags was the local haunt of gamblers, roisterers, curious farm boys out for a night of adventure, and painted ladies of the evening, among its other colorful denizens.

Stone found Jerd's Tavern and hesitated. He looked around and saw no one in pursuit, but he knew Sir Borus wouldn't rest until he'd tracked him down. Stone had told Gart where he was headed, and he knew Sir Borus would threaten the innkeeper—and anyone else—to get the information he wanted. What Stone didn't know was what awaited him inside Jerd's. For now, Brook had decided to trust this Kaemon fellow, but for all Stone knew, Kaemon might be in league with Sir Borus. Or he might be an honest man who held the key to their identities. There was only one way to find out, and besides, he couldn't stand outside Jerd's all night weighing his options. He pushed open the door of the tavern and stepped inside.

The place was small and appropriately dim, lit by a few torches in sconces on the walls and thick white candles on a dozen or so mismatched tables. Brook was sitting with three men at a rough pine table toward the back, and she glanced up briefly when Stone entered but gave no sign of recognition. When Stone strode to her table to make his presence known, she stared at him in surprise. There was no time for explanations or pleasantries.

"Sir Borus Renovar is here in Drumkin," he said to Brook. "He saw me at the Stream's End, and he'll be coming for me."

Brook stood up, and the three men sitting with her rose to stare at Stone.

"How do you know Sir Borus?" asked the man who seemed to be the leader.

Before Stone could answer, they heard the sound of horses slowing down outside. The front door flew open, and Sir Borus stepped inside, sword in hand. Three knights followed him in. They spread out and faced Stone.

"I want no trouble," said the man behind the bar. "Take your argument outside."

Sir Borus ignored the barkeep and started forward. When he spotted the three men who had been speaking to Brook, he stopped and stared. "You," he growled to Kaemon. "I shouldn't be surprised that a traitor to his country would be in league with this scoundrel."

Kaemon drew his sword. "Call me a traitor again and I'll put this through your black heart."

Kaemon's two friends drew their swords, and Stone drew his. Brook drew her dagger and held it in front of her. The five spread out to face Borus and his three. The other patrons had fled at the first sign of trouble, and the barkeep was retreating to a back room.

"If you plan to make a move, do it now," Kaemon said.

Sir Borus seemed to consider. "I have other men on the way," he said. "You won't get away. None of you will."

"Make your move or be gone," Kaemon said.

"You'll regret this day," Sir Borus said. "All five of you." Then he backed up toward the door and left, followed by his men. Moments later, they heard the sound of four horses galloping away into the night.

Stone let out a long breath, glanced at Brook, and then nodded at Kaemon. "It appears we have an enemy in common."

Stone and Brook, accompanied by their three new acquaintances, left Jerd's and took a circuitous route back to the Stream's End Inn, where a distraught Gart Daver told Stone that Sir Borus and his men had confronted him, demanding information about Stone.

"He asked me if I knew you," Gart said. "I told him you worked here as a stable hand, but that I knew next to nothing about you, which is true, isn't it? The knight accused me of lying and aiding a criminal."

"I'm sorry, Gart," Stone said. "But I'm no criminal."

"They left to go find you, but they came back again," Gart continued. "The big fellow said they were leaving Drumkin for now but would return with a whole company of knights to take you and anyone conspiring with you into custody—including me."

"I'm sorry," Stone said again.

"What's going on, Stone?" Gart asked. "What's this dreadful business about?"

"A simple misunderstanding, nothing more," Stone replied. "Besides, he's a hired knight and has no authority here in Misheroon."

Gart frowned and told Stone that his services as a stable hand were no longer required. He paid him what he owed him, and Stone and Brook and the three Redmonders moved on to the Pilot's Wheel. They ascended a rickety back staircase and entered Brook's tiny room in the attic, where there was barely room enough for all five of them. Stone and Brook sat on the bed, Kaemon took the straight-backed wooden chair, and his two friends sat on the floor.

Stone spoke first, addressing himself to Kaemon. "I am Stone Falconer. I've no doubt you've introduced yourselves to Brook, but I would also know your names."

Kaemon stood and extended his hand, which Stone took. "My name is Sir Kaemon Krowe, First Knight of the Kingdom of Ruxland, and these are my friends and fellow knights Sir Elling Bolger and Sir Panwer Ronn."

Stone stared at the man as if he had just claimed to have flown there from the moon. "First Knight, eh? I'd have taken you and your friends for factors or the sons of middling farmers."

"We're traveling discreetly, I confess," Kaemon said.

"Why is that?"

"I was about to explain it all to Brook when you arrived at Jerd's."

"And now your audience has doubled," Stone replied. "Say on."

Kaemon nodded and took a breath. "The tale begins about five weeks ago, in the Red City. Panwer and Elling and I had just returned from Blaewick, the province on Redmond's northern border. King Harrin, who is my cousin, had sent us there three weeks earlier. He wanted me to investigate firsthand the so-called "farmer's rebellion," then in its second week, and I had returned just in time for the king's weekly parlay with his counselors. I was thirsty and dust-ridden from my journey, and I walked into the king's council room just as the meeting was getting under way …"

Chapter 6 - The Red City

Kaemon Krowe, First Knight of the Realm of Ruxland and cousin to King Harrin, strode into the king's council room for the weekly meeting of the king's counselors. The walls of the room were decorated with large portraits of Ruxland's kings and queens, but another, larger decoration immediately caught Kaemon's eye. It was a huge tapestry hanging on the back wall behind King Harrin, who sat in an ornate oak chair at the head of the long council table.

"Ah, Kaemon," King Harrin said as his cousin approached. "I was afraid you wouldn't make it back in time. I was worried that our good farmers of Blaewick might have given thought to taking you hostage or doing you some other harm."

Kaemon smiled. "I took Sir Elling and Sir Panwer with me, Your Grace."

"Good men, certainly, but thirty farmers with pitchforks can accomplish a deal of damage, if they've a mind to."

"I was in no danger, Your Grace," Kaemon said. "These farmers want only to be treated fairly."

That brought a snort from Lord Vadd Marnum, Keeper of the Royal Coffers and Master of the Mint, a short, rotund man with a florid face and two chins. Kaemon gave him a sidelong glance and then turned back to the king. "I see you've a new wall-hanging, Your Grace."

King Harrin smiled and gestured toward Vadd Marnum. "A gift from the Keeper of the Coffers. It captures all of Ruxland's history. Magnificent, isn't it?"

Kaemon gave the tapestry a long look, slowly scanning its length from left to right. It depicted yeoman farmers working their fields, great castles and elegant manor houses—including a few owned by the Marnum family—gleaming under blue skies, smiths working at anvils, armorers making swords and shields, weavers and chandlers and other guildsmen plying their crafts. One scene showed knights charging into battle, another depicted ships of all sizes sailing up the Farro River or putting in at the Red City docks, some flying the Marnum banner. It was a dizzying panorama, with a hundred other colorful scenes, but to Kaemon the tapestry looked more like a glorification of Lord Marnum than a celebration of Ruxland.

"It's lovely," Kaemon said. He glanced around at his fellow counselors and saw that one was missing. A tall ginger-haired man who Kaemon had never seen before was sitting in his place. Kaemon looked at King Harrin. "Where is Jole Arrick? I thought he would be here."

"The good wizard seems to have taken ill," said Sir Damrick Brunville, the king's justiciar. Sir Damrick had short blond hair, no beard, and a mirthless smile that had sent chills down the spines of many an accused man or woman.

Kaemon stared at him. "Virrlings don't become ill, sir."

"Yet I'm afraid he has done so," said the ginger-haired newcomer. "He asked me to attend the session in his stead."

Kaemon looked at the man who had spoken, this time giving him a closer look. He had on a long gray tunic made of fine cloth and wore a round pendant on a short gold chain. The pendant seemed to be some sort of insignia, a grouping of triangles on a gray circle. Three upright black triangles of equal size touched at the corners to form a gray, upside-down triangle in the middle, and another, smaller, black triangle seemed to float atop the gray one. It reminded Kaemon of a throg's eye.

Kaemon looked at the ginger-haired man and tried to give him a friendly smile. "And you are?"

"My apologies," King Harrin said to his cousin. "Allow me to introduce the Ordseer. The good man arrived from the Eastern Islands by ship shortly after you left for Blaewick." The king turned to the stranger. "Sir, meet my cousin Kaemon Krowe, First Knight of the Realm."

"And the youngest among your counselors, it appears," the ginger-haired man said.

The king smiled. "We're of an age, Kaemon and I, but my cousin is wise beyond his years. I depend not only on his military skills but also on his sage counsel in other matters."

"Has the Ordseer a name?" Kaemon asked.

"I've been Ordseer so long I've nearly forgotten it," the man said. "And besides, I prefer Ordseer, an indulgence which I'm sure you'll forgive in an old man."

Kaemon thought the Ordseer looked far from old, but he just nodded. "How came you to be visiting our kingdom?"

"I've taken to traveling the wide world, occasionally aiding other kings and counselors, and yet I had never been to Ruxland. Now that I'm here, perhaps I can help sort out your little problem in the north."

"How do you know Jole Arrick? Are you also of the virrling clan?"

"He and I are old friends," the Ordseer said.

"He's my friend as well," Kaemon replied, noting that the man who called himself the Ordseer had not quite answered his question. "I hope I may be able to see him."

The Ordseer shook his head. "I'm afraid that won't be possible."

"Why not, if you please?"

"He's more gravely ill than I first thought. He's aboard my carrack, the *Skyte*, being cared for by my own wistlord."

The news about Jole Arrick was dire, and it was an effort for Kaemon not to let his alarm show on his face. The news also made him suspicious. Though virrlings could be killed in battle and affected by spells and enchantments, they were immune to the illnesses suffered by mortal men, and Kaemon had never known Jole to be anything but hale, healthy, and strong. Something was amiss, and Kaemon was determined to discover what it was. He was surprised that the king's other counselors hadn't already been investigating the matter.

"I'll have a word with Markram Meest, Jole's assistant," Kaemon said.

"I'm afraid the young man has disappeared," said the Ordseer. "No one knows where he's gone to."

Kaemon frowned and turned to Thig Grennell, the king's wistlord, a short, wiry man with thinning brown hair who served as King Harrin's personal sage, healer, and advisor.

"There's a rumor that Markram fled to Misheroon," the wistlord said.

"Why would he do that?" Kaemon asked.

"Use your head," Vadd Marnum said. "Jole Arrick takes ill, and his assistant flees. It shouldn't be difficult to guess what happened."

Kaemon refused to believe that Markram Meest would ever do harm to Jole Arrick, even supposing he could, but he decided to let the matter rest for now and deal with the subject at hand. He turned to King Harrin. "Our little problem in the north, as the Ordseer calls it, is easily solved. The farmers in Blaewick own nothing beyond their land and their good names, and when they have a poor year, they find it difficult to pay their taxes on time. But, as they expect a good crop come this harvest time, they need only a bit of leeway. That's all they ask."

"They've had time," said Vadd Marnum. "Now they're late."

"They'll make it up," Kaemon replied. "Bad seasons occasionally happen, and we should make allowances for them."

"Too many such allowances will bankrupt the kingdom," Lord Marnum said.

"I think not," said Kaemon. "Bad seasons are rare. Besides, the king's mines are still producing handsomely."

"Nevertheless, your Blaewick farmers are breaking the law," said Sir Damrick.

"Not by choice," Kaemon said.

"It sets an unfortunate precedent," said Sir Doville Pery, a laconic man with flowing iron-gray hair and a matching beard. He was First Lord of the Realm, the official who saw to it that the king's decrees were promulgated and enforced.

"I disagree," Kaemon replied. "Showing restraint and working with these men to solve the problem sets an excellent precedent."

"It invites disorder," said Sir Damrick. "If Blaewickers are allowed to bend the law, what's to stop the other provinces from following their lead? We all know that dreams of rebellion stir the sleep of more than a few Misherooners and Braanters. And with nearly all the realm's knights kept here in Redmond ..."

The usually placid King Harrin shot Damrick a baleful glance.

"Begging your pardon, Your Grace, I just meant ..."

"I know what you meant, Sir Damrick," the young king said. "Most of the knights of the realm stay here in Redmond Province, because we—because I—decided that the provinces were best left to rule themselves as long as they remain loyal to the greater realm. I retain that view."

"I question whether Blaewick can be said to remain loyal," Lord Marnum muttered.

Kaemon turned to Thig Grennell. "What say you, Master Wistlord?"

The wistlord looked thoughtful for a moment. "Both views have merit, but I believe that accommodating these farmers may be worth considering, so long as they understand their obligations."

Everyone turned to the king.

"Yes, well, I find myself agreeing with all my counselors."

Kaemon suppressed a sigh. The comment was typical of King Harrin, who had a good heart but, it had to be admitted, no head for deciding complex matters. Some even wondered if he had the stomach for rule. Kaemon thought he saw Sir Damrick begin to roll his eyes, but the others remained as expressionless as he did.

"What if we have them sign the fastle pledge that your other subjects have been signing?" Sir Doville said.

Kaemon frowned and looked at Sir Doville. "What pledge do you mean?"

The others glanced at the Ordseer, who smiled and turned to Kaemon. "Shortly after I arrived here, I suggested that, given the unrest in your northern province, it might be advisable for the people of Redmond Province to renew their pledges of fealty to king and realm. A simple way to remind them of their duties and obligations. It's called a fastle pledge."

"Redmonders are loyal," Kaemon said. "They need no reminders of their duties and obligations."

"And yet the people here in the Red City and near about have been happy to sign these fastle pledges," said Vadd Marnum.

Kaemon's frown deepened. "How many have signed?"

"Nearly all our farmers and merchants and tradesmen on the coast and along the Farro River have done so," said Sir Damrick. "Once all the people in Redmond Province have signed, we'll send men with pledges to the outer provinces as well. It only makes sense to include everyone."

Kaemon was shocked at the news but tried not to let it show. "I'm surprised the people didn't take it as an insult. They might have thought the king doubted their allegiance."

"You overstate the case," Sir Doville said. "It's not unlike when a husband and wife renew their marriage vows to remind themselves of what each owes the other."

"Yes," said Thig Grennell. He glanced quickly at the Ordseer and then back to Kaemon. "Of course, in the case of our citizens, certain promises were also made to them."

"What promises?" Kaemon asked. Once again, the group glanced at the Ordseer.

"I have some ideas to help King Harrin and Lord Marnum with the kingdom's finances. With the proper investments, riches such as you already possess here in Redmond Province as well as in the entire Ruxland Realm can beget even greater riches. King Harrin agreed that it was appropriate to let the people share in any newly gotten wealth derived from my notions, if they're fully put into effect. I daresay even your recalcitrant northern farmers might be induced to take part."

"I see you've all been busy since I left," Kaemon said. "But these pledges—there's something distasteful about them."

"We all signed," Damrick said.

Kaemon stared at him, surprise written on his face.

"As leaders, we felt we should set the example," Lord Marnum added.

Kaemon looked at Thig Grennell. "You, too, sir?"

Thig shook his head. "No. Long ago I swore an oath to my order, which is the last oath I'll ever make. I'm one of the few hereabout who haven't signed."

"What about you, Kaemon?" Damrick said. "Surely you'll sign the pledge to your king."

"My allegiance to the king and the realm is not in question, and I find the notion of a pledge offensive. I'll remain with Thig among the few who don't sign."

The Ordseer opened a leather case sitting on the table in front of him and removed a sheet of parchment with words written on it. He looked at Kaemon. "Should you not at least read it before passing a perhaps too-hasty judgment?" He slid the sheet across the table, and Kaemon picked it up.

The parchment was as fine as any Kaemon had ever seen and felt like silk in his hand. It was so white it seemed nearly to glow. He looked at the writing on the sheet, and blinked. The lines of ink seemed to waver for an instant, and he squinted against the brightness of the parchment. He set the sheet down and looked away from it.

"What do you think?" Damrick asked.

Kaemon folded the sheet without looking at it and stood up. "I'll read the thing later. I've had a long ride, and I need food and rest. And strong ale."

Kaemon saw the others staring at him, and he thought he detected a vague smile on the Ordseer's face. He felt as if his head was floating on the ocean, with swells rising and falling under it.

"Why not sign now?" Doville asked. "We all did, except for Master Grennell. Even the king signed."

Kaemon stared openmouthed at King Harrin. "What can he mean? What did you sign?"

"A loyalty pledge to myself," the king replied with a sheepish grin. "What do you think of that?"

"Begging your pardon, Your Grace, but it makes no sense."

King Harrin, a lopsided grin still on his face, shrugged. "The Ordseer thought it was a good idea. A king who leads by example is a king who keeps the allegiance of his subjects, as my good father and king before me used to say."

"I never heard him say that," Kaemon replied.

King Harrin's grin vanished, and he looked perplexed. "I thought he did," he murmured.

Kaemon's vision was roiling like a stormy sea, and his head felt as if it were expanding. "Pardon me, Your Grace," he said. "I'm feeling unwell. Please excuse me." He turned to walk out, stopped, and turned back to King Harrin. "You'll think about allowing the Blaewick farmers to bring in their harvests before they have to pay their taxes, won't you?"

The king smiled and waved a hand dismissively, but he gave no firm answer. Kaemon nodded, turned, and strode out of the meeting room, the folded parchment in his hand. As he left the chamber and entered a long hallway, he saw a burly knight with a monstrous dark red beard staring at him with obvious displeasure. The knight, a man unknown to Kaemon, wore all black, and the insignia on his breastplate was of the same design as the Ordseer's pendant. He was obviously part of the Ordseer's retinue. As Kaemon strode past the black-clad knight and continued down the long corridor, he felt the man's eyes on him.

Once outside the castle wall, the fresh air and warm afternoon sun calmed his churning mind. He headed for the Roose and Roop Alehouse, where he had arranged to meet his friends and fellow knights Elling Bolger and Panwer Ronn, who had accompanied him to Blaewick. He found them at a table along the inn's front wall, between two large windows, which let bright sunlight into the front part of the room, though the back half of the alehouse was dim. Elling was holding a sheet of parchment, scrutinizing it closely. As Kaemon joined them at the table, the barkeep, Skurt Yingmer, appeared with a tankard of ale, which he set before Kaemon.

"What are you reading that's so interesting?" Kaemon asked Elling, gesturing toward the parchment in his hand. "Another love letter from sweet Shareen?"

As Panwer snickered, Elling looked up and said, "It's a loyalty pledge to the king. Skurt gave it to me." He picked up a sharpened quill sitting next to a small pot of ink, dipped the quill into the inkpot, and set the point on the parchment.

"No!" Kaemon shouted, and he reached out and swept the quill away from the parchment, knocking over his tankard of ale and sending the inkpot flying. The ale foamed over the table, wetting the parchment and spilling onto the laps of Kaemon's two friends, who leaped up from their chairs as the cool ale soaked their breeches.

"Are you mad?" Elling shouted.

A moment later, the parchment burst into flames. The three men stared at it in astonishment as the flames coalesced into a single orange flame that turned yellow and then blue and then black before dying out. The parchment was gone, leaving behind no trace, not even a speck of ash. Only the charred tabletop gave evidence of what had happened.

The other patrons began murmuring in low tones, and Skurt Yingmer, the barkeep, frowned from the other side of the bar. The man's eyes were cold, and he was staring at Kaemon the way a guard dog trained to attack might stare at a trespasser. It sent a chill down Kaemon's spine.

The three knights looked around and then at one another.

"What's going on?" Elling said in a hushed tone.

"Let's go," Kaemon said, and they quickly left the Roose and Roop.

They made their way through narrow side streets and back alleys to Elling's lodging at the edge of the city, not far from the docks. On the way, Kaemon told them about the meeting in the king's council chambers. When they were safely inside Elling's small but tidy house at the end of a narrow lane, Kaemon produced the folded-up parchment the Ordseer had given him and showed it to his friends.

Panwer took it gingerly in hand and read it aloud. "I, the undersigned, do swear perfect fealty and allegiance, for now and forevermore, to the Ordseer."

"Let me see that," Kaemon said. Panwer handed it back, and Kaemon stared at it in disbelief. "That isn't what was written on it before. It said, 'allegiance to King Harrin and the Realm of Ruxland.'"

As he stared at it, the parchment shimmered and the words written on it faded to gray. He set it on the floor and pushed it away with his booted foot.

"Let's spill some ale on it," Panwer said. "See what happens."

Elling frowned. "Take it outside first. I'll not have my floor and fine Tothan carpet stinking of ale."

Panwer sniffed the air and wrinkled his nose. "Too late to worry about that, friend."

Elling looked at Kaemon. "What do you suppose any of this means? And what can we do?"

"We need to talk to the other knights and soldiers, get to them before they have a chance to sign this blasted pledge," Kaemon replied.

"It may already be too late," Panwer said. "Did you see those people in the Roose? The way they were staring at us?"

"I wish we could talk to Jole Arrick," Elling said. "I can hardly believe he's really ill. Perhaps we should sneak aboard the Ordseer's carrack and find him."

"And then what?" Panwer asked.

"Take him someplace safe."

"If he's ill, it could be dangerous to move him."

"He isn't ill," Kaemon said. "If this Ordseer is able to trick people into signing a loyalty pledge to himself, then he obviously has powers of enchantment. He may have put Jole under a spell— or killed him, it pains me to say."

"I still think we should get onto the Ordseer's carrack and search it," said Elling. "If nothing else, we'll have caught the Ordseer in a lie."

Kaemon nodded, but his face was grim. "Panwer, go to the barracks and talk to the other knights, tell everyone you see that no one is to sign any pledges, and that's by my order. I'll write it down and sign it for you to show anyone who has any doubt."

"What of those who've already signed?"

"Let's hope they're few, but be on your guard. Meanwhile, Elling and I will take his skiff and try to slip aboard the *Skyte*. We'll meet you back here."

After a quick meal, Panwer left for the knights' barracks at the Rose Castle, and Kaemon and Elling walked to a small wooden dock not far from the house, where Elling kept a skiff for occasional fishing excursions and, more often, for rowing his lady friends to a small, secluded island in the Farro River Bay.

By the time they rowed upriver to the major docks, dusk had fallen. They rowed along a forest of masts until they spotted the *Skyte*, a three-masted carrack, docked among the other merchant ships and fishing vessels, its name painted on the stern. The *Skyte* was deep and wide, with a high aftcastle and forecastle looming above the main deck like the towers of a stone fortress. Kaemon estimated the vessel was a hundred feet long and more than thirty feet wide.

They saw only two men on the deck, and Kaemon figured the Ordseer's other men had been given rooms in the castle, possibly in the barracks— just where Panwer was heading. He cursed himself for a fool for sending his friend to the castle by himself and hoped Panwer would be safe. Then he tried to put his worries out of his mind. He and Elling had their own mission to complete.

They put in on the sparsely populated east shore and waited for full dark. Before long, lights on the other side of the river began to wink on as proprietors of inns and taverns and alehouses prepared for guests seeking food and drink and whatever entertainment was on offer. Kaemon had watched the city change over from day to night a thousand times before, but on this night he thought the town looked different, even from a distance— more ominous he would have said, but he kept the thought to himself. He wondered how many people had already been persuaded to sign fastle pledges.

They waited until near midnight, and then rowed to the *Skyte*. The plan was for Kaemon to get off amidships, between the high aftcastle and forecastle, and wait for Elling to row the skiff to a nearby pier, tie up under it, and then approach the *Skyte* from dockside and try to distract the guards. If Elling was successful, Kaemon would climb to the deck and begin his search.

Kaemon stepped onto a timber that projected six inches out from the hull above the waterline and crouched down, waiting. After a while, he heard Elling hailing the men on the *Skyte*'s deck, heard their footsteps and their muttering as they went forward to confront the boisterous young man who was bellowing at them. Hugging the mahogany hull, Kaemon hoisted himself up to another projecting timber, then another, and then he was climbing over the gunwale. He ducked low and headed toward the stern, where the Ordseer's cabin would be. He hurried belowdecks, encountering no one, and began his search. The main cabin was empty, as were all the other cabins and berths. He climbed a ladder back up to the main deck and heard Elling, acting the perfect drunken fool, calling from the pier, insisting to the two guards that the ship was his, that he had left it "right here, at this very pier," and needed to go to his cabin for a change of clothing. The guards alternated between laughing at him and heartily abusing him. Kaemon finished his search. Jole Arrick was not aboard the *Skyte*.

Kaemon found a length of rope and went to the stern to lower himself down. Elling had outdone himself arguing with the two guards, and by the time he left them and disappeared into the night, a half hour had passed. Elling took a roundabout way back to where he had left the skiff and finally picked up Kaemon.

It was well into the small hours by the time they returned to Elling's abode, where Panwer was waiting.

"What news?" a relieved-looking Panwer asked Kaemon as soon as they stepped inside the house.

Kaemon shook his head. "Jole isn't onboard the *Skyte*. The Ordseer lied. I hope you had better luck with your mission."

Panwer looked grim. "I didn't. Nearly all the knights have signed. Whenever one signs, he gets others to sign as well. It's like a fever spreading among them. I've never seen anything like it. And they didn't take kindly to my prying. I thought more than once that someone would try to stop me from leaving the castle grounds or try to force me to sign one of those damnable parchments. I wound up retreating to my quarters in the barracks and hiding out like a craven child. I waited a while, with the door locked tight, not even daring to light a candle. I finally left the barracks and the castle grounds with as many of my possessions as I could carry and all the coin I own. I'll not return there."

"Ill tidings," said Elling.

"It gets worse," Panwer replied. "The people are in a tizzy of pledge signing. As I made my way here, I passed knots of people arguing about these

83

fastles. Those who've signed were haranguing and threatening those who hadn't. I saw a throng marching down Pepper Street like a mob on its way to a lynching, and there was pushing and shoving and ugly threats. I saw looks of pure fear and horror in the eyes of those being harangued, and I saw more than one family heading out of the city with whatever possessions they could carry on their horses or in carts and wagons. The signers had their eye on me, too—it's as if they can tell if you haven't signed, and I must have had a hundred of the things thrust in my face—but I avoided the mobs as best I could and took the long way round to get back here."

"What are we to do?" Elling asked.

"We may have to leave Redmond Province as well, or at least head to the countryside," Kaemon replied. "But first I want to go to Jole's house. If he's still alive, the Ordseer may be holding him there."

"If so, then he'll have soldiers guarding the doors," Panwer said.

"I'm going to try anyway. I may learn something."

"And if you're not allowed in?" Elling asked.

Kaemon hesitated. Finally, he said, "I know another way. Jole showed it to me once, though he made me swear never to reveal it to anyone else."

"Perhaps he was expecting some sort of trouble," Panwer said.

"Perhaps he was," Kaemon replied.

***

Jole Arrick's abode stood by itself on a parcel of wooded land on the northern outskirts of the Red City. Kaemon went alone, promising to return to Elling's house as soon as he was finished with his business there, no matter which way it went. When he arrived, just after dawn, he saw that the front entrance was guarded by two knights whom he knew, Sir Nevil Munfrid and Sir Tommick Tasher. The two were part of the King's Guard, a special contingent of knights sworn to protect the king. The twenty members of the company were under Kaemon's direct command but by long tradition took their orders from the king.

Kaemon dismounted and approached the wide wooden porch, where the two knights were standing on either side of the front door. Sir Tommick, a newly minted knight who had served for less than a year, glanced quickly over his shoulder at the door, as if he were expecting someone to come out. Sir Nevil, a gray-haired man who had served in the King's Guard for twenty-three years, walked across the porch and down the steps to greet Sir Kaemon, who stopped and waited to allow some distance between them and the house. Sir Tommick followed a moment later.

"Good morning, Sirs," Kaemon said. "I'm here to see Jole."

The two knights exchanged a quick glance. "Jole isn't here," Sir Nevil said in a low voice. "They've told us he's on the Ordseer's carrack."

"I just searched the Ordseer's carrack," Kaemon said. "Jole isn't there."

"Bastards," Sir Nevil muttered. "I knew they were lying."

"Are you sure Jole isn't here?" Kaemon asked.

Sir Nevil shook his head. "We can't be sure of anything. They don't let us inside. We stand guard at the door and sleep in an outbuilding. We take our meals there as well."

"Who told you to come here to stand guard?"

"We received a written command from the Ordseer, who's acting in the king's name," Sir Nevil said, still speaking softly.

"Before that, we received an order signed by the king stating that we should follow the Ordseer's commands as if they came from King Harrin himself," Sir Tommick said, as if he felt the need to explain the highly unusual state of affairs. When he was finished, he glanced quickly over his shoulder again.

"Who else is here?" Kaemon asked.

"Three Black Cloaks," Sir Nevil replied. He looked as if he had something bitter-tasting in his mouth and wanted to spit it out. "Sir Figa, the leader, and two jumped-up stinkards named Minniel and Trevo."

Kaemon looked from Sir Nevil to Sir Tommick and back again, trying to read their eyes. Finally, he asked, "Have either of you signed a fastle pledge?"

The two shook their heads.

"Have you been asked to sign?"

"Aye, we have," Sir Nevil replied. "So far, we've put it off."

"Do not sign any pledges, no matter who tells you, no matter if they claim to be acting for the king, no matter if the king himself demands it," Kaemon said, his voice a harsh whisper. "That's by my order, and you can tell anyone who asks that it's by my order."

"The Black Cloaks won't care," Sir Tommick said. "If we don't sign …"

Kaemon nodded. "If you don't sign, you'll be in danger. So I'm ordering both of you to leave Redmond Province at your first opportunity. If you find others who haven't signed, take them with you. My orders."

"With all due respect, Sir Kaemon, I'm not inclined to run from a fight," Sir Nevil said.

"I've a feeling there will be plenty of fighting to do soon enough," Kaemon said. "But for now we need to regroup and prepare. We're dealing with dark sorcery."

Sir Nevil was about to reply when the front door opened and a black-clad knight stepped out onto the porch and stared down at Kaemon. "Who are you and why are you here?" the Black Cloak demanded.

Kaemon gave a quick glance to Sir Nevil and Sir Tommick and then looked up at the Black Cloak. "Sir Kaemon Krowe, First Knight of the Realm. I'm here to see my friend Jole Arrick on a matter of some importance."

"Ah, well, Jole Arrick isn't here, is he?" the Black Cloak replied.

"This is his house."

"I know, but he took ill, and he's on the Ordseer's carrack."

"Is he?" Kaemon said.

"I said so, didn't I just?"

"So you did. I would know your name, sir, if you please."

"Sir Figa."

"Well, Sir Figa, perhaps you know the whereabouts of Jole's young assistant, Markram Meest."

"I hear he left Redmond when Arrick took sick. Heartbroke he was, or so I'm told. Couldn't bear to stay around and watch the virrling ..."

"Yes, go on, watch the virrling what?"

"Watch him die," Sir Figa said. "The Ordseer says it only a matter of time. He's as good as gone now. I doubt they'll let you see him there on the *Skyte*."

"How is it that you're guarding Jole's house?"

"By the Ordseer's command. He's acting in the king's name."

"I see," Kaemon said. "Thank you for your information."

When Kaemon turned to walk back to his horse, Sir Figa called out, "You there, First Knight of the Realm, have you signed a fastle pledge to your king?"

Kaemon kept walking and made no reply.

***

By the time Kaemon returned to Elling's house, the Red City was in a frenzy. Mobs were roaming the streets, smashing down doors and dragging people out of their homes, shoving fastle pledges at them and threatening to hang them if they didn't sign.

Kaemon and his two companions took their horses, weapons, traveling clothes, money, and enough food to see them to the border with Misheroon Province, if it came to that, and rode through the darkness to a hidden cave a mile inland from the west shore of the Farro River, which led to the secret entrance to Jole Arrick's house.

They dismounted and made their plans. Elling, who had never been to Jole's house, would remain at the cave entrance with the horses. Kaemon, who had visited the house numerous times, and Panwer, who'd visited there on perhaps a half dozen occasions, would sneak into the house through the secret entrance. While Kaemon searched the place, Panwer would remain out of sight and wait. If Kaemon didn't return to him after an hour, Panwer would go back the way they had come and rejoin Elling. The two would wait another hour for Kaemon, and if he hadn't shown up by then, they would leave and proceed to the village of Wanlee in Misheroon Province. They would take rooms at the Sword and Gourd Inn and wait there for a week. If there was still no sign of Kaemon, they would search for Markram Meest and try to find allies to join with them against the Ordseer.

Kaemon and Panwer lit torches and entered the cave. A mile in, they came to a side passage whose opening was barely wide enough for them to slither through. The narrow passageway rose gradually but steadily and eventually took them to a door, the secret entrance to the subbasement of Jole Arrick's house. Kaemon found a fist-sized rock that seemed to be half-buried in the floor and picked it up. He turned it over and undid a metal latch, revealing a key. He inserted the key into the door's lock, lifted the heavy iron handle, and pulled. The door creaked open, and they stepped through the entranceway.

They crossed the stone floor of a cavern-like chamber to a stairway carved into the rock. They climbed it to another subterranean level, a large space that contained Jole's workshop, herb room, and wine cellar along with storerooms and a small armory. Wooden stairs led up from there to the main floor of the house. They stepped lightly on the wooden treads to avoid creaking and climbed to a landing. Another set of stairs took them to another landing, where a low door, barely four feet high, was set into a wall. They stopped and listened, heard nothing. Kaemon crouched down, opened the little door a few inches, and peered through. The door, disguised on the other side as a storage crate, opened into an unused closet half filled with barrels and boxes and various oddments. Kaemon handed his torch to Panwer and then slid through the opening and into the closet. He opened the outer door and peered down a short hall that he knew led to the main hallway of the ground floor. He signaled Panwer, who closed the disguised door, and then stepped out into a hallway, closing the closet door behind him. He proceeded down the short hall to its end, where he stopped and peered around the corner into the long corridor. He saw no one.

Staying close to the wall, he walked slowly down the corridor, watching and listening. He heard muffled voices coming from the dining room, near the front of the house, and stopped, hardly daring to breathe. Save for the dining room, the ground floor was deserted. He retraced his steps and took another short hall to a back stairway. He climbed it to the second floor and began searching the rooms. There were four bedchambers, a small sitting room, and Jole's library, which had a small alcove with a desk, a chair, and a low cabinet. Kaemon searched them all, and then climbed another stairway to a half attic, which had chests and trunks and pieces of furniture—but no wizard. Jole Arrick was nowhere in the house.

Kaemon was descending the stairway from the attic when he heard the sound of voices from below. He turned and headed back up, then thought better of it and quickly descended to the second floor. He ducked into the library, just as two men in black tunics reached the top of the stairs.

"It's in the library," Kaemon heard one man say, and his heart nearly stopped. He dashed into the alcove and hunkered down under the desk, in the kneehole space between two stacks of drawers. He pulled the chair close and cursed himself for a fool when it scraped against the hardwood floor. He held his breath.

"The Ordseer won't like it if you go stealing his books," one of the men was saying as they entered the library.

"I'm just borrowing it," the other man replied. "Who's to mind? Come to think on it, who's to know?"

"Well, I know, don't I," said the first man.

"Was that a threat?"

"No, never a threat, Sir Minniel, just an observation."

"Don't *sir* me, Trevo, I'll not be mocked."

"Come along, then, there's the book over there."

Kaemon heard footsteps crossing the library and then silence.

"It's only a history book, not a book of spells," the man called Trevo announced with a hint of glee in his voice.

"Never mind, I still want to take a look."

"You've outsmarted yourself again," Trevo scolded.

"You'll be smarting soon enough if you don't hush yourself. Come on, over there, in that alcove."

"You're wasting your time."

"I'll have my look-see, make no mistake," Minniel said, and Kaemon heard footsteps approaching the alcove. He unsheathed his dagger and prepared to launch himself at the first man who came in. He'd wield the chair with his left hand and the dagger with his right.

Someone entered the room, and Kaemon tensed. He heard another voice, muffled, from outside the library.

"It's Figa," Trevo said. "He's wanting us. Best put your book back where you found it and come along."

The men left. Kaemon let out a long breath. He waited five minutes and then went back to where Panwer was nervously waiting for him.

Chapter 7 - Dreaming

"And so we rode here to Misheroon Province to begin our search for Markram Meest and see what might be done to save Redmond, and maybe the entire realm of Ruxland, from the Ordseer."

"If it isn't too late," Elling added.

"One question remains unanswered," Brook said, and everyone turned to her. She held up her right hand, displaying her ring. "When you saw my ring yesterday, Sir Kaemon, you seemed to recognize it. Perhaps you'll explain its significance."

Kaemon nodded. "The virrling Jole Arrick has an insignia, unique to him, or so I thought. Jole's mark is the very same emblem that's on your ring."

Stone and Brook looked at one another, and then Stone glanced at his own ring. The others noticed.

Panwer Ronn cut to the heart of the matter. "What is your connection with the virrling Jole Arrick?"

After a moment's hesitation, Stone said, "We don't know."

"Then how did you both come to own rings with Jole's emblem?"

"We don't know that, either," Stone said.

Panwer stood up and glared at Stone. "You expect us to believe such arrant nonsense?"

Stone rose to his feet and glared back. "Believe what you like, Sir Knight, it makes no matter to me."

Kaemon raised a hand to restrain his friend, and Panwer sat back down, still seething. Stone sat down a moment later. Kaemon looked from Brook to Stone and then said in a quiet voice, "I've told you our tale. It's time you told us yours."

***

By the time Stone and Brook were finished telling their stories, the sun had risen. They went to the dining room of the Pilot's Wheel and broke their fast on boiled eggs, dark bread, and flauns topped with honey. Brook left the group to begin her workday, and the four men repaired to Kaemon's room on the third floor to discuss what they should do.

Once inside the room, Kaemon locked the door and then arranged four plain wooden chairs around a small table near the window, which looked out over the street. As they talked, each man kept a wary eye on the comings and goings below.

"Finding your virrling friend may be the key to Brook and me finding out who we are," Stone said. "If he's still alive."

"And the key to finding Jole Arrick may be finding Markram Meest," said Kaemon.

"If he's still alive," Elling added.

"But now that the Ordseer has taken over Redmond Province, he seems to have his eye on Misheroon," Panwer said. "I don't doubt that Borus Renovar fellow will soon be back with a company, as he threatened."

"The Misherooners are a hardy people," Stone said. "They have their own men-at-arms and soldiers. They won't give in easily to an attack."

"It won't be an attack, at least not of the usual kind," said Kaemon. "The Ordseer will make his promises and weave his enchantments, and the people will sign his vile fastle pledge and become his thralls."

"And more than a few Misherooners would be just as happy to declare their independence from the realm," Panwer said. "The outer provinces have always been a bit restive."

"What's to be done?" Elling asked.

"Warn the Misherooners," said Kaemon.

Stone shook his head. "We're too few to warn them all, and they may not believe such a tale. Anyway, I can't stay here in Drumkin. I've lost my job, and when word gets around, which it will before the day is done, I'm not likely to find another. And Sir Borus wants my blood. I don't intend to hang around and let him have it."

"Borus wants our blood as well," Kaemon said.

"I ask again, what's to be done?" said Elling.

"Markram may be in Misheroon, perhaps even here in Drumkin," Kaemon replied. "We need to search the town and the rest of the province, before Sir Borus returns in force."

"Your virrling's assistant isn't in Drumkin, and I doubt he's anywhere in Misheroon," Stone said. "I've been all over the town, and the surrounding farms as well, and I've heard no word nor seen any sign of the youth you've described."

"He must be somewhere," Elling said.

Suddenly Stone sat up straight, his brow furrowed as if he were deep in thought.

"What is it?" Kaemon asked.

Stone sighed. "I'm just wondering if he may have been with the caravan we told you about. Most of the children and young people were interested in the two strangers who had stumbled upon them, and I was happy to entertain them with some frivolous nonsense talk. One young man was of middling height, slender, with brown hair that hung straight nearly to his eyes, and a freckled face."

"That does fit Markram," Panwer said. "It may have been him."

"That describes a thousand young men," Elling said. "Doesn't mean it was Markram Meest."

"Where did you say the caravan was headed?" Kaemon asked.

"I didn't," Stone replied. "We never asked them, and they didn't tell us."

"Bad luck, that," said Elling.

"Did you get any names?" Panwer asked.

Stone nodded. "Two. The man who seemed to be the leader told us his name was Pemquist. He was in his middle years or older and had a face that reminded me of a weather-beaten mountain peak. His wife's name was Sova."

The three knights looked at one another. Panwer closed his eyes and frowned. "Pemquist, Pemquist," he murmured. "The name is familiar somehow. Yes, yes, I think it's the name of a farm family in the west of Redmond Province. Markram may have sought shelter with them and even persuaded them to leave Redmond before the Ordseer's minions came calling."

"The caravan could be anywhere by now," Elling said.

"Anywhere but Misheroon," said Stone. "We should leave before Sir Borus returns and search elsewhere for the lad."

"I agree," said Kaemon. "Can you and Brook ride?"

Stone shrugged. "Probably."

"I'll purchase horses and saddles and supplies. We'll head west and try to catch that caravan or get news of it."

"What of Misheroon?" Panwer asked.

"All we can do is warn a few of the prominent people hereabout and hope they take our warnings to heart and spread the word. It will be up to them to protect themselves. But the only real hope for Redmond, if not the entire realm, lies in finding Jole Arrick, which means we must find Markram Meest."

***

After the meeting, Kaemon and his two companions left to purchase two horses and saddles. Stone went to the dining room and informed Brook of their decision. Brook told Heggott, the Pilot Wheel's proprietor, that it was necessary for her to leave Drumkin. He was sorry to see her go and wished her well. By the time Kaemon and the others returned with the horses, Brook had changed into riding clothes. As the three Redmond knights looked on, she and Stone mounted the horses. The two rode as if they'd been born to it.

"It's as if our bones and sinews still have some of our memories, even if our minds no longer do," Stone said after they dismounted.

Stone wanted to take a room in the Pilot's Wheel, but they were all occupied, and he had to settle for a straw pallet in the kitchen, which was a separate building from the inn proper. Heggott allowed Brook to keep her attic room for one more night. The five allies planned to leave Drumkin the next morning after breaking their fast, intending to head west to the next village, Garnuff, and thence north to Blackpond, in neighboring Braant Province. They met at a small alehouse called the Monk's Pate to share their last meal in Drumkin and then went off to their separate rooms.

Stone slept fitfully on his straw pallet in the kitchen of the Pilot's Wheel, dreaming of companies of armed knights riding him down, cats the size of ponies chasing him across a cloud, and shining swords that spawned whirlwinds. The visions rose up suddenly and sharply, like leaping fish glistening in the sunlight, and they faded just as quickly, one replacing the other in a long stream of images. One moment a black-clad knight was preparing to strike off his head, and in the next, Cregg's daughter Bellanna was chasing him through a garden of roses and bellflowers. But the dream of Bellanna continued uninterrupted, as if the dream maker inside Stone's head had decided that she was to be the favorite that night.

Bellanna giggled behind him, only a few yards away. He could feel her breath on his neck, but his legs felt like anvils, and he had to drag them forward, one slow step at a time. He heard Cregg calling out from somewhere behind him, and he tried to answer, but he couldn't find his voice. Still giggling, Bellanna ran into him, knocking him to the ground. He twisted as he fell and landed on his back. She fell on top of him and began kissing him. He felt her long hair on his face as he struggled to catch his breath. He tried to tell her to stop, but he couldn't get the words out. She began licking his face and nuzzling her head against his neck, little purring sounds burbling from her throat. He tried to take a breath, but she was squeezing the air from his lungs. She licked his face again, her hair tickling his nose, and he reached up and clasped her shoulders, trying to push her away from him.

He heard a low growl, and his eyes snapped open. He gasped, and his heart nearly stopped. One of Bennald's cat-a-mountains was sprawled on top of him, licking his face.

When the big cat saw him awaken, it stopped licking and backed away. It sat on its haunches and lowered its head briefly, as if it were nodding at him.

Stone didn't move a muscle, but he could practically hear his heart hammering in his chest. He stared at the cat, who was staring back. He forced himself to breathe. His eyes still on the creature, Stone slowly sat up.

"Well then," he murmured, still eyeing the creature.

Stone thought the cat smiled at him.

"Where's Bennald?" Stone asked.

The cat's ears swiveled forward, and it opened its mouth and made a whimpering sound.

"Where's Bennald?" Stone repeated.

The cat got up on all fours and headed for the door, turning once to look back at Stone.

Stone rose, dressed quickly, and followed the beast outside, into the cool early-morning air. The sun was just rising, and the eastern sky was streaked with pink. The cat began trotting away from the courtyard, heading for an alley. Stone followed it through a series of back alleys until they came to a long, narrow passage between buildings near the southern edge of town. The alley led to Lown Street, a main thoroughfare through Drumkin. The alley was lower than the street level, and a series of steps at the far end led up to the street. The cat padded down the alley to the steps and climbed them, keeping its head low and its long body stretched out. Stone advanced behind it and watched as the beast peeked out at Lown Street. A moment later, the cat turned to look back at Stone and made a crying sound. Stone climbed the steps and took a position next to the cat, his heart thudding.

Stone waited, listening to the big cat breathe, feeling its warmth, hoping it wasn't hungry. As the sun rose over the woods east of town, he heard voices. He peered out from the alley and saw a party of three mounted Black Cloaks enter Lown Street. Just behind them, a fourth Black Cloak was at the reins of a horse-drawn cart.

The cat stood up and gave a low growl, but he stayed where he was. Stone coaxed him back down a couple of steps and then peered out again, lying against the steps and keeping his head low so he wouldn't be seen. The mounted Black Cloaks passed, and the cart came into view. In the back of the cart, behind the driver, another man was kneeling, his hands manacled behind him. The man was Bennald.

When Stone and the cat-a-mountain returned to the other end of the alley, the other three cats were waiting there. Stone swallowed and looked at them. They were looking at him expectantly, or so it seemed to him. He looked at the first cat. "What are we going to do with you and your friends? I don't think they'll give you rooms at the Pilot's Wheel."

The cat looked east, toward the forest.

"Yes, wait there, in the woods. Get some rest and something to eat, perhaps a few fat rabbits or the odd milkmaid or baker's apprentice."

The big cat purred.

"That was a jape. I mean about the milkmaid and the apprentice. Be off now before someone comes along. I'll, uh ... talk to you later. In the woods."

The cats crept stealthily out of the yard at the back of the alley and then took off for the forest.

Scarcely believing what had just transpired, Stone hurried off to tell Brook about it.

She and the three Redmond knights were in the dining room of the Pilot's Wheel, breaking their fast, when Stone arrived. He sat down and waited until the serving maid had put bacon and bread and sliced fruit in front of him. It was still early, and, except for the serving maid, the five were the only people in the room.

"We have an unexpected development," Stone announced in a low voice.

Everyone stopped eating and looked at Stone.

Stone looked at Brook. "Bennald has been captured by a group of Black Cloaks. I saw them bring him into the village no more than fifteen minutes ago. They have him in chains. They're probably bound for the lockup on Farrier Street."

Brook closed her eyes. "We can't leave without him." She opened her eyes and looked at Kaemon. "You have to help us free him."

Kaemon sighed and nodded, a slight frown marring his handsome features.

"A most unfortunate development," Elling said.

"We had better move fast," said Panwer. "And we'll need to buy another horse and saddle."

"How do you propose we free your Bennald from a locked jail?" Elling asked.

The others were silent for a moment, but then Stone smiled and said, "I think I may have an idea."

Chapter 8 - Constable Hollawill

It was still early when Stone and Brook left the Pilot's Wheel and headed for the woods east of the town, the same woods in which they had hidden their raft when they first arrived in Drumkin. Every few minutes, Stone looked over his shoulder to make sure they weren't being followed, but their luck held. They walked quickly and entered the woods a half hour after setting out. When they were deep enough into the forest that they couldn't be seen, Stone stopped and glanced around. The smell of moss and wet leaves and damp earth hung in the air.

"Now what?" Brook asked.

"We wait," Stone replied.

They didn't have long to wait. A few minutes after they entered the forest, the cat-a-mountain leader appeared and purred at Stone. The beast approached and rubbed against Stone's leg.

"He likes you," Brook said.

"A good thing, that."

A moment later, three more cats appeared, but these hung back slightly, as if they were uncertain.

"Can you communicate with them?" Brook asked.

"No, not exactly, not like Bennald. But they know we're connected to him, and they'll help us. At least I think they will."

"You'd better let them know your idea."

Stone nodded and looked at the cat-a-mountain standing in from of him. "All right, friend, here's what we plan to do …"

***

When Stone and Brook returned to the Pilot's Wheel, they saw Kaemon, Elling, and Panwer sitting at a table in the common room with two men they had never seen before, a brown-haired man about Kaemon's age and a gray-haired man in his middle years. Kaemon looked up as Stone and Brook entered and waved them over. Elling slid two more chairs to the table, and they sat down.

Kaemon introduced the other two men as Sir Nevil Munfrid and Sir Tommick Tasher, both knights of Redmond, though they were dressed as plainly as Kaemon.

"You may remember my telling you that Sir Nevil and Sir Tommick were the two knights guarding Jole Arrick's house," Kaemon said. "They, too, escaped the Ordseer's treachery."

"And there are others as well," Elling added.

"Fair tidings," Stone said.

Kaemon nodded. "A group of free Redmonders, knights and citizens both, have established an encampment, and riders are searching for more to bring into the fold. Sir Nevil and Sir Tommick want us to return with them to the camp, where I would lead the free Redmonders—at least until someone of higher rank is found." Kaemon lowered his voice. "I explained that first we must help you free your friend."

Sir Nevil, the older of the two newcomers, cleared his throat. "Sir Kaemon, you're the First Knight of the Realm, and we will follow your orders. But consider how ... unseemly it might appear for a leader such as yourself to be breaking captives out of a town jail."

"I promised our new friends I would help them," Kaemon replied. "I understand your concern, but I'll not go back on my word."

"Then let us help your friends instead," said Sir Tommick. "That way, should anything go amiss at the jail, you'll be able to disavow any knowledge of the scheme."

Kaemon shook his head. "It smacks of cravenness and deceit."

"One moment," Stone said. He looked at Kaemon. "You should go with your fellow knights as soon as you can. Brook and I can deal with the other matter."

Kaemon frowned. "Just the two of you?"

"Not quite," Stone replied.

Kaemon's frown deepened.

"Stone is right," Brook said. "You should go with your knights and lead your people."

Kaemon stared at Brook for a moment and then looked at Stone. "Surely the two of you could use help."

"We have help," Stone said. "In fact—and I mean no disrespect, Sir Kaemon—we have all the help we need."

"Very well," Kaemon said. "We'll go to the Redmonder camp and see how the people are faring.

If all is well, we'll find you again, to help in the search for Markram Meest."

"Perhaps by then we'll have found him," Brook said.

Stone rose to his feet. "In the meantime, Brook and I have some work to do to prepare."

***

It was nearly dark when Brook entered the constable's office in the front room of the building that housed the jail, which was in the northwestern part of town, a half block from The Lags. Constable Hollawill, a quiet widower who occasionally took a meal at the Pilot's Wheel and who seemed to fancy Brook, was the only one there, and Brook asked if she might speak with him.

"Of course, good lady," Constable Hollawill said. He stood up from behind a massive oak desk and fetched a chair for her. "Would you care for a cup of lemon water or some wine?"

She accepted the offer of lemon water and sat down. She saw Bennald's staff leaning against a corner, its orange gemstone glinting dully in the low light of a torch attached to a sconce just above it. The constable went to a sideboard and poured water from a pewter jug into a tankard. He handed it to her and then poured a cup of wine for himself before sitting down again behind his desk. "What brings you here tonight, Mistress Brook?" he asked.

Brook hesitated for just a moment. Stone had concocted a tale for her to tell, a gossipmonger's delight meant to distract the constable with its luridness. According to the story, the jail's new prisoner, Bennald, had once been Brook's betrothed, but her wicked sister, a fallen woman, had seduced him away from her. Brook had listened to Stone's fable and immediately rejected it. She knew Hollawill was sound and solid and a lot smarter than most people gave him credit for. He had no taste for gossip, and she had her own ideas about how to engage him in conversation.

She took a breath and began. "Early this morning, a group of black-clad knights brought in a prisoner."

Hollawill furrowed his brow. "Aye, they did. They'll be taking him back to Redmond Province tomorrow."

"I know the man."

"I confess that surprises me," Hollawill said. "I would not have expected an upstanding woman such as yourself to be associated with outlaws."

"He's no outlaw," Brook said.

"His captors claim he is."

"Do you trust these Black Cloaks?"

Hollawill hesitated a moment before answering. "They have a writ from King Harrin granting them certain authority."

"But do you trust them?"

"Whether or not I trust them is of no matter—they have their writ from the king, and if they say this prisoner is an outlaw, then I must assume he's an outlaw."

"He isn't," Brook insisted. "He's a … he's a kind of shepherd."

"So you say. And what is your connection with this shepherd?"

"We have a … a family link."

Hollawill raised an eyebrow.

"Cousins," Brook said. *Close enough*, she thought.

"Best not tell the Black Cloaks," said Hollawill. "You should go back home now and forget about your cousin."

"I won't."

"If you've come to talk to him, I must tell you that these Black Cloaks have forbidden anyone from doing so."

"I haven't come to talk to him," Brook said. "I've come to talk to you. I hoped you might be able to help in some way."

The constable shook his head. "There's nothing I can do, Mistress Brook. If you want to speak for your cousin, you'll have to go to the Red City."

"I fear he won't get there alive."

"I'm sorry, Mistress Brook."

"Do you know Sir Kaemon Krowe?"

Hollawill seemed surprised by the question. "I've met him a time or two. Why do you ask?"

"He was here in Drumkin. He and two other Redmond knights, Sir Elling and Sir Panwer, only recently left."

Constable Hollawill smiled. "I don't think so, Mistress Brook. Surely, I would have known."

"They weren't traveling as knights."

"Why not?"

"Have you heard about the trouble in the Red City?"

"I've heard rumors of trouble."

"The trouble is real and very likely spreading, even to Misheroon. Sir Kaemon told my friend Stone Falconer and me about it. If you know Sir Kaemon, you know he's an honorable man. I believe he told it true."

"Sir Kaemon is most certainly an honorable man," Hollawill said. "But this news that the First Knight of the Realm is traveling in disguise and secretly confiding in you and your friend is, I confess, difficult to credit."

"I know. But it's true, nonetheless."

"What did Sir Kaemon tell you of the troubles in Redmond?"

Brook told the constable a quick version of the story Kaemon had told her and Stone. Hollawill frowned, opened a desk drawer, and pulled out a bright white parchment. "This pledge Sir Kaemon told you about—did it look like this?"

Brook felt the blood drain from her face. "Where did you get that?" she asked Constable Hollawill.

"From the leader of the four Black Cloaks who brought in the prisoner, a man who calls himself Sir Marman. He called it a fastle pledge and said people were signing them to renew their oaths of fealty to King Harrin."

"Did you sign the thing?" she asked.

Hollawill shook his head. "No, not yet. I didn't like the look of those Black Cloaks or the notion of this pledge. They didn't take kindly to my not signing it, said they'd be talking to me about it again."

"Don't sign," Brook said. "And don't let anyone else sign them."

Constable Hollawill gave her a long look, as if he were trying to come to a decision. "That Black Cloak will tell me I'm showing disrespect to the king. And maybe I will be."

"Sir Kaemon told us the pledges were the products of dark sorcery from the Ordseer."

Hollawill stared down at the parchment and read what was written there. "I, the undersigned, do swear perfect fealty and allegiance, for now and forevermore, to …"

The constable's face had turned the color of boiled milk. He stared at the parchment a moment longer and then looked up at Brook. He looked down at the pledge again and began reading, in a low voice. "I, the undersigned, do swear perfect fealty and allegiance, for now and forevermore … to the Ordseer." He looked at Brook again. "That isn't what it said before."

Brook stood up. "May I see it?"

The constable handed it to her across the desk. She glanced at it briefly and then rolled it up and dipped one end into his wine cup, which still held an inch of wine.

There was a sound like a demon being tortured, and Brook pulled her hand away quickly. The parchment flamed, lighting up the room as a finger of red fire shot nearly to the ceiling. Just as quickly, the flame flickered and died. The parchment was gone, not a scrap or even an ash to mark its presence, only a wisp of smoke that soon faded and disappeared.

"I wouldn't drink the rest of that wine," Brook said to the astonished Constable Hollawill.

***

Stone rode west from the forest where he and Brook had met with the cat-a-mountains. He skirted the town proper, riding through an open field south of it as the sun was setting. By the time he and the four beasts reached the small grove where he planned to leave his horse, it was nearly full dark. He dismounted and took four lengths of rope from his saddlebags before heading on foot toward the west end of town, the infamous Lags. The cats padded behind him in single file.

He avoided the street, walking instead behind the buildings on the south side of Longboat Lane, which shielded him from the view of any people on the street. But to reach the jail, he and the cats would have to traverse a half block in the open. The Lags was dark, with only dull light coming through a few tavern windows or an occasional splash of illumination when a door opened. But the moon was three-quarters full, and no one who passed by would fail to see the cats unless he was exceedingly drunk.

Stone came to an alley and held up a hand to halt his four companions. The alley led to the short street that would take him to the jail, where he would duck down another alley to reach the rear of the building. He signaled to the cats and then crept quietly down the alley. He stopped at the end and looked around. There was no one about. He couldn't believe his luck. He stepped into the street and the cats followed him, two by two, turning their heads and peering into the darkness, seeing what he couldn't. He heard a skittering sound and stopped. A large gray rat dashed across the street and into another alley. One of the cats gave a low growl.

"Hush, boy," Stone whispered, and he began walking again. A door opened, and two young men, farm boys by the look of them, stumbled out. From around the corner, two ladies of the evening appeared. When they saw the young men, they licked their lips and flashed well-practiced smiles. Stone kept walking, past the young men and then past the women, to whom he nodded. They turned their smiles on him, but then he saw their painted faces freeze. One swore an oath that would have done a sailor proud, and then the two women spun around and bolted down the street as if a squadron of demons were chasing them.

Stone kept walking.

"Oiks, what're those?" he heard one of the farm boys say in a loud voice. He heard the tavern door open behind him. He glanced over his shoulder and saw a group of four men exit. They spotted the running whores a moment before they spotted the cats.

Stone kept walking.

He heard voices behind him as he crossed the street that marked the end of The Lags and headed for the jail. He heard another tavern door open and close again, and more voices were added to the hubbub. He and the cats ducked into the alley next to the jail and ran to the rear of the building. He heard footsteps running down the street they had just left and more voices. He and the cats crouched in the shadows and waited. The voices died away, and the footsteps soon faded. Stone wiped the perspiration from his brow and stood up. The rear of the stone building had four windows a foot above ground level. Each window had three iron bars set vertically. The cats ran to the last window and began purring and crying.

A face appeared at the second window and Stone heard a man swear. A pair of meaty hands grabbed the iron bars from inside the cell, and a face with a huge red nose and tiny dark eyes appeared at the window.

"Quiet," Stone hissed as he crouched down again and looked over his shoulder toward the alley.

"What in blazes is going on?" the prisoner inside the cell snapped.

"I'm here to talk to Bennald," Stone whispered, hoping the prisoner might feel some comradeship with a fellow prisoner. "Quiet down."

"I won't quiet down, you furgy wretch," the man shot back. "I'll call the constable."

"Don't do that," Stone said.

"Why shouldn't I?"

Stone produced a handful of coppers and shook them in his hand. "These are yours, and you can have more if you tend to your own business."

The man reached a hand through the bars, and Stone dropped the coppers into his sweaty palm. The man started to count them out loud.

"Quiet," Stone said, and the man muttered something under his breath.

Stone went to the window where the cat-a-mountains were congregating and saw Bennald on the other side, talking to them. When Bennald saw Stone, he nodded as if he'd been expecting him. Apparently, the cats had told him Stone was there.

"There's no time to explain," Stone whispered. "Brook is inside, trying to distract the constable. We have horses waiting."

Stone quickly tied each of the four lengths of rope around one of the iron bars. Each cat took the looped end of a rope in its mouth and started pulling. Stone watched the ropes go taut, saw the cats' muscles straining under their tawny coats. He went to the window, grabbed the bar, and started pulling with all his strength. Inside the cell, Bennald placed his waste bucket upside down below the window, stood on top of it, and pushed on the bar from inside.

Stone's mouth formed into an involuntary sneer and his upper lip trembled as he strained. His muscles felt as if they might snap. He heard Bennald grunting, heard the cats' low growls and skittering feet as they tried to gain solid purchase on the bare ground.

The bar gave way, and Stone fell backward and hit the ground. He scrambled back to the window and knelt down in front of it. "Can you squeeze through?" he asked Bennald.

Inside the cell, Bennald placed his hands on the stone windowsill and hoisted himself up. As he did, the bucket fell over, making a clanging sound as it banged against the stone floor and rolled all the way to the wall.

114

Both Brook and Constable Hollawill started at the noise. Constable Hollawill, still shaken from seeing the fastle pledge burn, rose from his chair frowning. He gave Brook a hard stare. "You should go now, Mistress Brook. I'm going to check on the prisoner."

"Don't," she said. "Please."

The outside door opened, and four black-clad knights entered the room. "We've come to question our outlaw," the leader announced.

"No one told me anything about questioning him tonight, Sir Marman," Constable Hollawill replied.

"He's our prisoner, isn't he?" Sir Marman said. "We'll question him now, if you please."

Hollawill gestured toward Brook. "As you can see, I'm busy at the moment. You'll have to come back later."

"How much later?"

Hollawill glanced quickly at Brook and then looked at Sir Marman. "Forty minutes should do. Go across the street to the sign of the Yellow Mountain and have yourselves some of their fine ale."

"And who will pay for these fine ales while you waste our time?"

Hollawill dug into a pocket and then flipped a coin to Sir Marman. "They're on me, to compensate for your trouble. There's enough for two ales each."

"What if we each want three ales?"

Hollawill flipped another coin. "Have four."

Sir Marman caught it and nodded. "Forty minutes," he said, and then he and his men left.

When they were gone, Hollawill opened the door that led back to the cells. "Come with me, Mistress Brook," he said, and then he pointed at Bennald's staff. "You had better bring that."

She picked up the staff and followed the constable through the doorway. The second cell in the row was the only one occupied; the last cell had a bar missing from its window. Hollawill unlocked the back door of the building, which opened onto a small yard, and he and Brook stepped outside. Bennald was there with the four cat-a-mountains. Brook saw Bennald's eyes go wide when he saw Hollawill and heard Hollawill's sharp intake of breath when he saw the cats.

"It's all right," Brook said. "Where's Stone?"

Bennald pointed toward the other end of the alley, where Stone was peering out. Brook went to fetch him. "The constable will help us," she told him, and they returned to the yard.

"You've put me in a pickle," Hollawill said, still eyeing the cats nervously. "But perhaps you'll help me get out of it."

"We'll do anything we can," Brook said. She looked at Stone. He nodded.

"Wait with me in my office," Hollawill said. "When those four Black Cloaks return, I'm going to arrest them and confiscate the rest of those pledges. I'll need your help."

"Bennald and I will need swords," Brook said.

"I have them," said Hollawill. "And daggers and crossbows as well." He looked at the cat-a-mountains. "Although their teeth and claws may be all the weapon we'll need."

In the end, the four ale-soaked Black Cloaks were no match for the constable and his odd band of deputies. By the time Stone, Brook, and Bennald left Drumkin, the Black Cloaks were locked up in Drumkin's cells, and the other fastle pledges that the Ordseer men had with them had been burned. The next morning, word went out throughout Drumkin that no one was to sign any pledges of any kind, and Black Cloaks found anywhere in Misheroon were to be arrested on sight.

Chapter 9 - On The Run

Despite their temporary alliance with the constable, Brook, Bennald, and Stone decided to follow through with their plan to leave Drumkin and head north in search of any sign of Markram Meest. Still wary of Black Cloaks, especially Sir Borus Renovar, they rode all night, slowly making their way over fields and farmland and eventually coming to a rough road. Just before dawn broke, they spied a wooded area a half mile from the road and made for it, intending to rest and break their fast. They dismounted and entered the woods, stopping when they came to a small clearing. Brook got some bread and salted beef and a flagon of wine from a saddlebag, and they ate a quick meal as the sun turned the sky pink.

"Where did your friends go?" Stone asked Bennald when he realized the cat-a-mountains were no longer with them.

"Hunting," Bennald said. "They're hungry, too."

"Will they be back?" Brook asked.

Bennald shook his head. "Not unless there is some need. They prefer to keep their distance from men."

"Just like you," Stone said.

Bennald gave a wry smile and nodded. "Like me. But I'll see them again one day."

They finished their meal and mounted the horses. They rode west through fields and farmland and picked up the road that led north from

Misheroon to Braant, another of Ruxland's outer provinces. They rode all morning, and just past noon they rested in a shady grove of fingen trees nestled between two farms, where they took another small meal. As they ate, Bennald told his story.

"After you left the forest, I was content enough to be by myself, with only the wild animals for company. But something—I can't explain it—nagged at me from time to time."

"You want to know who you are," Stone said. "Same as us."

Bennald shrugged. "Perhaps so. All I know is that it was an uneasy feeling that cropped up now and then that I couldn't comprehend. And then I had a dream."

Bennald paused, as if he were trying to decide something.

"Go on," Brook said softly.

"I dreamt about the two of you. It was shadowy and vague, but you were in trouble somehow, and it was up to me to help you, to rescue you."

"An odd dream, considering it was us who rescued you," Stone said.

"Yes."

"You're welcome," Stone said, but Bennald just stared at him.

"You were telling us about your dream," Brook said.

"Yes, I had the feeling that I should help you somehow, but there was someone else as well who was supposed to help."

"Who?" Stone asked.

Bennald shook his head. "In my dream, I never saw his face. We were on top of a mountain covered in mist, and he was running away. I tried to catch him, but I could not. I would get close to him, but then he would disappear into the mists again. The dream troubled me. I still don't know what to make of it."

"Perhaps it was just a dream," Stone said.

"I had the strong feeling that I should find you," Bennald said. "I began to follow the path to the stream where you put in the raft, but before I got there, I was accosted by those black-clad horsemen. They said they were from the Ordseer and wanted to question me. I told them they had no business with me, and I made to walk away. One of them drew a sword, and Taekon appeared out of the woods."

"One of the cat-a-mountains?" Brook asked.

Bennald nodded.

"A good friend to have in a sticky situation," Stone said.

"When the Black Cloaks saw him, one of them raised a crossbow," Bennald said. "Without a thought, I swung my staff and knocked the weapon out of his hand. They arrested me. Taekon would have attacked them, but I was afraid he'd be killed, so I told him to run. He didn't want to go, but he finally did."

"Good boy," Stone said.

"I was wrong not to join you two when we first met," Bennald said. "But I confess that I have no idea what we should do now."

"I'd say we have two options," Stone said. "Continue due north into Braant Territory and beyond, if necessary, and try to glean news about Pemquist's caravan or any other sign of this Markram Meest fellow. Or veer east and try to find Kaemon and his people."

"Who's Kaemon?" Bennald asked.

"Kaemon Krowe, the First Knight of the Realm of Ruxland. He's from the Red City in Redmond Province, the capital of the realm. He told us the Ordseer took over Redmond through dark magic and now has his eye on the rest of Ruxland. Kaemon and two of his friends escaped from the Red City before the Ordseer could enthrall them, and they're trying to find other fugitive Redmonders."

"I met him in Drumkin," Brook said. She held up her right hand, and the green gemstone on her signet ring flashed and sparkled. "He recognized the insignia on my ring. He said it's the mark of a virrling named Jole Arrick, also of Redmond Province, and a counselor to Ruxland's king. Kaemon said the Ordseer told him Jole Arrick had taken ill, but when Kaemon tried to locate the virrling he was nowhere to be found. Kaemon believes the Ordseer has either killed Jole Arrick or imprisoned him or has him under some enchantment."

Bennald looked at his own ring and frowned. "Why would our rings and our swords and daggers and staffs bear the insignia of this virrling?"

"That, my friend, is the question of the hour," Stone said. "Kaemon believes that to solve the puzzle and discover who we are, we must find a lad named Markram Meest, who was Jole Arrick's squire. He may have escaped from Redmond Province. He might even be with the caravan that Brook and I encountered."

"Then we must follow the trail of the caravan," Bennald said.

"I agree," said Stone. He glanced at Brook.

She nodded. "Kaemon has his quest, and we have ours."

***

Stone figured it would take about ten days to reach Blackpond, a prosperous town in Braant, the province north of Misheroon. Worried about how fast news of their recent crimes might travel, as well as who might be chasing them, they skirted towns and avoided inns, sleeping under the sky in bitterfruit groves and kepple orchards and forest clearings. Twice they purchased hay from small farms for the horses, but mostly the horses ate grass. The small store of food they had brought for themselves was soon exhausted, but Bennald knew every edible plant in field and forest, and they found enough roots and berries and wild greens to sustain them. Under Bennald's tutelage, they uprooted piles of dragonweed, mallowsill, goatsweed, and other plants and picked ripe berries and seeds and nuts from bushes and trees. The bulbous roots of the dragonweed were nearly as filling as roasted fowl, and its wing-shaped leaves tasted like baby greenleaf. The leaves, stems, roots, seeds, and flowers of the goatsweed were all edible without cooking, and the mallowsill leaves added a minty note to their meals.

Along the way, Stone and Brook told Bennald everything they had learned about Misheroon and Redmond and the other two of the realm's provinces, Blaewick and Braant, and the three cobbled together a story to tell to anyone they might encounter. According to the tale, Stone and Brook were siblings and Bennald was their cousin, the only son of their late father's late brother, and the three shared the family name "Falconer." They were on their way to Bennald's brother's farm in Hennisport, in the far north of Braant Province. This imaginary brother, who they decided to name Wilker, had recently lost his imaginary wife and their imaginary son and had invited his three imaginary blood relatives to live with him and help him run his imaginary farm.

Tutoring Bennald and perfecting their story helped to pass the time, but by the tenth day after setting out, Stone and Brook had shared with Bennald the total of their limited knowledge of civilization, and even the usually voluble Stone was tired of the sound of his own voice. After so long on the trail, their thoughts had turned to plates of roasted lamb and beef, tankards of strong ale, and beds with pillows and soft mattresses.

The trail wound through another sun-dappled forest, and by midmorning of their tenth day on the run, it had brought them to a flat plain. They continued due north, and an hour later the ground began to rise. In the distance they saw the gray outline of a low mountain range. When the ground finally leveled out again, they stopped to rest the horses before setting forth once more. Another hour's ride took them within sight of a copse of bokkin trees, where they rested and took a meal and let the horses graze. The sun was nearly overhead when they set out again, and they were soon climbing another rise.

"Where is this town of yours?" Brook asked Stone.

"Should be just beyond this ridge," Stone replied. "Or the next. Or perhaps the one after that."

"Perhaps we should invest in a map," Brook muttered.

They reached the top of the ridge and saw in the distance a town spread across a flat valley five miles to the north and slightly west. Stone grinned triumphantly and was about to say something when he spotted some movement below them. Brook and Bennald saw it at the same time, and all three quickly retreated back down the ridge and headed for a stand of trees fifty yards away. They dismounted and led the horses into the copse. Bennald petted the beasts and told them to stay calm. Stone peered out from behind a tree and scanned the ground they had just traversed. It remained empty.

"Do you think anyone spotted us?" Brook whispered.

"I don't think so," Stone replied.

"Who are they?" Bennald asked. "What are they doing?"

"I'm not sure, but it might be a military encampment," Stone said. "I think I saw weapons. I'm going up for another look."

"I'm going with you," Brook said.

Stone nodded and turned to Bennald. "You should stay with the horses."

Bennald nodded, and Stone and Brook left the grove and climbed back to the top of the ridge. They lay on their bellies and peered down the slope. Below them, five hundred yards across a shallow valley, was another, lower ridge, thinly forested. Beyond that was a half-mile-wide field that dipped and undulated and formed a shallow, rock-strewn swale before rising to form the front slope of yet another low ridge. The nearer valley was filled with thousands of milling men and hundreds of horses and wagons. Sunlight glinted off swords and pikes and battleaxes, and black-clad knights on horseback rode up and down the ranks, stopping to talk to knights clad in red and gesturing toward groups of archers and pikemen.

Stone focused on the knights clad in black. As he gazed, his vision became more acute, as if he could see with the eyes of an eagle or falcon. The shields and armor of the knights in black bore the same triangular device he had seen on the shield and armor of Sir Borus Renovar.

"Those black-cloaked rogues are Ordseer men," Stone whispered.

"How many?" Brook asked.

"I've counted sixty so far."

"What about the knights in red?"

Stone focused on a red shield leaning against a tree and saw the red star of Redmond Province in the center of the colorful roundel that signified the realm of Ruxland.

"Redmonders," Stone whispered. "In thrall to the Ordseer. There must be five hundred men-at-arms and at least ten thousand foot soldiers."

"We should warn Blackpond," Brook said.

Stone pointed to the second ridge, which lay on the other side of the quarter-mile-wide swale, opposite the Ordseer's encampment. "They already know."

Along the top of the second ridge, archers were setting up screens, men-at-arms were donning armor, and grooms and squires were preparing horses.

"There's going to be a fight," Brook murmured.

"Aye," Stone replied.

"Do you think this thrall army attacked Drumkin?"

Stone shook his head. "I'm guessing Constable Hollawill spread the word about the fastle pledges and the Misherooners were on their guard. I hope so, anyway."

"Let's go," Brook said. "We'll take a meal in Blackpond and be on our way before the battle is over."

Stone shook his head. "You and Bennald go to Blackpond, and I'll meet you there later. I want to see what happens here."

"Why?"

"Those are the Ordseer's men down there. The Ordseer may have something to do with us losing our memories. I want to see what unfolds."

"You're going to fight, aren't you?"

Stone shook his head. "No. I'm going to observe. You and Bennald go to the first inn you come to that has an animal or a flower in its name and wait for me."

Brook sighed. "All right. We'll wait."

"Be careful. The people will be on a war footing and may be suspicious of strangers."

"You be careful," Brook said.

Stone raised an eyebrow. "I'm touched by your concern."

Brook frowned and made her way back down the slope to rejoin Bennald.

Chapter 10 - Blaewick

Sir Nevil and Sir Tommick, the two Redmond knights who had found Kaemon, Elling, and Panwer in Drumkin, took them directly to a secret encampment at the northern tip of the Horn of Misheroon. The Horn was a long, narrow finger that extended north for three hundred miles along Misheroon's eastern border with Redmond and Blaewick, bordering Braant Province on the west. The camp was in the Pallopey Mountains, a low range of hills that rose from the plains of Toth and extended northeast through eastern Misheroon, up into the Horn, and thence into the eastern part of Lower Braant before flattening out again in the Great Northern Wilderness.

The camp, an array of tents and pavilions and hastily constructed shacks, was just west of the border between Misheroon and Blaewick Province and also near the border with Braant. Blaewick, the province Kaemon had visited a few months earlier, was only eleven miles away, directly to the east. Kaemon had met there with a group of frustrated farmers not long before and persuaded them to cease their nascent tax rebellion. Many of those farmers had fled with their families after the Ordseer's takeover of Redmond, and most · had sought refuge in the camp. The camp was also home to nearly three hundred Redmond knights, a hundred or so pikemen, and a few dozen archers, all of whom had escaped from the realm without signing fastle pledges.

The arrival of Sir Kaemon Krowe, First Knight of the Realm of Ruxland, sparked excitement approaching jubilation among the people in the camp. Knights, soldiers, and farm families alike welcomed him as their leader. His first action was to form the three hundred knights into three companies, one under his direct command, one under Elling, and the third under Panwer.

His second action, five days after arriving, was to take fifty knights from his own company across the border into Blaewick Province on a scouting mission. He reasoned that if he could secure that remote region, it might serve as a foothold for retaking Redmond Province. He also knew that three hundred knights, a handful of foot soldiers, and five hundred farm families were hardly enough to secure an entire province, even one as small as Blaewick. But occupying even a part of it might give the refugees some hope. Besides, the people needed to eat, and the camp was already on short rations.

Kaemon, the fifty knights, and a young farmer named Drisser Neff, who knew the area well and claimed he could handle a sword, set out for the border just after sunrise. They crossed into Blaewick Province two hours later. There was no sign of dark sorcery, and nothing seemed amiss as they followed a stream through a wooded area. Sunlight filtered through the leafy canopy, birds sang and flitted through the trees, and squirrels went about their usual business, gathering nuts and chasing each other around trees. Nevertheless, it was difficult to relax knowing they were in an area that might be under the sway of the Ordseer's magic, and the men kept a sharp lookout for any sign of trouble.

Another hour took them to the end of the woods and into a meadow of green grass and tiny yellow wildflowers. A bright sun peeked in and out of slow-moving white clouds, but the pleasant day didn't obscure the fact that they had reentered a country under siege.

"This meadow is part of the Snaydon farm," said Drisser Neff, who was riding next to Kaemon.

"Toyne Snaydon?" Kaemon asked.

Drisser nodded. "He and his family made it out and are back in the camp. It's his cows been supplying most of the milk for the children. He sneaks back here now and again to steal a look at his property, but he won't go no farther than right where we are now. Speaking of which, Sir Kaemon, what will we do if we run across any Ordseer men? Or any … ah …"

"Thralls," Kaemon finished.

"Aye, thralls."

"We'll retreat. I want information, not battle. The men know my mind."

"What if thralls attack us and retreat is impossible?"

Kaemon looked the young farmer in the eye. "You have leave to defend yourself. We all do."

Drisser nodded and turned his gaze straight ahead.

The company rode at a trot across the meadow until they came to a sizable stone farmhouse and a number of smaller outbuildings. Kaemon ordered

130

half the men to dismount and told the others to spread out and keep watch. "We'll have a look around," Kaemon said to Drisser. "Look for any signs that the Ordseer's men have been here."

The dismounted knights spread out to check barns and stables and storage sheds, and Kaemon and Drisser and a young knight named Pitt Waulker entered the farmhouse to look around. The front door was unlocked.

"Toyne must've figured they'd get in one way or another, so he probably left it unlocked to save the door from being bashed in," Drisser explained.

"Have you been here before?" Kaemon asked as they stepped through the doorway and into the front hall.

"A time or two," Drisser replied. "Toyne's eldest daughter is a, um, acquaintance of mine."

Kaemon tried to suppress a grin. He cleared his throat and said, "You'll know if anything's amiss?"

"I'll know."

A thorough search found nothing amiss. They went back outside, and Drisser walked to the well behind the house and drew up a bucket of water. He tasted a drop, and then another, and then took a small sip. He smacked his lips like a wine merchant sampling a new vintage and pronounced the water free of poison or contamination. "I don't believe the Ordseer's men or any thralls have been here," he said.

"Do you think Toyne would be willing to return?" Kaemon asked.

Drisser shrugged. "Mayhap. But not without a hundred of your knights standing ready to protect him."

"How far to the next farm?" Kaemon asked.

Drisser pointed eastward. "Just over that rise. The Moalner place."

"Mount up," Kaemon ordered his men.

They checked more than twenty farms, all intact and undisturbed, before Drisser told them they were nearing the village of Timmery.

"That's where we met with the Blaewick farmers a month and a half back," Kaemon said. "It was outside, in the town square."

"I heard about your parley," Drisser said. "They said you were fair-minded, mostly. Said you promised to make their case to the king."

"I did. It was on the very same day I first met the Ordseer and found out about his fastle pledges."

A half hour later, they spotted Timmery, a sizable village that sprawled on the other side of a stream. A wooden bridge crossed the stream, and a narrow path wound from the far end of the bridge to the village, passing a cluster of large, half-timbered buildings on the left and a smaller group of thatch-roofed houses on the right before ending at the village square. Rows of one- and two-story structures bordered the square and included shops, a smithy, an inn, and a tavern. A small, open structure of dun-colored bricks stood in the center of the square. It was there that Kaemon had listened to the complaints and pleas of the Blaewick farmers only seven weeks earlier.

When they reached the bridge, Kaemon raised his hand to call a halt. Everyone peered at the village, scanning the streets and buildings. There was no one about.

"What do you make of it?" Kaemon asked Drisser.

"Some of the villagers came with us and are back in the camp. I don't know what might have become of the others."

Kaemon ordered half his company to remain where they were, and he led the other half across the bridge and into the village.

A search of the buildings took the men two hours. They found no people—not even a dog or a cat—but they discovered barrels of ale and some wheels of cheese that had been aging in the kitchen of the Iron Rose Inn. Kaemon posted guards and let the men eat and drink their fill. When the knights were finished, they returned to the opposite side of the stream and traded places with the men waiting there. As the newcomers poured their ales and sliced great wedges of cheese, Kaemon and Drisser pored over a rough map Drisser had drawn on a white cloth using splinters of charred wood from the inn's fireplace.

There was a commotion in the back room, and twenty knights leaped up from their chairs and drew swords. The door to the back room flew open, and two knights who had been rolling up a barrel of ale from the undercroft burst through, shoving another man in front of them.

"We found him lurking in the cellar," one of the knights said.

The man they had found was short and slender, with brown hair tinged with gray. He looked terrified. When he spotted Kaemon, his brown eyes went wide. "Sir Kaemon?"

Kaemon stood up and stared at him. "Thig? Thig Grennell?"

The man nodded.

"Let him go," Kaemon said. "This is Thig Grennell, the king's wistlord."

The two men holding the man shared a quick glance and then released him. "Beg your pardon, Sir Wistlord," one of the knights said.

"I didn't sign," Thig said to Kaemon. "I never signed. They tried to make me, but I wouldn't. I refused."

Kaemon took Thig's arm and steered him toward an empty table in the far corner of the dining room. "Come, Thig, we must speak."

They sat at the table, and the other knights returned to their ales and conversations. Drisser Neff brought a tankard of ale and a plate of food for Thig, and Kaemon introduced them.

"Thank you for your kindness," Thig said to Drisser.

"You're welcome, sir. I never met a wistlord before," Drisser said before returning to his table.

Thig took a long drink and then looked at Kaemon. "I'm glad to see you, Sir Kaemon. It gives me some hope. I had nearly run out of it."

"What's happening in Redmond?" Kaemon asked. "What are the tidings from the Red City?"

"The tidings are ill," Thig replied. "With few exceptions, only thralls and Black Cloaks remain.

The thralls go about their business like ghosts, with dead eyes and grim faces, and the Black Cloaks ride around looking for empty homes to loot and free people to intimidate."

"Ill tidings, indeed."

"I tried to find you the night the scales tipped, but the Red City was a maelstrom. People were waving those damned fastle pledges as if they'd lost their wits, threatening others with harm if they didn't sign. I've never seen the like of it. I saw people who refused to sign pledges cut down by their own neighbors. Others tried to escape with whatever they could carry in their carts or on their backs. Groups of resisters commandeered wagons and horses as they could. Pledge signers formed their own groups and fought them. It was ghastly."

"Elling, Panwer, and I barely escaped with our own skins in one piece," Kaemon said. "Before we left, we tried to find Jole Arrick. His house was guarded, but I sneaked into it to search. Jole wasn't there. Nor was he on the Ordseer's carrack. The Ordseer lied."

"Jole may be dead," Thig said.

"I know. Yet I have a strong feeling that he isn't."

Thig peered at Kaemon a moment, as if trying to read his thoughts. "Why? What else do you know?"

"Not long ago, we met two people, a man and a woman, who call themselves Stone and Brook," Kaemon said. "Both wear rings bearing Jole's insignia, and the man has a sword with the same symbol. The woman has a dagger with it."

Thig's eyes went wide. "Where are they? What's their connection to Jole?"

"We left them in Drumkin, in Misheroon Province. As for their connection to Jole, they have no idea."

"How can that be?" Thig asked.

"They have no memories of themselves, and they've never heard of Jole Arrick. They don't know why they bear his symbol."

Thig stared at Kaemon. "But this is astonishing."

Kaemon nodded. "There's more. A third member of their group, a man with no memory who calls himself Bennald, was captured by Black Cloaks and brought to Drumkin in chains while we were there. Stone and Brook were planning to break into the Drumkin jail to free him."

"The world is going mad," Thig murmured. "Do any of these three have any … abilities?"

"They didn't say, but there's something about them that makes me suspect they do."

"Wandremes," Thig said.

Kaemon cocked his head at him. "Wandremes?"

"There are ancient tales of wandering enchanters with no memories. They were called wandremes. Some of the old tales are comical, with a wandreme getting in and out mischief. In other of the tales, they perform heroic acts. In some of the stories, they do harm and evil."

"I have a strong sense that these three have good hearts," Kaemon said.

"Yet you also said that two of them were planning to break into the Drumkin jail to free the third."

"Aye, but I count enemies of the Black Cloaks as friends of the realm."

"What else were they planning?" Thig asked.

"If Stone and Brook succeeded in freeing Bennald, they'll be heading north, looking for Markram Meest. More than one person told us of seeing a lad who looked like him on the road. If we can find Markram, he may have knowledge of what happened to Jole."

Thig closed his eyes for a moment. When he opened them again, he looked as if he might weep. "Sir Kaemon, I have tidings about Markram Meest. Ill tidings."

Kaemon felt the bottom drop out of his gut. "What is it?"

"He's dead. Markram Meest is dead. I saw him killed. He had been hiding, but the Ordseer knew he was Jole's squire and was determined to find him. Some Black Cloaks did find him, and they tried to make him sign one of the fastle pledges. He refused. They tried again, too insistently, and he drew on them. They cut him down. It was in the courtyard of the Rose Castle, and I witnessed it from my quarters. That's when I decided to leave. I packed some things and headed here the next evening."

Kaemon was stunned. He had placed a great deal of hope in finding Markram and perhaps discovering what had become of Jole Arrick. With Markram dead and Jole seemingly vanished into the air—or dead himself—hope was dwindling.

137

"We must find these three who bear Jole's insignia," Thig said.

Kaemon looked at him and raised an eyebrow. "We?"

"I'd like to go with you."

Kaemon nodded. "Perhaps a wistlord can solve the mystery of what happened to them. If they freed Bennald, they'll be in Braant by now. They meant to travel from Drumkin to Blackpond on lesser-used roads, and then to Sevnpools, and Greenport after that."

"What if they failed to free their companion?"

"I have a feeling they didn't fail," Kaemon said. "But I'll send Elling and Panwer to Sevnpools and thence to Greenport. You and I will ride directly to Greenport, make our inquiries, and wait for them. If neither party has any luck, we'll continue north and try to pick up the trail."

Kaemon finished his ale and stood up. "We should go. There's a camp on the other side of Redmond's border with Misheroon, with three hundred loyal Redmond knights, two hundred foot soldiers, and two thousand Blaewickers. We'll make our plans and leave as soon as we can. One way or another, I won't rest until we've brought the Ordseer down."

Chapter 11 - Battle

Brook and Bennald entered Blackpond through the town's south gate and looked for an inn with a flower or animal in its name. They soon came across the Hare's Hollow, where they took rooms and stabled the horses, figuring Stone would enter the town from the same direction and spot the place. They took a meal in the common room, and as they were enjoying their ale and meat, a man dressed in a blue cloak entered by himself and took a table adjacent to theirs.

The man was large, taller than Bennald, with too much weight on his bones, as if his belly was out of proportion with his small head and short legs. He had a hairless skull and a pale complexion, as if he avoided the sun. After he was served, he turned to Brook and Bennald and flashed a smile.

"Greetings," he said in a hearty voice. "My name is Melkin Rantolle. I'm passing through Blackpond on my way to Grymstone."

Brook wanted to remain as inconspicuous as possible and had no desire to make conversation with strangers, but ignoring him might have seemed rude and drawn more attention. "My name is Brook, and this is my cousin Bennald," she said before turning back to her meal.

"Travelers are you?" Melkin asked.

Brook smiled and nodded, as politely as she could manage.

"Where are you coming from?" Melkin asked.

"From near Drumkin," Brook said after a moment's hesitation. She wished Stone, a far better storyteller than she, were there to mislead their troublesome new acquaintance. She was glad they had rehearsed their tale, and she told Melkin they were on their way to Bennald's brother's farm in the far north of Braant. "We're waiting for my brother. Then we'll be off."

"Let's hope the coming battle goes well for the locals," Melkin said. He glanced around at the other patrons and shrugged. "Though no one hereabout seems much worried, do they?"

"No," Brook said.

"Don't you think that's odd?"

Brook shrugged. "I wouldn't know."

"Perhaps they have confidence in their soldiers. I hear the numbers are evenly matched, which will give the Braant defenders an advantage."

Brook focused on her meal and said nothing.

"Did you say you came here from Drumkin?" Melkin asked.

"I said near there," Brook replied.

Melkin leaned toward Brook and said in a low voice, "You must have heard about the dark sorcerer who escaped from Drumkin's jail a week and a half ago, eh?"

As Brook was about to tell him they hadn't heard any such thing, Bennald blurted out, "He was no dark sorcerer," before Brook could reply.

Melkin eyed Bennald with a curious squint and a vague smile. "Who was he, then?" he asked at length.

Bennald's ruddy face turned a shade ruddier. "I, I, I don't …"

"What my cousin means is that we pay no mind to idle rumors," Brook said.

"The escape in Drumkin was no rumor," said Melkin.

Brook shrugged. "Perhaps not. But we heard the same tale from another traveler, only in his telling the escaped man was an innocent shepherd, falsely accused."

"Was he?" Melkin said. "Well, we all like a good story, don't we?"

Brook stood up. "Now it's time for us to take our leave and get some rest."

Bennald, his face still flushed, pushed away from the table and stood next to Brook.

"Do stay a while longer," Melkin said.

"I think not," Brook replied.

"I may be able to help you."

"Good night to you, sir," Brook said quickly, and she made to move off.

"Wait," Melkin said. "I said I may be able to help you."

"We need no help, thank you."

"Yes, you do, whether you know it or not." He gestured toward the chair Brook had been sitting in. "Please. Sit a while and hear me out."

Brook clenched her fists, wishing she were clenching her dagger in one of them. "We'll hear you out, but we'll stand, thank you, so say your say and be quick, if you please."

"Very well," Melkin said. "Here's how I can help you …"

***

After watching Brook and Bennald ride northwest toward a gap in the ridgeline that would take them to Blackpond, five miles away, Stone mounted his own horse and rode east. He rode two or three miles, turned north, and climbed the ridge again. He descended the other side of the ridge, continued north for another three miles, and then turned west. He planned to approach the Braant defenders' camp from the rear. Despite what he had told Brook, he was prepared to offer his sword to the Braanters to help defend Braant Province against the Ordseer.

He spotted a two-horse cart heading south from Blackpond to the defenders' ridge and rode toward it. When the driver saw him coming, he stopped and drew a sword. Stone held up a hand to signal his peaceful intentions and dismounted. He saw that the cart was filled with sheaves of arrows.

"Who are you and what do you want?" the driver demanded.

"My name is Stone Falconer, and I want to talk to one of your captains. I know something about the enemy across the way."

"And how might that be?"

"Some of the enemy knights, the ones in black, are loyal to a sorcerer who calls himself the Ordseer. I fought one of these Black Cloaks a few months back. The foot soldiers and the other men-at-arms are Redmonders who are thralls to the Ordseer."

The cart driver furrowed his brow and took a moment to ponder what Stone had told him. Then he picked up a loaded crossbow and pointed it at Stone's chest. "You ride ahead of me, and not too fast. Don't do anything I won't like, or I'll put a bolt through your neck."

Stone spurred his horse and positioned himself a few yards in front of the cart, and then he and his escort proceeded to the north slope of the ridge, which was crowded with nearly as many foot soldiers and men-at-arms as the invaders' encampment less than a mile to the south.

When they arrived at the camp, Stone stood by while the cart driver and a pair of squires unloaded a couple of hundred sheaves of arrows. When they were finished, the driver, whose name was Zamp, took Stone to see a captain, whose name was Nollup. When Zamp told Nollup what Stone had told him, the captain took Stone to a small tent to hear his story.

The captain sat behind a small field desk, and Stone sat on a low stool in front of it. Stone accepted a tankard of wine from the captain and related the tale that he and Brook and Bennald had concocted before telling him a quick version of what Kaemon had told them about the trouble in Redmond. He concluded by telling the captain that he had come to warn the Braanters that they were facing sorcerer's men and soldiers who had been placed under a dark enchantment.

Captain Nollup was skeptical. "As it happens, I know Sir Kaemon," he said when Stone was finished. "Describe the man to me."

Stone did, to Captain Nollup's grudging satisfaction.

"We had heard there was some trouble in Redmond," Nollup said. "There was no shortage of rumors about it."

"What I told you came directly from Sir Kaemon," Stone said. "He met the Ordseer and saw the results of his sorcery. He and his two friends barely escaped. He's trying to find more of his knights who might have gotten away. They mean to take back Redmond and try to protect the other provinces."

"The other provinces can take care of themselves," Nollup said. "We have our own fighting men here in Braant, and they're as capable as any Redmonders. The other provinces do as well. Except for Blaewick, of course."

"Your soldiers may be no match for dark sorcery. And your men, though they're Braanters, will be fighting their own countrymen, thralls though they are."

"There's not much friendliness between Redmond Province and Braant," Nollup said.

"Still, you're all part of Ruxland."

"Perhaps that will be changing now that Redmond has marched into Braant."

Stone had a sudden thought. "Perhaps that's what the Ordseer wants. To create trouble between the provinces."

"We'll see," Nollup said. "What do you mean to do?"

"I mean to observe. If I may."

Nollup glanced at the sword hanging at Stone's side. "No stomach for fighting?"

"Not this time. I promised my … sister that I would only watch."

Captain Nollup stood up. "Come along then. We expect the enemy to attack within the hour. I'll take you to a place where you can observe. You'll remain there until the battle is done. Then we'll talk again. Do you understand?"

"I understand," Stone said. "Thank you." He resisted the urge to ask the captain what the Braant troops would do if the battle didn't go their way, but there wouldn't be much choice but to retreat to Blackpond, man the city's walls, and wait for help to arrive from the Braant capital, Baymont, fifty miles to the north.

Captain Nollup found some bread and cheese and a flagon of water for Stone and then led him to a rise on the far left of the Braant position, where the ridge curved slightly toward the enemy ridge and rose sixty feet above the main ridgeline, forming a lightly wooded hillock. The knoll was aswarm with a two-hundred-strong company of archers wielding longbows, and hundreds of sheaves of arrows were neatly stacked or leaning up against tree trunks. Some of the archers had descended partway down the southern slope of the hillock to take positions behind large boulders that were strewn there.

The archers, who were also armed with swords and daggers, eyed Stone suspiciously when he arrived with Captain Nollup, but after the captain explained that the visitor was there only to observe, they mostly ignored him. Stone found a position behind an unclaimed boulder and waited. The archers finished their preparations, setting screens and heavy stakes where there were no trees or boulders to stand behind, and waited with him.

They didn't have long to wait. It was three hours past noon when they heard the sound of drums booming from the south. Stone, who had been sitting atop his boulder and bantering with one of the younger archers, stood up and peered at the opposite ridge. Moments later, six hundred red-clad Redmond knights, armed with swords and lances and protected by chain mail, rode down the slope and formed three lines of two hundred men each. The lines were stacked one behind the other, their men spread out in the center of the nearly mile-long field that lay like a giant trencher between the two opposing ridges. When the Redmonders were in position, two lines of heavily armored Black Cloaks emerged from the woods and streamed down the shallow slope, riding two by two on armored mounts. One group of Black Cloaks, thirty strong, rode to the far left flank of the position, and the other group, equally manned, rode to the far right. The Black Cloaks in both groups waved their swords in the air, but as far as Stone could tell, none was armed with a spear or lance.

At a signal from a man who must have been the leader, the two squadrons of Black Cloaks at the flanks spurred their mounts forward at a walk. When they had traveled twenty yards, the first line of mounted Redmonders started forward. The second line followed at a ten-yard interval, and then the third.

146

On the Braant side, the archery captains gave orders, and the bowmen took their positions behind trees and screens and boulders, unfastening sheaves of arrows and planting them in the ground within easy reach. Stone looked to the west from his position on the far left flank and saw what must have been two thousand Braant archers ranged along the ridge in fortified defensive positions. Behind them were six thousand pikemen, ready to step forward to blunt a mounted charge or repel enemy foot soldiers should any survive the storms of arrows that were about to rain down on them. In the flats behind the ridge, squires and pages were helping knights and men-at-arms don their armor, and grooms were readying their horses. Stone looked at the advancing Black Cloaks and Redmonders and wondered what magic the Ordseer intended to deploy to aid them. But except for the strangely impassive demeanor of the Redmonders, there was no sign of sorcery. The Ordseer was probably still in Redmond, tending to his thralls there and letting his Black Cloaks manage events here. Stone wondered if the Black Cloaks also were thralls.

When the mounted Redmond knights had advanced five hundred yards, about halfway across the swale, the flanking Ordseer men stopped, and the two squadron leaders each raised a hand. The Redmonders behind them halted, maintaining their orderly triple line. One of the Black Cloaks cantered out to the middle of the field and turned to face the first Redmond line. He raised his sword over his head, looked right and then left, and swung the sword down. All three lines of Redmonders surged forward at a quick walk, passing the Black Cloak who had given the order to advance. They soon switched to a trot, and moments later they spurred their horses to a canter.

When the knights were three hundred yards from the defenders' ridge, the Braant archery captains gave the order to fire. A cloud of two thousand arrows rose up from the Braant side and fell on the oncoming Redmonders seconds later. The bodkin-tipped arrows penetrated leather and cloth and chain mail, and men and horses tumbled to the grassy swale. Five or six seconds after the first volley of arrows, a second volley darkened the sky before dropping into the Redmond lines. Horses whinnied and reared and went down, thrashing and tumbling and crashing into the earth and sending their riders sprawling and rolling like rag dolls hurled by wanton children. The noise from injured and dying horses sent a shiver down Stone's back, but not a sound was heard from the Redmonders, and not one of them turned back.

The Black Cloaks on each flank spurred their horses and galloped up to the Redmonders, pointing and shouting orders and urging them on. The Redmonders closed ranks, filling gaps left by their dead and wounded comrades, and then charged forward at a full gallop. Another volley of arrows rained down, piercing chain mail and horseflesh, but the missiles bounced off the heavy plate armor of the black-clad Ordseer men, who once again fell behind the storming Redmonders.

The three lines of horsemen dissolved into a long, ragged blur, its lead elements now only a hundred yards from the Braanters' defensive position. A final massed volley of arrows fell, taking out more men and horses, and then the Braant archers began to aim at individual targets. Stone watched as thousands of arrows were loosed at the remaining few hundred Redmond knights. The twanging of bowstrings and the hissing of arrows filled the air and mingled with the sound of bodkin points penetrating chain mail and flesh and the ongoing din of the terrified horses.

The company of archers that Stone had joined was out in the open, no longer feeling the need to hide behind trees or screens or boulders. The surviving Redmonders had coalesced toward the middle of the swale, too far for accurate shooting by Stone's group, but some of the archers had climbed atop the larger boulders and were still loosing arrows.

And then it was over. A few dozen Redmonders had made it partway up the slope, but none had made it to the top. The Braant archers had cut them down as they came, completing the slaughter. A half dozen or so had been hit but were still alive, and these were taken to the physician's tent to be treated. Horses still able to run headed for the Braant side, where they were captured and tended to.

A cheer went up from the Braanters, and the archers clapped one another on the back and began regaling one another with tales of prowess and numbers of arrows shot. Pages brought up jugs and

149

small casks of wine and ale for the parched longbowmen, and the fletchers' boys brought up more sheaves of arrows. The battle had lasted fifteen minutes.

Stone looked down at the field and the hundreds of dead men-at-arms and horses. He thought about Kaemon, who had led these men before the Ordseer placed them under his dark enchantment. He wondered how many others were under enthrallment and ready to do the Ordseer's bidding. Perhaps it didn't matter. The hardy Braanters had proven that the Ordseer, for all his sorcery, could be defeated in conventional battle.

Stone saw the black-clad Ordseer knights heading back to the opposite ridge. None had come close to the Braant position, and their heavy armor had protected them and most of their horses from the volleys of arrows shot by the Braant archers. The Black Cloaks rode up the slope of the other ridge and disappeared into the woods.

Stone accepted a tankard of wine from one of the archers, and then pages brought platters of crusty bread and wedges of hard cheese. The archers were laughing and boasting like boys, and any suspicions they may have had regarding the armed stranger in their midst seemed to have evaporated.

Stone finished his wine and walked halfway down the south-facing slope before climbing on top of a boulder. He scanned the field of battle, trying to blot out the awful sounds from the dying horses. He saw movement among the fallen, but none of the wounded men made a sound. He saw something stirring on the far ridge and waited. The Redmonders would no doubt be sending wagons under a flag of truce to collect their dead and wounded.

He caught the glint of sunlight off metal. Moments later, he saw Redmond pikemen emerge from the trees and head down the far slope. The mounted Black Cloaks reappeared and spread themselves along the bottom of the ridge, gesturing and shouting orders, as they had done before. Under the direction of the Ordseer men, the streams of Redmond pikemen flowing down the slope arranged themselves into four battalions of about two thousand men each. Each battalion consisted of two ranks, and together the mass of foot soldiers formed two lines of four thousand men each, spread evenly across the mile-long field. Stone peered at the battalion on the enemy's right flank and saw that half of its front rank was made up of archers. That meant about five hundred bowmen were there, and most likely another five hundred were on their far left flank. That made one thousand archers and around seven thousand pikemen armed with twelve-foot-long, iron-tipped pikes along with short swords, daggers, and small shields.

The Braant side, which had suffered virtually no casualties in the cavalry assault, had two thousand archers in defensive positions, six thousand pikemen behind them, and a thousand men-at-arms. Stone was baffled. Unless the Ordseer or his minions deployed some kind of magic, the oncoming fight would be another slaughter. Stone looked up, half expecting to see a squadron of fire-breathing dragons. But all he saw was a near-cloudless blue sky and a bright sun shining down and illuminating the swale, which was strewn with dead and wounded Redmonders. Their freshly let blood was seeping into the earth and turning patches of grass red.

As their still-fresh comrades formed behind them, some of the wounded Redmond knights crawled forward toward the Braant side. When a number of them were close, small groups of Braant knights rode down the slope, followed by groups of litter bearers. As the knights stood by, ready to protect them, the litter men put the wounded Redmonders on stretchers and hauled them back up the slope and then down the other side to the physician's tent. A few more wounded crawled forward and were collected by the Braanters, but by then drums on the other side of the swale had begun to boom.

Stone walked back up to the top of the ridge and saw the Braant archers picking up sheaves of arrows and scurrying back into position.

"We'll have more fine hunting today," one of them said, not very enthusiastically.

No one responded. The Braanters looked grim. They gathered their sheaves of arrows, took up their positions, and waited. Stone went to his boulder and waited with them.

By now the Redmond battle lines were formed, the men standing nearly shoulder to shoulder in two ranks, with small gaps between the four battalions. The scarlet pennons of Redmond fluttered against the blue sky, and other flag bearers raised the colors of the four battalions and the forty individual companies they comprised. The sixty black-clad Ordseer knights formed into five groups and rode to their positions, fifteen Black Cloaks on each flank, and ten filling each of the three gaps between the Redmond battalions. One of the Black Cloaks shouted an order, and the drummers changed their rhythm.

The front rank of Redmonders stepped out, keeping pace with the drums, and moments later the second rank followed, eight thousand men marching toward the waiting Braant defenders, their swords and pikes glinting in the bright sunlight. It took them five minutes to advance five hundred yards, halfway across the swale. On the Braant side, the archers picked up arrows and fit them to bowstrings. Another minute passed, bringing the Redmonders within four hundred yards. Stone felt a thrill run down his spine. Despite the horror and bloodshed that was only moments away, the sight of eight thousand red-clad archers and pikemen striding forth under a bright sun in perfectly dressed ranks was a stirring sight.

A minute later, the Braant archery captains gave the order to fire. Clouds of arrows sprang forth from the longbows and descended on the marching ranks. The pikemen raised their scarlet shields to protect their faces, but some of the two thousand arrows found their marks. As before, the missiles bounced off the plate armor of the Ordseer men and their horses, but the Redmond pikemen lacked even chain mail, although chain mail had done little to protect their knights during the first assault. With the Redmonders stretched out in two long, thin lines, and the distance still too far to allow aiming at individual targets, many of the arrows overshot or landed in the gaps between the battalions. But not all. Each time a volley flew, Redmonders went down. Yet still they came—until the Ordseer men stopped them.

Stone let out a breath and relaxed his muscles. Perhaps the attackers would retreat and head back to Redmond. Perhaps the Ordseer would take to his ship and return to whatever cursed land he came from.

The Black Cloaks cantered forward and then turned toward the Redmonders and called a halt. The red-clad archers and pikemen stopped, even as Braant arrows continued to rain down on them. Stone climbed up to the top of his boulder and surveyed the scene. The Black Cloaks were directing the foot soldiers to close ranks and dress the lines. The men moved sideways to fill the gaps, but the unrelenting Braant arrows made more gaps. The Black Cloaks shouted and gesticulated as arrows shattered against their plate armor, and the Redmonders sidled again, holding their shields in front of them.

Stone turned his gaze to the far right of the Braant position, a mile west of where he stood. The ridge was somewhat lower there, and it curved slightly in toward the swale. A company of two hundred Braant archers was pouring down the slope where it hooked in. As the Redmonders continued to dress their lines, the Braant archers set stakes and screens along the lower section of their slope while

154

fletchers' helpers brought them more sheaves of arrows.

As Stone watched them deploy, a large wagon drawn by a team of oxen appeared at the top of the ridge above them. Two men unyoked the oxen and led them away while a dozen other men, holding ropes tied to the vehicle, slowly let it roll down the slope. When it reached the bottom, the men positioned the eighteen-foot-long wagon with one side facing the swale. Thick, foot-wide oak planks had been bolted to that side, and now a half dozen bowmen were climbing aboard and taking positions behind the planks. Another wagon appeared and was lowered in the same manner. It was positioned next to its mate but slightly further out, creating a small salient from which the Braant bowmen could shoot arrows into the Redmonders left flank.

As a third wagon was positioned, the Black Cloaks gave the order to advance, and the Redmonders resumed their march. Thousands had already been cut down, and the two lines had contracted toward the center. But their ranks remained straight, and the marchers stepped out briskly, changing pace or direction only to step around a dead horse or over a downed knight from the earlier assault.

Stone marveled at the lack of noise. There must have been hundreds, maybe thousands, of wounded, but the Redmonders were all silent. No wounded man begged for mercy or called for his mother or cried out in pain. Stone could hear the massed footsteps of the marchers and the voices of the Black Cloaks shouting orders, but his hearing had not attained the acuteness that his vision had, and he couldn't make out what the Ordseer men were yelling. He looked behind him, but no war wagons appeared at the top of the ridge. The Braant left was higher than the right, and the attackers would be hard-pressed to climb the rocky slope below without being shot.

Or so he hoped. He made a fist and then opened his hand and spread his fingers a few times. He unsheathed his sword and cut the air with it. It felt good in his hand.

"You going to run down there and skewer one of those Redmonders or one of those Black Cloaks?" one of the archers asked.

Stone shook his head. "I'll let you and your mates do the skewering. But just in case any of them make it this far ..."

"They won't," another archer said.

Stone nodded, sheathed his sword, and turned his attention back to the field.

The rain of arrows continued unabated. As color bearers fell, another man would pick up the banner or pennon until he went down in his turn. Stone saw one flag fall and rise again five times as the Redmonders swept forward.

They were now close enough for the Braant archers to fire at single targets, but the Redmond archers on both flanks had set their screens, and they were shooting back at the Braant men from behind them. As archers on the flanks of both sides exchanged shots, the Braant archers in the middle of the ridge concentrated their fire on the attackers' center. On the Braant right, the archers on the slope of the incurving ridge and in the three wagons at the bottom fired into the Redmonders' left flank, quickly taking out the opposing archers and dropping pikemen by the score.

A company of Braant men-at-arms swept down the west slope and joined the archers, who left their defensive positions on the lower slope and inside the wagons and headed toward the Redmond left flank. A section of Redmond pikemen turned and charged the archers, but the men-at-arms met their attack with swords and lances. A dozen horses went down, and the unhorsed men-at-arms continued the fight with swords, slashing at the enemy pikes as the Redmonders thrust at them. The Braant knights still on horseback swung swords or jabbed with their long lances. The Redmond pikemen kept coming, fighting until they were either dead or too grievously wounded to fight on.

The Braant men-at-arms still on horses spotted the Black Cloaks that had been covering the Redmonders' left flank. They had sat their horses at a distance and hadn't come to the aid of their pikemen. The Braant men-at-arms gave chase, but the Black Cloaks turned and fled toward the center, and the Braanters didn't press the attack.

More archers and men-at-arms on the Braant right joined their fellows on the swale to harry the Redmonders' left flank, forcing a shift in the Redmond lines to the right, toward Stone's position on the Braant left. The Braant archers around Stone were trading shots with enemy archers, and bowmen on both sides were being hit. Stone's eagle-like vision allowed him to see oncoming arrows as if they were flying at half speed, and he ducked away from more than one. A Braant archer near Stone went down with an arrow through his thigh, and Stone dragged him behind his boulder. The man was screaming with pain, and other Braanters were shouting and bellowing and crying out in rage or anguish. Stone picked up his man and carried him up to the top of the ridge, where litter bearers were waiting to take him down to the physician's tent. He felt the breeze from a hissing arrow tickle his ear as he went, and he nearly dropped the Braanter. It was one thing to have enhanced vision when you were facing your enemy, quite another when your back was to him.

Stone went back to his position. The Redmond lines, still harried on their left, were moving rightward even as they continued to march forward. Braant archers all along the line were cutting them down, but still they came, now only a hundred yards from the slope. Companies of Braant pikemen were forming at the top of the ridge behind Stone, ready to charge down the slope and blunt the attack. The enemy archers on the Redmond right were still firing up the ridge, still doing damage, even as the Braant archers matched them shot for shot.

The twenty Black Cloaks on the Redmond far right flank, joined by twenty of their fellows who no longer had gaps to fill, spurred their horses and galloped to the aid of the Redmond archers. Five hundred pikemen followed them at a run. A Black Cloak gave an order, and the pikemen charged up the slope, quickly overrunning the forward Braant archers. A company of Braant pikemen charged down the slope to meet the attackers and a wild melee broke out. Stone unsheathed his sword, but he was reluctant to fight the Redmonders. A Braant pikeman went down near him, and he stepped out from his boulder and dragged the man behind it. More Braant foot soldiers were flowing down the slope, but the Redmonders fought like men possessed. A company of Braant knights appeared at the top of the ridge, but the slope was too rocky for the horses to charge down. The knights dismounted, grabbed their lances, and charged on foot. The Redmonders were thinning out, all but spent, their dead and wounded littering the slope.

"Yield, you fools!" one of the Braant knights shouted.

The other Braanters took up chant. "Yield! Yield! Yield!"

But the remaining Redmonders kept coming, shambling and crawling and weaving up the slope like drunken ghosts. The Braanters took pity on them. They aimed their sword and pike thrusts at the Redmonders weapons, if they carried any, and took the few survivors prisoner.

Stone looked at the swale and saw the sixty Black Cloaks, all unscathed, galloping back to the south ridge.

The battle was over.

Chapter 12 - Aliya

The Braant army collected their dead and treated their wounded and did what they could for the dead and wounded Redmonders. The Braant commander sent a contingent of archers and knights to occupy the Redmonders' now-abandoned camp on the opposite ridge, and a company of knights rode south to hunt for the fleeing Black Cloaks. But the Ordseer men seemed to have vanished, and Stone figured they were slinking back to Redmond after their crushing defeat.

A defeat, Stone mused, that seemed deliberate. The Redmond army had been destroyed, but no Black Cloak had suffered so much as a scratch. And now the Black Cloaks were gone, leaving behind thousands of dead thralls. Stone wondered what kind of deranged strategy would call for such an action. Perhaps the Ordseer was willing to sacrifice thralls by the thousands because he figured he could always get more. Stone was eager to discuss the matter with Brook and Bennald.

He went looking for Captain Nollup and found him sitting on a camp stool outside his tent. Nollup was trying to question one of the few captured Redmonders, a young archer who was sitting cross-legged on the ground. Two Braant pikemen stood just behind the Redmonder, keeping a close eye on him. The young man was staring vacantly, his eyes blank and his mouth hanging slightly open. Nollup looked up when Stone arrived and gave him a nod.

"I heard you rescued a couple of Braant men," Nollup said.

Stone nodded back.

"I thank you for that. Might be I'll stand you and your friends a round of ales."

Stone gestured toward the Redmonder thrall. "Has he said anything?"

"Not a word," Nollup replied. "His body's well enough, but his mind is sick."

"The Ordseer's work," Stone said.

At the sound of the word *Ordseer*, the thrall gave a little start and fixed his gaze on Stone. Stone squatted down opposite the man and stared into his empty eyes for a few moments before turning to Captain Nollup. "Mind if I have a go?"

Nollup shrugged and got up from his stool. "Have at it."

Stone sat down on the stool and leaned forward, his hands on his knees. "What's your name?" he asked the thrall.

The thrall stared back but said nothing.

"Where in Redmond do you hail from?"

He got no reply.

"Were you a soldier?"

The thrall blinked and then looked down and spotted Stone's ring. He gave a little gasp and then looked at Stone and then back at the ring. Stone lifted his arm and held his right hand out so the Redmonder could see the ring clearly. The man was transfixed by it.

Stone was startled when he felt his right hand begin to vibrate. Something tugged at the back of his mind. He closed his eyes and searched for a deep memory, but he couldn't draw one out. He saw shadows flitting through a fog and heard voices whispering, but he couldn't catch the words. He heard Brook's voice, and then Bennald's, and then another voice, unfamiliar to him. His muscles had tensed, and his hands were clenched. He took in a long breath and forced himself to relax. He focused his inner gaze and peered through the fog that filled his mind. His vision stretched, and he saw a tiny glow, far away but coming closer. The world began to spin, but he kept his sight focused on the spark of light in the distance. He felt his heart beating, heard the sound of blood running through his veins. He was running like the wind, tiny twisters of fog swirling in his wake. He came to the edge of a cliff and hurled himself forward, spread his arms, and soared like an eagle.

He opened his eyes and stared into the still-dead eyes of the Redmonder thrall.

"Look at me," he whispered. "Look at my eyes."

The thrall blinked once and stared at Stone. Stone locked eyes with the man. He felt as if he were falling into the Redmonder's eyes.

He was in a vast, dark cavern. Nooks and alcoves lined the walls, and passages led off from it. Sparks of light and flashes of color burst in the air, like sparks shooting up from a smoldering log in the dark of night. As sparks and flashes appeared, threadlike lines of pure white light shot from one spark to another, creating images. Stone followed a darting white light into a passage, saw it float and rise and then fall and disappear into another passage. A butterfly made of red and yellow jewels fluttered past, and he followed it through another passage and into a small room. The room had a bed and a chest, a small table and two chairs. A book lay on the table, open. Stone peered at it. The room disappeared, and Stone was plunged into darkness.

He opened his eyes. The Redmond thrall was staring at him.

"What's your name?" Stone asked in a steady voice that seemed not quite his own.

"My name?" the thrall murmured.

"Yes. Tell me your name. Think back and remember."

"I ... my ... my name is ... "

"Your name is Larmon," Stone said. "Say it."

"Larmon. Larmon Sprole." The man blinked twice and took in a sharp breath. He furrowed his brow and peered at Stone. "Where am I?"

"Just outside Blackpond," Stone answered.

"Blackpond? In Braant?"

"Aye," said Captain Nollup, who had been watching.

"Why am I in Braant?" the Redmonder asked. "How did I get here?"

"What do you remember?" Stone asked.

Braanters who had been standing nearby were watching intently, and others were joining them.

The Redmonder frowned. "I was in the Red City, in my quarters in the barracks. One of my mates gave me a parchment. A fastle pledge, he called it. Said it was a pledge to the king and I should sign."

"So you signed it," Stone said.

The man nodded.

"What else do you remember?" Captain Nollup asked.

The Redmonder shook his head. "It's all so muddled, I can't fix my mind on anything. I feel as if I've been asleep for weeks."

Captain Nollup turned to one of his men. "Take him to the healer's tent and have Master Traik see to him. And get him something to eat. You others go about your business and stop your gaping." As the men shuffled off, Nollup looked at Stone. "I'd like to talk to you inside my tent, if you please."

Stone nodded and they entered the captain's tent. Nollup sat behind his camp desk and Stone sat on a low stool.

"Are you a mage then?" Nollup asked Stone. "Or a sorcerer of some kind?"

Stone shook his head and thought fast. "No, but I'm a … I'm a cousin—a distant cousin—to a virrling."

Nollup raised an eyebrow. "Oh, aye? Which virrling might that be?"

"I'd rather not say."

"How did you cure that Redmonder of his thralldom?"

"I don't quite know," Stone said.

The captain frowned. "A bit more to you than I first thought. You sure you're not a mage or a sorcerer?"

"I'm as sure of that as I am of anything," Stone replied.

Nollup's frown deepened as he gazed at Stone and considered his answer. "Never mind," he said.

164

"But perhaps you should ride into Blackpond with me and some of my men."

"I'd like to try to disenthrall the other survivors first," Stone said. "With your permission, of course."

Nollup shrugged. "Why not? There are only a handful of the poor buggers, so you may as well have a bash at it."

Stone succeeded in disenthralling the other surviving Redmonders, only six in number, and then he rode to Blackpond with Captain Nollup and a group of ten Braant knights. The sun was five hours past noon when they set out, riding two by two on a narrow road that cut between farm fields and pastures. Nollup rode next to Stone, the last pair in the twelve-man column.

"Where do you mean to meet your friends?" Nollup asked after they set off at a canter.

"I should find them at the first inn we come to with an animal or flower in its name."

"That would be the Hare's Hollow," Nollup said. "Good ale there."

They rode in silence for a while, and the men ahead of them were also quiet, unusual behavior for soldiers who had just won a resounding victory. Stone looked over his shoulder, as if he expected the Black Cloaks to reappear or the Redmond army to rise from the dead and resume its attack.

"An odd battle, that was," Nollup said, shaking his head. "And an odd aftermath as well. I'd still like to know how you broke the spell on that Redmonder."

"I'm not entirely sure," Stone confessed.

165

"I once saw a street player who claimed to be a mage put someone under a spell of some sort, or so he claimed," Nollup said. "He did it by holding up a small, polished silver cup and telling a young man to stare at it. The young man seemed to enter into some kind of dream, and yet he was awake—yet not fully awake, either. It seemed as if his mind had blocked out all the noise from the crowd and was set solely on whatever the mage told him."

"And what did the mage tell him?" Stone asked.

"The mage told the young man to walk and squawk like a chicken, which he did, much to the delight of the people watching. Most of them, anyway."

"Perhaps the young man was in league with the mage," Stone said.

"I don't think so," Nollup replied. "What you did back there reminded me of it."

Stone wasn't sure how to reply, but he knew he had to say something. A disciplined soldier like Captain Nollup might not want a suspected mage wandering around in one of Braant's towns.

"When I looked closely at that thrall, a notion suddenly sprang to mind, so I followed my instinct," Stone said. "Like your street mage, I thought perhaps if the Redmonder could set his mind intently on something outside himself, perhaps he could break away from the spell on his own."

Stone knew he was spouting nonsense, but his explanation seemed to satisfy Nollup. As to what had actually taken place, he needed to discuss it with Brook and Bennald.

"This Ordseer fellow you mentioned—what else do you know about him?" Nollup asked.

"Only what Sir Kaemon said."

"The Ordseer's magic didn't help his side in the battle we just fought."

"No," Stone replied. "That battle gives me an uneasy feeling."

"It does me as well," said Nollup. "There's something amiss, something off, even apart from fighting thralls. I'm glad we won, but I don't like it."

An hour later, they passed through the south gate of the wall that surrounded Blackpond. They entered Pond Street, the town's main thoroughfare, and when they came to the Hare's Hollow, Stone bade Nollup and the others farewell. The captain shook his hand and promised to find him later and make good on his promise to stand him and his friends to a round of ale.

Stone took his horse to a nearby stable and then entered the Hare's Hollow's common room and looked around. There was no sign of Brook or Bennald, but he hadn't expected to see them straightaway. He asked the innkeeper, a man of middle age with a mop of stringy black hair, if a young, dark-haired woman and a sturdy sandy-haired man had shown up earlier. The innkeeper shook his head and asked him if he wanted a room or a meal.

"I need to find my people first," Stone replied, and he left the inn.

He walked along Pond Street, stopping at every inn or tavern with a flower or animal in its name to inquire after Brook and Bennald. Nobody had seen anyone meeting their descriptions. Stone continued his search, block by block, to no avail. As dusk fell, he gave up and went back to the Hare's Hollow to take a meal and get a room. He ate a quick dinner, washed, and collapsed on the bed in his small room. He was asleep within seconds.

He awoke early the next morning and went to the dining room to break his fast. He planned to resume his search for Brook and Bennald, but he decided that if he hadn't found them by noon, he'd leave word with the innkeeper and head north to the next town on their itinerary, Sevnpools. If he couldn't find any trace of them in Sevnpools, he'd proceed to Greenport and wait for them there.

He went to an empty table in the back corner. A few minutes later, the innkeeper brought him a tankard of ale and a plate of warm buttered bread, two hard-cooked eggs, and a slab of bacon. The dimly lit room was about one-quarter full, and the conversations were muted, which suited Stone. He was frustrated that he had lost his friends and still troubled by the carnage he had witnessed the previous day. He was also unsettled by his apparent ability—assuming he could harness it again—to break the Ordseer's fastle spell, which had sparked an idea he wanted to discuss with Brook.

He finished his meal and called for another ale. As the innkeeper set down a fresh tankard, the door opened and a young woman in a dark green dress and a matching hooded cloak entered. She looked around the room, drawing admiring stares from the dozen men who were scattered about, until her eyes found Stone. His eyes met hers, and he thought she gave him a slight nod. He frowned. She was a stranger to him, and yet she was looking at him as if she knew him. His surprise mounted when she made her way to his table and sat down opposite him.

"Are you Stone Falconer?" she asked.

He picked up his tankard and took a long pull. He set the tankard down and stared at her. "And who might you be?"

"You haven't answered my question," she said.

"You haven't answered mine."

She considered a moment. "I'm Aliya Greenmantle."

Stone doubted it. "What's your business with this Stone Falconer fellow?"

"Are you he?"

"Depends. What's your business with him?"

She glanced over her shoulder and then turned back to him. "I've come to take you to your friends," she said in a low voice.

That got his attention. He tried to act casual, but when he saw the glimmer of a smile cross her face, he knew his own face had betrayed him. Nevertheless, he meant to continue his charade. "What friends do you mean?" he asked.

She threw back her hood and gazed at him. Even in the dim light of the tavern, her dark eyes glittered. She was beautiful, Stone thought, but so were the flowers of the deadly serpent plant, he reminded himself.

"Your friends Brook and Bennald," she said.

"You mean Falco Stoner's friends."

She sighed. "If you insist on playing this game, then yes, Stone Falconer's friends Brook and Bennald."

"Why should I or this Stone fellow believe that you can take me—take him—to these friends of his?"

"Because you'll never find them otherwise."

Stone didn't know if that was a threat or a warning, but he was determined to find out. "Let's suppose, just for the moment, that I'm possibly considering believing you," he said. "How do I know I can trust you?"

"You don't, but I can't help that."

"Where are these friends you mentioned?"

"Somewhere safe, not far from Blackpond. They're with my sister. We can be there before night falls."

"Why are these mysterious friends where you say they are?"

"I was in the Hare's Hollow yesterday, waiting for my sister. We're leaving Blackpond and getting away from Braant before the Ordseer takes over. I overheard your two friends talking about him, about the Ordseer. I could tell they were on the run. I decided to help them before the Ordseer's men found them. I hate the Ordseer."

Stone let out a breath and smiled. "You won't have to worry about the Ordseer taking over Braant," he said. "Your brave Braant soldiers just routed his army of Redmonders."

The door opened again, and Stone looked up to see Captain Nollup enter. The man's eyes were bloodshot, and his face was pale and drawn. He spotted Stone and quickly strode to his table. "I see you found your sister," Nollup said, nodding toward Aliya. Stone didn't correct him.

"You look troubled," Stone said to Nollup. He was eager to return to the discussion with Aliya, but Nollup's uneasy demeanor had sent a rush of anxiety surging through him.

Nollup pulled a chair to the table and sat down. "Late last night, as some of the men were celebrating and taking their ease at the various taverns, a number of proprietors showed them parchments inscribed with some sort of pledge to King Harrin. They called them fastle pledges."

Aliya started at the mention of the fastle pledges, and when Stone glanced at her, he saw her face go pale. "Don't let your men sign," he said to Nollup. "It's the Ordseer's work."

"It's too late," Nollup said, wiping perspiration from his brow. "The first ones to sign took scores of these parchments and persuaded others to sign. When I asked who had told them to make pledges to the king, those who had already signed threatened me. I was lucky to get away. I hid all night in a shed in a back alley I know and made my way here at first light, hoping I'd find you. I saw men and women carrying parchments and knocking on doors, trying to get more people to sign. Some are resisting, and fights have broken out. I was hoping you might be able to help."

Aliya stood up, her face still ashen. "There's no help for it. We need to go."

The door opened, and a group of four Black Cloaks walked in and sat at a table. Stone felt the blood drain from his face.

"What's wrong?" Nollup asked.

"It can't be," Stone whispered.

"What can't be?"

"Black Cloaks. They just took a table near the door. I don't understand."

Nollup glanced over his shoulder and then turned back to Stone, fear written on his face. "They're carrying those damned parchments."

"But you defeated them," Stone said. "You routed them and the Redmond army. You destroyed them."

"It was a trick," Aliya whispered. "We must leave now."

Stone saw one of the black-clad knights spot them. The man whispered something to his friends and then stood up and approached.

Stone gripped his sword as he slowly backed his chair away from the table. Nollup stood up and faced the approaching Black Cloak.

"You, knight," the Black Cloak said to Nollup. "Have you signed the fastle pledge to good King Harrin?"

"Take your men and get out of Braant," Nollup said. "And take your false pledges with you."

"I said fastle pledge," the Black Cloak said. "If you won't sign a pledge to your king then perhaps it's yourself who's false."

Nollup drew his sword. The Black Cloak stepped back and drew his own, and his three companions stood up and approached. Stone rose and stepped away from the table. He drew his sword and stood next to Nollup, facing the four Black Cloaks. Aliya backed into the corner. The other patrons were heading for the door, the innkeeper right behind them.

"Who are you?" Stone asked the Black Cloak.

"Sir Gritten," the man replied.

"An Ordseer man," Stone said. "A trespasser and a thief, like the Ordseer."

Sir Gritten's face darkened, and he scowled at Stone. "Drop your weapons and sign the fastle pledges, all three of you. And utter no more insults against the Ordseer, or I'll run you through."

"The Ordseer is a blood-sucking viper," Stone said.

The Black Cloaks struck at the same time, but Stone used their fury at his words to his own advantage, sidestepping as they surged forward, ducking and spinning away while plucking his dagger from its scabbard with his left hand. He moved so quickly that he felt as if he had stepped into another level of time, like an eagle flying above a tortoise. He plunged the knife into the ribs of his nearest antagonist. As the knight fell, the man next to him swung at Stone, and their swords clashed. He heard Aliya scream and Nollup curse, and he laid into his man with lightning thrusts, dispatching him and rushing to Nollup's aid. It was too late. Nollup was on the floor, his sword arm bleeding, trying to scramble under a table. Sir Gritten was slumped against another table, bleeding from wounds in the neck and chest that Captain Nollup had inflicted. The Black Cloak still on his feet turned to face

Stone. With the odds suddenly changed, the man was reconsidering the new state of affairs. "I yield," he said after a moment.

"Drop your sword," Stone commanded.

The Black Cloak dropped his weapon. A moment later, Stone heard a thud and saw the man's eyes go wide. The knight fell forward, and Stone saw a dagger sticking out of his back. Aliya walked up to him, pulled out the dagger, and cut the knight's throat.

"He yielded," Stone said.

"I don't care," she replied. "He would have done the same to you. We must go. Out the back."

Stone knelt down by Captain Nollup and saw that he was bleeding from his chest as well as his arm. "Go," Nollup whispered. "I'm killed." He closed his eyes and lay still. Stone felt for a pulse. There was none.

Stone swore under his breath and closed Nollup's eyes. He stood up, and he and Aliya ran into the back room. They sped past the terrified innkeeper, who was cowering behind a barrel of flour, and fled through the back door.

Chapter 13 - The Querl

"My horse is in the stable across from the Hare's Hollow," Stone said to Aliya as they headed down the alley that ran behind the inn.

"That's where mine is," she replied.

They turned right at another alley and took it to a narrow street, where they turned left.

"Where are we going?" Aliya asked.

Stone pointed straight ahead. "That street crosses the one we want."

They turned left again, onto a wide street that was crowded despite the early hour. Knots of people stood outside doorways, peering at passersby, and small groups were striding up and down the street, eyeing each other. Two men on horseback cantered past, kicking up dust.

"What's happening?" Aliya whispered.

"Keep walking," Stone replied. "Don't look at anyone."

Stone looked straight ahead, avoiding others' gazes, but he felt eyes on him. When he realized he had unconsciously quickened his pace, he took a breath and slowed down.

"We should hurry," Aliya whispered.

"No. Walk at a normal pace."

They heard a commotion ahead of them. A group of five men had surrounded a group of three younger men and were shouting and gesticulating at them. As Stone and Aliya approached, he caught the eye of one of the young men. The youth looked away, but there was no mistaking the fear in his eyes.

"There," Stone whispered. "That alley up ahead."

"Those men …"

"Don't look at them."

Aliya nodded and took his arm. A shout rose up from the group in front of them, and one of the young men broke away and began running. Two men gave chase. The other two youths took off in the opposite direction, toward Stone and Aliya. Three men were chasing them. Stone lurched to his right, and one of the three pursuers crashed into him.

"Beg your pardon," Stone said. The man swore and shoved him aside and continued the chase.

A group of three men standing together on the other side of the street witnessed the collision. They crossed the street and approached Stone and Aliya. "You there," one of them called.

Stone and Aliya ducked into the alley and ran to the stable. "Go in and saddle your horse," Stone told Aliya. "If there's any trouble, yell." Then he drew his sword and turned to face the three pursuers.

The men, who had spread out as much as the narrow alley would allow, stopped and drew their own swords. "Have you signed the fastle pledge?" Stone barked at them.

"Of course we have," one of the men shot back.

"Then why are you following us?"

"You've signed?"

"Aye, we have."

"Both of you?"

"Of course, both of us," Stone said.

"Where are you off to, then?"

"There's a whole countryside that needs to sign," Stone told him.

The man narrowed his eyes at Stone. "Where are your fastle pledges?"

"In our saddlebags, you fool," Stone shouted.

"He's lying," one of the other men said.

Stone pointed his sword in the man's direction. "Call me a liar again and I'll slice off your ears before I cut out your heart."

"None of that, now," the third man said. "You won't mind showing us your pledges, then."

Stone made an exaggerated sigh and rolled his eyes. "I'll mind all right, but if it's the only way to get you three scoundrels to bugger off, then let's get on with it." He sheathed his sword and turned away from his antagonists before heading into the dimly lit stable. The three men followed him inside. "Tack room is in the back," Stone said. "I'll get my saddle."

"We'll come with you," one of the men said.

"Where's the woman?" another asked.

Stone heard a scream and spun around, drawing his sword. He kicked the closest man in the groin, sending him to the floor. The man who had been last into the stable was lying on the floor with a pitchfork sticking out of his back. The man still standing lunged at Stone and made a quick thrust with his sword, but Stone parried and knocked the weapon out of his hand. Aliya was about to throw her dagger when Stone shouted, "No!"

The man flung himself at Stone and tried to strike at him with his fists. All of Stone's senses heightened. It was as if he could read the man's eyes and see where his fists would strike before he threw the punches. He blocked his antagonist's blows and delivered one of his own, connecting with the man's jaw and sending him sprawling. He strode to the man who was writhing on the floor and kicked his head, knocking him out and putting an end to his groaning. He pulled the pitchfork out of the back of the third man and flung it aside before kneeling down to check on him. He looked up at Aliya. "He's still alive."

"I should cut their throats."

"Save your knife work until we need it."

They saddled their horses and led them toward the rear entrance. Stone held up a hand before peering out for a look around. The alley was filled with men pushing and shoving and trying to squeeze past one another. He turned back to Aliya and shook his head. "Out the front. Quickly."

They led the horses through the front entrance of the stable and out to Pond Street. It was seething with people. It seemed as if the entire town had gone outside to quarrel. A noisy scuffle broke out across the street. Two men threw another man to the ground. People were running up and down, and the dust rising up from the street swirled and eddied in their wakes.

A woman screamed. Two black-clad knights wheeled around a corner and swept down the street at a canter, scattering the crowd. Someone threw a bitterfruit at one of the knights, striking his back.

The knight halted, dismounted, and drew his sword, looking around at the milling people.

Stone gazed at the chaos that was swirling up and down the street like a sudden tempest and felt a flush of panic. He had to keep his wits about him. He looked at Aliya. Her face was pale, and she was clutching her throwing dagger in her right hand. "Let's go," Stone said. "We'll take it slow, but be ready to fly."

Aliya nodded, and they mounted their horses. Stone thought Aliya had been wearing a dress, but when she got on her horse he saw that her garment was divided into two loose-fitting legs, like a pair of very baggy trousers. *Clever girl*, Stone thought.

"Which way?" Aliya asked.

Stone pointed up the street. "Stay close. Be ready to bolt."

Twenty yards ahead of them, a red-bearded man wearing a leather apron ran into the street from a tannery and hurled a stack of gleaming white parchments into the air. The parchments scattered like leaves in a gale and fluttered to the dusty street. The tanner turned and ran back inside his shop, slamming the door behind him just before a crossbow bolt struck it. One of the Black Cloaks dismounted and strode toward the pile of parchments. A young man dashed out from a doorway and plunged the tip of a sword into a parchment before the knight could pick it up. There was a shrieking sound, like metal rubbing hard against metal, and the parchment burst into flames. The knight drew his sword and swung it at the young man, who darted away, leaving his own sword behind.

The knight gave chase. A tavern door swung open, and a huge man carrying an empty ale cask ran out and flung it toward the Black Cloak. It hit the street and rolled, and the black-clad knight barely got out of the way in time. The youth who had skewered the parchment escaped down an alley.

Stone and Aliya continued down the street. A Braant knight on horseback appeared from around a corner and shouted, "The army is coming. They've signed the pledges." And then he was gone, headed into the raging conflict that Stone was trying to flee.

Three blocks on, the crowds were thinner, and no one attempted to stop them. The next block was even calmer, and in the one after that, the street was quiet, though they could still hear shouting and clamoring behind them. They made for the north gate, riding at a canter. A half hour later, they were leaving the city behind. Stone looked over his shoulder to make sure no one was following. In the distance, a plume of black smoke was curling up from somewhere near the town center.

***

Stone should have been relieved that his new ally hated the Ordseer enough to kill one of his men without blinking, but he was troubled. As he and Aliya rode northwest from Blackpond toward an unknown destination, he became ever more skeptical of the tale she had told of overhearing Brook and Bennald whispering about the Ordseer in the common room of the Hare's Hollow Inn. He was convinced she was either lying or there was more to the story, but he didn't know how to discover the truth. Meanwhile, his course was set, and he would follow any path that might take him to his friends.

At midday, they left the road and headed for a nearby cluster of trees to rest the horses and take a light meal. The sky was overcast, and Stone smelled a hint of rain in the air. A steady breeze from the west ruffled the grass and sent leaves tumbling along the ground. Aliya was leaning against a tree, nibbling on a crust of dark bread from a loaf she'd had in her saddlebag. Stone was crouched a few yards away, facing her. The horses grazed nearby. "Tell me more about this place we're headed toward," he said. "And tell me why you hate the Ordseer."

"We're going to a querl between Blackpond and Meerpool," she replied. "The head freykon is a distant relation of my family. We should be there just before nightfall."

"How did my friends come to be in this querl of yours?"

"I directed them there."

"Because you overheard them discussing the Ordseer."

Aliya nodded. "Anyone who talks about the Ordseer but who hasn't signed one of his damnable pledges is in danger from him."

"How did you know they hadn't signed one of his damnable pledges?"

"I can tell."

"How?"

She pointed to her eyes. "The mazies' eyes are empty, like an unfilled bucket. Their faces have no spark to them, no life. The Ordseer sucks their will out of them, like a skeeth sucks the marrow out of a bone. Then he bends them to his own will."

Stone thought about the Redmonders' suicidal assault against the Braant defenders. He had no doubt the Ordseer had bent those men to his will, but for what purpose besides self-destruction he couldn't fathom. He put the thought aside. For now, he had to focus on his friends. "Why should you care what happens to strangers?" he asked.

"I'll help any enemy of the Ordseer, strangers or no," Aliya said. She made no effort to hide the bitterness in her tone.

Stone squinted at her, but she looked away. "The Ordseer did something to you—or to someone close to you," Stone said.

Aliya clenched her jaws and nodded. "He destroyed Redmond with those pledges of his."

"You're a Redmonder?"

"Aye."

Stone wondered if she knew Kaemon Krowe or either of his companions, but he decided not to ask her yet. First he'd find out if her story of what took place in Redmond matched Kaemon's.

"What happened there?" he asked.

"The Ordseer happened," she replied with the same bitter tone she'd used before. "My sister and I lived with my mother and father in Banderry, a town not far from the capital. After the mazies took over the Red City and most of the other towns along the river, they headed inland for the farms and villages. They came to Banderry a week after Maze Night."

He frowned at her. "Maze Night?"

"The night the Ordseer used the mazies—his thralls—to take over the Red City for good and all. That's what we call it."

Stone nodded. "Go on."

"Banderry had fair warning, but we didn't heed it. A man who met a man who escaped from the Red City told the village elders about Maze Night, but few believed that dark sorcery had set Redmonder against Redmonder or that the Red City had fallen to thralls. When the mazies came to Banderry, we were ill prepared for what was to come."

"How many mazies came?"

"Only a few at the start, no more than a half dozen."

Stone thought again about the dead-eyed thralls who had attacked the Braant position. "You said the thralls' eyes are empty. Could you not tell they were thralls?"

Aliya shook her head. "The ones who showed up first were posh worldly-wise types, and it takes longer for them to go dead-eyed. But make no mistake, they were thralls."

Stone recalled Kaemon's description of the king's council meeting. Except for the king's wistlord and Kaemon himself, the counselors had all signed fastle pledges, yet Kaemon said they had acted normally. "So your people were fooled."

Aliya nodded. "The mazies' words were soothing, and they smiled like they were your best friend. The elders met with them, and the tricksy bastards told them the pledges were only a gesture, a tribute to our king. They said all of King Harrin's counselors had signed, and they let slip that his new counselor, the Ordseer, was going to see to it that Redmond became rich beyond all reckoning. They hinted that those who signed would share in the wealth."

"So they signed."

"Aye, most of them. I didn't and neither did my father or mother. But in the end, Banderry had its own Maze Night. It was horrible."

She gazed into the distance as if she were looking for something far away or remembering something she'd sooner forget. Stone heard a distant rumble of thunder. She closed her eyes and leaned back against the tree.

"You said you lived with a sister."

She nodded, her eyes still closed. Stone waited.

"Her name is Jannela. Someone persuaded her to sign a fastle pledge, or forced her to. Now she's a thrall, a mazy. Now you know why I hate the Ordseer."

"I'm sorry for all your troubles," Stone said. "Thank you for helping me find my friends." He paused a moment and added, "Do you know a Redmond knight named Kaemon Krowe?"

Her eyes opened. "I know of him. He's the First Knight of the Realm and a cousin to the king."

"We met him and two companions of his in Drumkin," Stone said. "They went off to join other Redmonders who escaped from the Ordseer. Maybe we'll find them again, and you can join them."

"To what end?"

"To be with your own people. They want to take the battle to the Ordseer. You could help them."

"I wish them luck, but they're likely doomed. We're all likely doomed."

Stone wondered at her willingness to help him but not her own people, and a cold rill of fear ran through him. He shook it off and rose to his feet. He gazed a moment at the darkening sky, smelled the oncoming rain. "We should go."

They reached the querl grounds as dusk fell and a light rain began. They left the horses with a groom in a nearby stable and walked across a dusty yard toward the querl. The front of the structure was a square tower five stories tall with a flat roof surrounded by a crenellated parapet, like a corner tower of a castle. A heavy oak door in a high archway served as the main entrance. The rest of the querl was a long low structure with a steeply pitched roof.

When Aliya continued past the main entrance, Stone asked, "Where are we going?"

"Around the side," she replied.

They walked around the front and continued past a series of buttresses, eleven in all. High, narrow windows were set in the spaces between the buttresses, but no light shone through any of them. They proceeded to the rear of the querl, where a series of steps led down to a low door below ground level.

"Wait here," Aliya whispered, and she descended the steps. She rapped on the door. A few moments later, three loud raps from inside answered her. She looked up at Stone and nodded.

"Tell my friends I'm here," he said, his voice louder than he'd intended. He looked around, felt his heart begin to beat faster. He stretched his fingers and then brushed his hand across the grip of his sword.

"You must come inside," she said.

"I'll wait here."

"You've nothing to fear. But the freykon would meet you and hear your tale. Come. Please."

Stone let out a breath. "All right."

She pushed open the door and stepped inside. Stone looked around once more and then descended the steps and followed her in, leaving the door open an inch. A single candle in a sconce on the back wall revealed a large, empty room. Stone could barely make out the figure of Aliya a few yards in front of him.

He heard the door close behind him and then a rustling sound, like someone quickly donning a long silk cape. He spun around, but his feet went out from under him, and something hard struck him a blow to the back of his head, sending him into dark oblivion.

Chapter 14 - The Ordseer

Stone dreamed he was outside, lying in the same field he had awakened in without his memory. He was surrounded by darkness, and a starless, moonless sky loomed overhead. Slowly, gradually, the edge of the sky lightened, and the first splinter of dawn appeared, revealing shadowy silhouettes in the distance.

Stone opened his eyes and groaned. A blurry candle flame flickered and hissed in a sconce set in a stone wall some yards away. He sat up slowly, and a shard of pain pierced his skull. He checked himself for broken bones, found none. He touched the back of his head and felt a bump. It hurt, but he'd live. He was in a small, windowless cell. The scent of damp earth and mold tainted the air. There were other smells he preferred not to think about. He felt for his sword and dagger, but they were gone, as he knew they would be.

He stood up slowly, and the pounding in his head swelled. Three steps took him to the cell's heavy iron door. It was made of thick iron bars, like those on the window of Bennald's jail cell in Drumkin. He tried the door, with no expectation that it would open. It didn't. He looked out through the bars, but all was darkness, pierced only by the lone candle flame. He turned around.

Along the back wall of the cell was a narrow wooden pallet with a worn, filthy blanket on top. In one corner was a bowl of greasy water and a dented metal goblet. In another was a foul-smelling bucket obviously intended as a receptacle for human waste. He lay down on the pallet to wait for whatever would happen next, cursing himself for a fool and thinking of all the things he would do to Aliya if he ever saw her again, which seemed unlikely. He wondered how much gold she had been paid to betray him. He wondered who had paid it. He thought about Brook and Bennald and hoped they were still alive.

He thought back to his first encounter with the Black Cloak Sir Borus Renovar and recalled his brief duel with the man. He had wielded his sword as if he'd been born to it. He smiled at the memory, shook his head at the strangeness of it. He was no stranger to strangeness. He had worn a sword and a ring with the insignia of a powerful virrling, run like the wind when need demanded, observed with the eyes of an eagle, disenthralled a thrall. Yet he had no memory of himself and was now imprisoned like a common thief, the victim of a beautiful but treacherous woman. If he did have powers of sorcery or wizardry, now would be a fine time to learn how to use them.

With such thoughts swirling through his mind, he fell into a deep sleep. He dreamed of whirlwinds and black-cloaked knights riding him down. He dreamed of cat-a-mountains that talked and of raven-haired women who lived underwater. He dreamed of thralls marching to battle and falling by their thousands.

He was awakened by a harsh screeching sound as the cell door opened. He turned toward the door and saw three Black Cloaks standing there.

"On your feet," one of them said.

Stone got to his feet. "Who are you?" he asked the Black Cloak.

"Shut your gob," the Black Cloak replied.

"Funny name for a knight," Stone murmured.

The Black Cloak delivered a blow to the side of his head that sent him sprawling. "My name is Sir Lempter. See that you don't forget it."

Stone picked himself up and faced his captors.

"Turn around and face the wall and put your hands against it," Sir Lempter said.

Stone leaned over the pallet and placed his hands against the wall.

"Higher."

Stone put his hands higher on the wall. He heard footsteps behind him, and then someone placed a hood over his head. He felt a moment of panic until he realized the hood had breathing holes. There were no eyeholes.

"Turn around."

He turned around, and someone shoved him out of the cell. He felt hands grab his arms and shoulders, and then the Black Cloaks pushed him forward. He tried not to stumble as they swept him along, and he tried to picture the route in his mind. They stopped after a few minutes, and he heard the sound of another door opening. They pushed him through, and he heard the door slam shut behind him. Someone took off the hood, and he saw a ginger-haired man in his middle years sitting on a wooden chair behind a small table.

"Sit down," the man said.

A Black Cloak kicked a rickety chair toward him, and Stone sat down and faced the ginger-haired man.

"Do you know who I am?" the man asked.

Stone shrugged. "By the look of you, some petty thief or murdering scoundrel is my guess. Or perhaps you're a spider that's been turned into the semblance of a man by some dark sorcery."

The man's expression didn't waver. "Save your sorry japes. They'll have no effect on me."

Stone shrugged again and gave the man an even look. "Do you know who I am?"

"No, but I will soon enough. That's why I had you brought here. So you can tell me."

Stone nodded. "I'm the high exalted king of go bugger yourself." He detected the faintest glimmer of a twitch on the man's face.

"I am called the Ordseer," his interrogator said.

Stone barked a brief laugh. "I thought the Ordseer was a mighty sorcerer. You look to me like a trifling knave. If you're the famous Ordseer, do something sorcerish."

"All in good time," the Ordseer said. "First I want to know who you are and what you're about."

I wish I knew, Stone thought. What he said was, "My name is Stone Falconer, and I'm about six feet tall."

"I told you to save your japes. Do you know a virrling named Jole Arrick?"

"Never heard of him," Stone said.

"And yet your sword and your ring bear Jole Arrick's insignia. How do you explain that?"

"Ask him."

"I'm asking you."

"Then you're wasting your time."

"I think not," the Ordseer said.

"You're wasting my time as well."

The Ordseer shot Stone a mirthless smile. "Time is all you have, and if you don't tell me what I want to know, you'll have little enough of that." He looked at one of the Black Cloaks. "Take him back to his cell."

The Black Cloak dropped the hood over Stone's head and hauled him to his feet.

"Don't give him any food," the Ordseer said. "Beat him if he gives you any trouble. And bring him back here tomorrow at the same time."

***

The sound of men talking and horses whickering awakened Aliya just before dawn. She slipped out of bed and went to the window of her small room, which was on the top floor of the querl's tower. She peered down into the dim courtyard and saw a dozen Black Cloaks mounting their horses. She gasped when she saw her sister, Jannela, get on a horse behind one of the knights. It was all she could do not to call down to her.

Aliya backed away from the window and closed her eyes. Tears welled and she let them come. She took a breath and went back to the window. She couldn't quite make out what the men were saying, but she thought she heard the word "Greenport" uttered more than once before the knights headed off at a canter.

Aliya lay down again. She stared at the ceiling and thought about what to do. She had intended to leave with her sister as soon as she delivered Stone Falconer into the hands of the Ordseer, but he had put her off, explaining that he needed more time to undo the odd spell that Jannela had unwittingly inflicted on herself. Aliya had protested, but there was little she could do but wait. She had hoped the Ordseer would be as good as his word, but that had been a foolish hope. She had spent the first two nights in the room she occupied now, locked in and not allowed to see her sister. And now her sister was gone, and she was little more than a prisoner.

She slipped a hand under her long tunic and felt for the slim blade she had secreted in a special pouch sewn into her riding dress. The Black Cloaks had taken her other weapons—her throwing knife and a fine dagger—but they had not found this one. It gave her some comfort.

The door opened, and Aliya looked up to see the Black Cloak who called himself Sir Tacken enter the room.

"Knock before entering a lady's chamber," Aliya snapped.

"What lady?" Sir Tacken said.

For the briefest moment Aliya thought about reaching for her blade, but her better judgment prevailed. "What do you want?"

"The Ordseer is ready to see you now. You're to come with me."

Aliya thought fast. She wouldn't let on that she knew her sister had left. She would play the ignorant wench and try to learn what she could. "Is my sister ... better?"

Sir Tacken made no answer. Aliya went with him, and he took her to a large sitting room that appeared to be part of a suite of rooms. It looked comfortable enough, if not ostentatious, and it was decorated with paintings depicting the gods as well as a few small statues. Aliya assumed the suite was the high freykon's quarters, but she had seen no sign of any freykons or even novices, only Black Cloaks and a few servants, probably thralls.

"Sit," Sir Tacken said, gesturing toward a bench.

"I'll stand," Aliya said. "I don't intend to remain long."

A door located in an alcove opened, and the Ordseer stepped into the room.

"Where's my sister?" Aliya asked.

"Ah, she isn't quite ready to leave with you yet," the Ordseer replied.

Aliya clenched her right hand into a fist, wishing it were enclosing a sword or throwing knife. "Have you not cured her?"

"Sadly, she is still as she was," the Ordseer said.

"You said she would be better."

"Yes, so I did."

"Well then?"

The Ordseer shrugged. "It's a much more delicate thing than I had at first assumed. I believe ..."

"You lied," Aliya barked, interrupting him.

"Watch your tongue, bitch," Sir Tacken said. "Or I'll cut it out for you."

Try that, and you'll find a blade between your ribs, Aliya thought. She took a breath and then said to the Ordseer, "I want to see Jannela. Now."

"That's quite impossible," the Ordseer replied.

She took a step toward him, and Sir Tacken put a heavy hand on her shoulder. She shrugged away from him and approached the Ordseer to within striking distance. "You lied to me."

"Yes," he said. "It's of no matter. I need to keep your sister here with me to … study her a while longer. She'll come to no harm, and perhaps one day, she'll be as she was. Or perhaps she'll choose to sign a fastle pledge properly and devote herself to me—as you should do. As everyone should do."

It took all of Aliya's strength of will not to strike the man down where he stood. She would happily have given her life in exchange for his, but she had to stay alive for the sake of her sister. She let out a breath and took a step back. "If you won't give me my sister, then give me gold. I brought that fellow to you, as you asked, and I'm not leaving with nothing in return. I want five gold pieces."

The Ordseer looked at Sir Tacken, who was standing behind Aliya. "Go to Sir Waltick and tell him to give you ten silvers for the lady."

"Sixty silvers," Aliya said. "I risked my life."

"Twenty," the Ordseer replied.

"Fifty," Aliya said. "And that's my final offer."

The Ordseer's eyes went wide, and then he laughed. "Your final offer, is it? You're in no position to make final offers. But I'm glad to know you'll abandon sweet Jannela for the right price. All right, fifty silvers it is." He nodded toward Sir Tacken. "See to it."

Aliya sat down to wait. Her heart was hammering in her chest. She looked around the room, willing herself to stay calm, determined not to give away the game she was playing.

Sir Tacken returned with a leather pouch filled with coins. Aliya dumped them out onto a table and counted them, trying hard to keep her fingers from trembling. Finally, she put the coins back in the pouch and stood up. "I'll be off then. I'll need my horse, and I want the knives your man took from me."

"You'll get your horse," the Ordseer said. "The knives I'll keep."

"I need to protect myself. It's a dangerous world out there."

"One of my men will escort you to Sevnpools."

"Those blades cost me. I'll need another ten silvers—otherwise I'll tell everyone I meet that the great and noble Ordseer is a thief."

A hand struck the side of her head and knocked her from the chair.

"I told you to watch your tongue," Sir Tacken said.

Aliya stood up and faced the Ordseer. "My knives or ten more silvers, if you please, Sir Ordseer."

The Ordseer sighed and then looked at Sir Tacken. "Have Sir Boknale return her precious knives to her after he sees her to Sevnpools. And

195

tell Boknale to take care she doesn't use any of those blades on him."

***

Stone's stomach rumbled as two Black Cloaks, Sir Lempter and Sir Ogger, escorted him to the interrogation room for a second go-round. The Ordseer was waiting there behind his little table. Stone sat down and faced him. The two Black Cloaks stood behind him.

"Hungry?" the Ordseer asked.

"Aye," Stone replied. "I'd like some roasted beef, a loaf of fresh bread—still warm from the oven, if you please—and a mess of cooked greens, any kind will do. And a tankard of your finest ale."

"I told you yesterday to save your japing," the Ordseer said.

"Who's japing? Go on, you're a famous sorcerer, conjure me up a meal. Or are you a fraud and a cheat?"

The Ordseer reached into his cloak and removed Stone's signet ring. He placed it on the table.

Stone gave the Ordseer a bright smile. "Ah, so you're a thief. I'll have my ring back now, thanks very much." He stood up and approached the table, but Sir Ogger shoved him back into the chair.

The Ordseer produced two more rings bearing the same insignia, one with a green stone, the other with an orange one—Brook's and Bennald's. Stone stared at them.

"Nothing to say?"

196

"Did you steal those others as well, or did you have them made? It's a foul thing that you would steal some artisan's design, but I can't say I'm surprised."

"Your constant japing grows tiresome."

Stone shrugged. "Have yourself a nice nap. I don't mind waiting."

"I have your friends, here, in this querl, as you'll know by these two rings. Tell me what I want to know, and no harm will come to them. Otherwise …"

Stone made a show of scratching his head and frowning. "What was it you wanted to know again?"

The Ordseer leaned forward. "Who you are, who your friends are, and why you have rings that bear the insignia of the villain Jole Arrick."

"Where is Jole?" Stone asked. "What have you done with him?"

The Ordseer sat back and smiled triumphantly. "I thought you said you didn't know Jole Arrick."

Stone shrugged. "I don't. What have you done with him?"

The Ordseer drew his mouth into a tight line, and a muscle under his right eye twitched. "You'll watch as I pluck out first one eye and then the other of your friend who calls himself Bennald. Or perhaps I'll start with the woman. Perhaps you'll enjoy watching."

Stone let out a long sigh, as if he were dealing with a particularly dull child. "All right, Sir Ordinary, if you must know, Jole Arrick is a distant cousin of mine, and the stout young man and lovely young woman who own those other rings you stole are also Jole's cousins. Cousin Jole called us here from the Northern Wilderness, where we live with a band of witches, because he suspected that you wanted to take control of Redmond, if not the entire Ruxland realm, and he was determined to stop you. As we speak, he's recruiting our witch friends as well as a tribe of giants from the Southern Islands to make war on you and your foul Black Cloaks. Your days are numbered. May I have my beef and ale now?"

The Ordseer stood up and glared. "You're lying."

Stone shrugged. "You'll find out soon enough if I am."

"Where is Jole Arrick now?"

"I told you, he's in the Northern Wilderness. He was, anyway. I suppose by now he's in the Southern Islands, parlaying with the giants I told you about. Great big strong fellows they are. They eat sorcerers for breakfast. As soon as they agree to help us, they'll attack you from the south, and the witches will attack from the north. May I have my beef and ale?"

The Ordseer stood up suddenly and drew a sword. He kicked the table out of the way and approached Stone, who stood up. When Sir Ogger made to grab him, he shot an elbow into the Black Cloak's throat and spun away. Sir Ogger swore and came at Stone again, but Stone delivered a quick fist into the man's nose, which cracked like a twig under a horse's hoof. As Sir Ogger howled and drew his sword, Sir Lempter drew his and placed the tip against Stone's throat.

"No!" the Ordseer shouted. "Put away your sword."

"The bastard broke my nose," Sir Ogger replied. Blood was pouring from his nose and dripping down his front.

"Get out and get it tended to. Send Sir Tacken here."

The Black Cloak left, and a few minutes later, Sir Tacken stepped into the room. Stone wondered how many Black Cloaks the Ordseer had with him. Not very many, it seemed, which was curious. The Ordseer sheathed his sword and gestured toward the overturned table. Sir Lempter picked up the table and placed it back where it had been. The Ordseer sat down. He wiped a bead of sweat from his brow and said to Sir Lempter, "Take him back to his cell."

"What about my beef and ale?" Stone said.

"Get him out!" the Ordseer yelled.

Back in his cell, Stone wondered if the Ordseer believed his tale about the northern witches and southern giants. He had heard stories about both but had always assumed they were fairytales to frighten children and make fun of the gullible. Was the great Ordseer gullible?

Sir Lempter brought him a plate of cold beef and a small loaf of stale bread, which he set on the floor inside the door as Sir Tacken and another Black Cloak looked on. "I hope you appreciate the Ordseer's kindness," Sir Lempter said after he locked the cell door again.

"Tell the Ordseer to marry a swine," Stone replied before taking a huge bite of beef.

Chapter 15 - Sir Boknale

Aliya left the querl the next morning, escorted by a Black Cloak named Sir Boknale. The early morning air was cool, and Aliya pulled her cloak tighter around her neck as they set out at a trot for Sevnpools, thirteen miles away. Despite the chill, a blue sky and twittering songbirds gave promise of a pleasant day.

Sir Boknale was in no hurry, and Aliya wondered if he was happy to get away from the Ordseer for the better part of a day. She gave him a sidelong glance but looked away when he glanced back. Were the Black Cloaks part of a clan that owed allegiance to the Ordseer, or were they merely hired swords? Perhaps they were thralls, bound to the Ordseer by some dark sorcery.

"A pleasant day, isn't it?" Aliya ventured. They had left the wooded area surrounding the querl and entered rolling farmland. Lush green meadows on either side of the road glistened with dew, and in the distance a group of farmhands were working fields planted with crops.

"Aye, it is that," Sir Boknale replied.

"How long till we reach the village?"

"A few hours. No point pushing the horses."

Aliya glanced at the knight's mount, a great black warhorse that could no doubt outrun her much smaller horse if she tried to give him the slip. "You're right. If we run into any brigands, we'll want the horses able to bolt."

Sir Boknale gave a sharp laugh. "You needn't worry about brigands. I've dealt with more than a few in my life, and they all regretted it."

"I'm happy to hear it. It makes me feel safer. Tell me, did you once serve a king or have you always been bound to the Ordseer?"

The Black Cloak's expression clouded over, and he set his mouth into a thin line. He made no answer.

"Do you know Sevnpools?" Aliya asked after a brief but uncomfortable silence.

"Not well, we only just passed through," Sir Boknale said. "The Six and One Inn was fair enough for a hot meal and strong ale."

"Perhaps I'll try it," Aliya said. "Will you be taking a meal there? Or do you need to get back to your ... back to the querl?"

"I brought hard cheese and bread," Sir Boknale replied. "We'll eat along the way. When we're within sight of Sevnpools, you'll be on your own."

"May I ask you a favor, Sir Boknale?"

"You may ask."

"Will you see that my sister is well taken care of?"

The knight made no reply.

***

Stone was awakened by something scrabbling in the darkness. He opened an eye and slowly turned toward the front of the cell. In the dim light cast by the single candle on the corridor wall, he saw a small shadow scurrying along the floor—a rat or a mouse or perhaps an industrious squirrel.

"Be gone," Stone muttered.

The creature stopped for a moment and then started again, heading for the cell.

"I said be gone, little beastie," Stone whispered. The animal ignored him and continued to approach. Stone sat up and peered at it. He couldn't be sure in the dim light, but it looked like a brown-tailed forest roke, a small woodland creature that had also adapted to town life. It was about the size of a small rabbit. Bennald had told him that forest rokes were known for building elaborate nests, using twigs and leaves if they lived in the woods, or bits of cloth and pieces of wood and leather if they lived nearer a town. They were especially fond of shiny things, and their nests were often furnished with links from chainmail, handles from metal tankards, small silver and copper coins, and similar items. They were intelligent creatures, and there were countless tales of rokes taking one item and leaving another in its place. One of Stone's farmer friends in Misheroon had sworn that a roke once left four matching wooden buttons in exchange for a bronze brooch.

"I wonder what raw roke tastes like," Stone said, but the small creature didn't hesitate. The candlelight caught something shiny as the creature approached, and Stone smiled. "You shouldn't let yourself be impressed by glittery objects," Stone said. "Someone might mistake you for a ..."

Stone jumped up and dashed to the front of the cell, leaning his head against the bars and squinting at the still-moving creature. "Bloody hell, is that a …?"

The creature scampered into the cell and dropped the four-inch kitchen knife it had been dragging. Stone picked it up and slipped it into his boot. He stared at the roke, which was staring back. For a brief moment, he thought it smiled at him. "Bennald," Stone whispered. "Great gods, Bennald sent you."

The roke scurried out of the cell and disappeared into the darkness.

Stone heard footsteps and quickly lay down on his pallet. The cell door screeched open, and a Black Cloak stepped inside. Two more stood outside the cell, one carrying a torch.

"On your feet, knave," the Black Cloak commanded. "The Ordseer would speak with you again."

Stone thought about what to do. He had a weapon, but it was a paltry one, and he had no way to contact Brook or Bennald. They were most likely in their own cells and unable to contact each other. Bennald would have armed himself first and then sent his roke to Brook's cell afterwards. They most likely had three kitchen knives among them to face Black Cloaks armed with swords and daggers and crossbows. But the Black Cloaks wouldn't expect them to have weapons, so if it came to a fight, surprise would be on their side. But first Stone had to get the three of them together in the same room.

"I said on your feet," the Black Cloak barked.

Stone yawned and swung his legs to the floor. "I'm quite sorry, my good fellow, but I was having a delightful dream about cutting the Ordseer's throat."

The Black Cloak grabbed Stone's arm and hauled him to his feet. He pulled him close and thrust his face to within an inch of Stone's. "I'm tired of your japing. When the Ordseer is through with you, it'll be your throat that's cut. And I'll be doing the cutting."

Stone resisted the urge to drive his knee into the man's groin. "What does the good sorcerer want?"

"You know what he wants, knave, and you had better tell him what he wants to know," the Black Cloak said, his face still only inches from Stone's.

Stone wrinkled his nose. "Tell your cook to use fewer onions. Your breath smells like a dung heap."

He was rewarded with a cuff to his head that sent him reeling. He exaggerated his motion and let himself strike the wall without doing any damage before crumpling to the floor. He eyed the three Black Cloaks, calculating his chances. He could slip the knife from his boot, gut the nearest one, and grab the man's sword. But one of the others would slam shut the cell door, and that would be the end of Stone's rebellion. He took a breath, waited for his racing heart to slow, and then stood up. The Black Cloak dropped the hood over his head and shoved him out of the cell, and they made their way once again to the Ordseer's interrogation room.

**

They came to a crossroads, and Aliya noticed that Sir Boknale glanced to his left as they passed the other road. She resisted the urge to ask him where it led, but she had no doubt it led to Greenport.

A half hour later, Sir Boknale pointed toward a stand of drumble trees just off the road. "We'll stop here to eat, over by those trees." He reined in his horse and dismounted, and Aliya followed suit. It was mid-afternoon, and the sun was shining in a clear sky. They led the horses to the trees and hobbled them.

"How far to Sevnpools?" Aliya asked as Sir Boknale opened a saddlebag and pulled out a cloth bundle.

"Another hour."

"Let me," Aliya said as she gestured toward the bundle.

Sir Boknale handed it to her and fetched his wineskin. Aliya opened the bundle and found a large loaf of dark bread, a wedge of hard white cheese, two metal plates, a wooden cutting board—and a dagger. Without looking at Sir Boknale, she spread the cloth on the ground under the shade of a drumble tree and began cutting chunks of cheese with the dagger. When she was finished, she stuck the point of the dagger into the cutting board and divided the cheese between the two plates. As Sir Boknale looked on, she tore pieces from the loaf and put them on the plates. She handed him a plate, and he took it and sat down. The cutting board with the dagger was between them.

"It feels good to have a man to serve," Aliya said.

Sir Boknale grunted, but she thought she detected a slight nod.

"Wouldn't you like a woman to … do things for you?"

"I've had women," he replied.

"A wife?"

He shook his head.

"A pity."

"Why?" he asked. "Why is it a pity?"

She shrugged. "A knight should have a lady, that's all I meant. It's in the natural order of things."

He stopped chewing and frowned. Above them, a redbird flitted from one branch to another, followed by its mate. As Aliya and the Black Cloak looked up, the female redbird hopped over to the male and placed a seed she was carrying in her beak into his.

"Are you saying I'm not in the natural order of things?" Sir Boknale asked. He pulled the dagger from the cutting board, sliced more cheese, and then slipped the dagger under his sword belt.

Aliya picked up a twig and stared at it, and then she broke it in half and tossed it away. She looked into the Black Cloak's eyes. "I'm not saying anything. I'm just wondering." She sighed and then lay back on the grass, her hands clasped under her head. She watched the redbirds fly off, and then sighed again.

In the next moment, Sir Boknale was standing over her, a hungry look in his eyes. He took a long pull from his wineskin. "I'm as natural as any man."

Aliya smiled. "Come down here and show me."

The Black Cloak swallowed, unfastened his sword belt, and let it fall to the ground. He dropped to his knees next to her, and she reached up an arm toward him. He bent down to kiss her. As his lips met hers, she turned slightly and slipped her thin blade from its hiding place. She murmured contentedly as he reached a hand under her tunic, and then she plunged the dagger into the back of his neck.

His eyes went wide, and he collapsed on top of her, paralyzed. She scrambled out from under him, holding her dagger in front of her. He was still alive, but his breaths were ragged. She picked up his sword belt and tried to buckle it on. It was too big, so she tied it on instead. She approached him cautiously, waiting until she heard no more breaths.

When she knew he was dead, she gathered her own knives, which he had been carrying, and searched his saddlebags. She took the remaining food and the wineskin and mounted her horse. Then she headed back toward the road that would take her to Greenport.

Chapter 16 - Witches

For the third time in as many days, Stone sat facing the Ordseer.

"I'm tired of your japes and your stubbornness," the Ordseer said. "Tell me who you are and what you have to do with Jole Arrick."

"And what will you give me in return?" Stone asked.

The Ordseer raised an eyebrow. "You're in no position to ask for something in return."

"Then you'll get no information from me."

The Ordseer glared. "What would you have?"

"My friends—I would see them, to know they're unharmed."

"I promise you they are unharmed—for now."

"Your promises are worthless. I'll see them, or I'll say nothing."

The Ordseer shrugged. "Very well. First tell me who you are and where Jole Arrick is."

"No. Not until I see my companions."

"Do you take me for a fool?"

"No. But if I tell you what I know, there's no guarantee you'll live up to your part of the bargain."

"You think I'm a cheat, do you?"

"I take you for a powerful sorcerer who wants information that I have and who will do anything to get it. So I make you an offer. I will give you a portion of my knowledge, and you will have one of your knights fetch Brook and bring her here, where I can see her. I will give you more, and you will fetch Bennald. And then I will tell you everything, and you will let us go on our way."

"Agreed," the Ordseer said, almost shouting. "Now talk."

Stone nodded. A hundred japes passed through his mind unsaid. He was done with japing. He had no illusions that the Ordseer would actually let them go, but if he could get Brook and Bennald in the room with him, they might have a chance—assuming the other two were armed, even if it was only with kitchen knives. Stone closed his eyes for a moment. The room was silent save for his own breathing and that of the Ordseer and the two Black Cloaks standing behind him. He opened his eyes again and looked at the sorcerer.

"When I told you that Brook, Bennald, and I were cousins to Jole Arrick, I spoke the truth," Stone lied. "We are of his own family, but cousins at a distance. We, too, are virrlings, but lacking in the great powers that Jole possesses. Our abilities are meager in comparison with his, though we can cast small spells when the need arises."

"Where do you hail from?" the Ordseer demanded.

"The wastelands of the far north."

The Ordseer gave Stone a mirthless grin. "Where your witch friends live."

Stone nodded. "That was true as well, but we have no alliance with them. We share the land as separate peoples, and the peace between us is fragile."

"Go on."

"When we heard ..." Stone stopped and crossed his arms in front of him.

"I said, go on."

Stone shook his head. "I'll see Brook now. Then I'll say more."

The Ordseer licked his slips and nodded to one of the Black Cloaks. "Bring the woman."

The Black Cloak returned a few minutes later with Brook. The second Black Cloak brought in a chair and set it down not far from Stone. As Brook sat down, she gave Stone the slightest nod.

"Tell me the rest of it," the Ordseer commanded.

Stone ignored him and looked at Brook. "Are you well?"

"I've been worse," she replied. "Though my head feels as if someone had stuck a *knife* in it."

"I know exactly how you feel," Stone said. "Exactly."

"Enough," the Ordseer barked. "You can see she's alive and well. Now tell me the rest of it."

Stone nodded. "Very well. When we heard ..."

"Stop," the Ordseer shouted. He stood up, his eyes blazing, a grotesque smile curling his lips into a trembling sneer. He pointed at Brook. "You. I would hear the tale from you. Who are you and what do you know of Jole Arrick? We'll see if your words agree with his."

Brook shrugged. "Never heard of him."

"It's all right," Stone said to her. "I already revealed to him that we're distant cousins to Jole. I plan to tell him the rest once I know Bennald is unharmed."

"Quiet," the Ordseer said. "Let her tell it. You hold your tongue."

"*Which is* just what I plan to do," Stone said, shooting Brook the briefest glance.

Brook gazed at him. "Are you sure it's all right?"

Stone nodded. "It's all right. I agreed to reveal everything we know about Jole and his allies if he agreed to let me see you and Bennald."

Brook nodded and turned to the Ordseer. "When we heard that Cousin Jole had gone missing, we determined to find him. We thought he might have taken refuge with the witches of the far north, but we learned that was not so."

The Ordseer gazed at her. "How did you learn it?"

"We asked the witches."

"With whom you supposedly have a fragile peace?"

"That's right."

"Go on."

"When we realized Jole was not with the witches, we …"

"Just a moment," Stone said. "Before we tell you more, we want to see Bennald."

The Ordseer waved a hand at one of the Black Cloaks. "Bring the oaf."

A few minutes later, the Black Cloak returned with Bennald, who remained standing. He was on Stone's left, Brook was sitting to his right, six feet away.

"Greetings, Cousin Bennald," Stone said to him. "Are you unharmed?"

"I'm well enough," Bennald replied. "Though I feel as if a herd of forest rokes has been stampeding through my brain."

"Very poetic, cousin," Stone said. "Brook and I have been telling the good Ordseer all we know of Cousin Jole. Brook was just explaining ..."

"Silence!" the Ordseer shouted. He stared at Bennald. "Tell me what you know of this virrling cousin of yours. From the beginning."

Bennald nodded. "In the beginning, Cousin Jole was born. His father was a powerful virrling prince, and his mother was a beautiful witch princess. As a child, young Jole ..."

"No, you fool!" the Ordseer barked. "I want to know your link to Jole Arrick, and I want to know where he is. I don't need his entire history."

"I'm Cousin Jole's cousin," Bennald replied. "As to where he is, I haven't a notion." Bennald squinted and stared past the Ordseer. He pointed to the corner where his staff was leaning. "There's my staff." He began to walk toward it, past the small table at which the Ordseer sat.

"Get back where you were, fool," the Ordseer snapped.

Bennald stopped and pointed again. "There's my staff," he said and started walking again.

The Black Cloaks had drawn their swords and started forward after him. When they strode past Stone, he reached down and pulled the kitchen knife from his boot. Brook pulled a paring knife from under her tunic, and they sprang forward at the same moment. The Black Cloaks turned, too late. Stone punched Sir Ogger's throat with his left hand

and plunged his blade into the knight's chest. Sir Ogger screamed and swung his sword, its edge just catching Stone's shoulder, tearing his tunic and nearly biting into the flesh. Stone spun away as Sir Ogger tried to swing again, but the man was teetering, screaming bloody oaths. As he fell to his knees, Stone kicked his sword hand, sending the knight's blade clattering against a wall.

Brook had plunged the paring knife into Sir Tacken's side and slashed him open. He had gone down like a sack of grain. He was still alive, clutching his stomach and moaning. Bennald had his left arm tight around the Ordseer's throat and a butcher's knife in his right hand. The Ordseer was beginning to turn blue.

Stone and Brook picked up the felled knights' swords and daggers. Stone was about to open the door and look out, when Sir Lempter and the Black Cloak named Sir Waltick burst into the room with swords in their hands. Stone and Brook jumped back, holding swords in front of them.

"Stop!" Bennald shouted. "Drop your swords or the Ordseer is dead."

The two Black Cloaks stared in horror at the Ordseer. His tongue was out of his mouth and his eyes were bulging. Bennald pulled his arm tighter around the Ordseer's throat. He raised his right hand just enough to let the Black Cloaks see the knife clutched in it.

"I'll cut his throat," Bennald said. "Drop your swords."

"If we do, how do we know these two won't run us through?" Sir Lempter said as Sir Tacken continued to moan from the floor. Sir Ogger had gone silent.

Bennald let go of the Ordseer's throat, grabbed a handful of his ginger hair, and wrenched back his head. As the Ordseer drew in a great, shuddering breath, Bennald put the point of the butcher knife against his throat. "If you don't drop your swords in the next three seconds, I'll slit his throat. One … two …"

Sir Lempter dropped his sword. A moment later, Sir Waltick dropped his.

"You two, go stand in the corners, noses against the wall, your arms raised high and pressed against the wall," Stone said to the two Black Cloaks. They did as they were told.

"How many more Black Cloaks are here?" Brook asked.

When there was no answer, Stone pressed the point of his sword against the back of Sir Lempter's neck. "Answer the lady, and don't lie."

"There are no more of us here than are in this room," Sir Lempter said.

Stone pressed his sword harder, and a drop of blood bloomed and ran down Sir Lempter's neck. "I told you not to lie."

"I'm not lying," Sir Lempter snapped. "Seventeen of us came here with the Ordseer. Twelve have left, and one is escorting the wench who brought you here."

"Escorting her where?"

"Sevnpools."

"What about the other twelve?" Stone asked. "Where did they go?"

"Greenport."

"Why?"

Sir Lempter hesitated a moment before replying, "They took the other wench."

"What other wench?"

"The sister."

Stone twisted the point of his sword against Sir Lempter's neck. "What sister? What's her name?"

"Jannelle or Jannela or some such."

"We need to go," Brook said.

Stone nodded. "Stay just as you are for the next hour," he said to the Black Cloaks. "Or we'll kill the Ordseer."

Brook went to door and looked out. "It's clear," she said and stepped into the hallway.

Bennald followed, pushing the Ordseer ahead of him, his arm still around the sorcerer's neck. Stone picked up the Black Cloaks' swords and left the room, closing the door behind him. "Remember," he bellowed through the door. "If we see any sign of movement from you lot, I'll rip out the Ordseer's entrails and use them to strangle him."

They made their way outside, passing a handful of terrified servants. When the stable boy saw them coming with the Ordseer, he tried to run, but Stone put on a burst of unnatural speed and caught him. "Get our horses ready. When you're finished, take one yourself and get as far away from here as possible. Take the other servants with you. And don't sign any parchments."

"Yes, milord," the stable boy said, and he set to his work.

"What'll we do with the Ordseer?" Brook asked when the horses were ready.

Stone went to where Bennald was holding the sorcerer and peered at him. The man looked terrified. "Ease up on him a bit," Stone said. Bennald loosened his grip and Stone put his face inches from the Ordseer's. "What do you know about us and our connection to Jole Arrick?"

The Ordseer's eyes went wide, and his entire lower jaw began to tremble.

"Why do we not have our memories?" Stone demanded. "What sorcery has been done to us?"

The Ordseer shook his head with tiny, rapid movements. His entire body was shaking.

"He doesn't know," Brook said.

Stone slapped the Ordseer's face. "Who are you?"

The Ordseer's jaw worked, but no sound came out.

"Are you really a sorcerer?"

The Ordseer nodded and then shook his head again.

"What'll we do with him?" Brook asked.

"We should tie him up and gag him," Bennald said.

"I think I'll cut his throat," Stone said, and the Ordseer whimpered like a lost puppy before fainting dead away.

Stone slapped the Ordseer's face again and shouted in his ear. He was about to slap him again when he noticed that the man's face had turned the color of boiled ashes. He put an ear to the sorcerer's chest. His heartbeat was barely perceptible.

"He's fading," Brook said.

"I know," said Stone. "I can barely hear his black heart beating."

"No, I mean he's really fading."

Stone stopped listening to the Ordseer's chest and stared at his face. It was like looking at someone at the bottom of a murky pond.

"Get away from him," Bennald yelled.

Stone jumped back, still staring at the Ordseer. The man was shimmering and rippling and growing fainter, like stars fading against the sky as the sun rises. A moment later, he was gone. All that remained of the Ordseer was his pendant and the short gold chain that held it. The three stared at the spot where he had disappeared. Then they stared at one another.

"What do you make of that?" Stone asked.

Brook shook her head. "I haven't a notion."

"We should go," said Bennald.

Stone picked up the Ordseer's pendant and dropped it into a pocket. Then they mounted their horses and headed for Sevnpools.

They were halfway there when they rounded a bend in the road and heard the sound of a single horse cantering. A moment later, they saw Aliya riding toward them.

"You!" Stone shouted.

Aliya reined her horse to a stop. The other three stopped as well. "Who is she?" Brook asked.

Stone drew his sword. "Put your hands high over your head," he told Aliya.

Aliya raised her hands high. "Please," she said. "You've got to help me."

"Help you?" Stone sputtered. "Help you? You're japing. You must be japing."

"Who is she?" Brook asked again.

"The lying wench who betrayed me to the Ordseer," Stone replied.

"I had to," Aliya said. "They have my sister."

"Ah, yes, the famous Jannela," Stone said.

"You've got to help me rescue her. A dozen Black Cloaks took her to Greenport."

"Get down from your horse, slowly, and keep your right hand high," Stone said.

"Please," Aliya begged. "We have to follow them."

"Get down now," Stone said. "The moment you dismount, lie on the ground with your feet apart and both arms out to your sides."

"I won't," Aliya said.

"You will," Stone replied. "Otherwise, we won't help you find your sister."

Aliya hesitated a moment, and then she slid off her horse and lay on the ground.

Stone looked at Bennald. "Take her left hand in both of yours and don't let go. I'll take her right hand. Brook, you search her for daggers. Search everywhere. Strip her naked if you have to. She has a talent for hiding blades. Throwing them as well. And she'd as soon cut your throat as look at you."

The three dismounted, and Stone and Bennald approached Aliya. They held her arms firmly as Brook searched her.

"An awful deal of trouble for one slip of a girl," Brook muttered. She was about to say something else when she found the first blade. She found two more before she declared Aliya bladeless.

"Are you sure?" Stone asked.

Brook nodded. "Check her for yourself, if you like."

"Never mind," Stone said. He turned to Aliya. "On your feet. We're taking you with us to Sevnpools, where you'll tell us the truth about yourself and this sister of yours."

Aliya stood up and brushed dirt from her tunic and leggings. A tear slid down her cheek, and a sob shuddered through her body. "Please," she said softly. "We have to hurry."

"Get on your horse," Stone said.

After Aliya mounted her horse, Stone took a length of rope from his saddlebag and tied her hands behind her. "Bennald will be in the lead," he told her. "You'll follow him. Brook and I will be right behind you. Don't try anything that you might regret."

They set off again at a slow trot. As they went, Stone asked Brook how she and Bennald wound up in the clutches of the Ordseer.

"After we left you, we entered Blackpond through the south gate and spotted the Hare's Hollow Inn. We took rooms there and stabled the horses, figuring you would enter the town from the same direction and spot the place. We were having a meal in the common room when a well-dressed man entered by himself and took a table adjacent to ours. I took him to be a merchant of some sort.

"After he was served, he began to speak with Bennald and me. I had no desire to talk to strangers, but ignoring him might have seemed suspicious. He asked us if we were travelers and wanted to know what news we had. I told him the tale we had rehearsed and mentioned that we had come from near Drumkin. At the mention of Drumkin, he asked if we had heard about the dramatic escape of a dark sorcerer from the Drumkin jail and the flight of this sorcerer and his two accomplices, a man and a woman. I was about to tell him that we had not heard of any such antics, when Bennald, the poor fool, spoke up and claimed the escaped man was no dark sorcerer."

"Ah, Bennald," Stone said, shaking his head. "The soul of innocence, bless him."

"The stranger claimed he wanted to help us, which made me suspicious, but I said I'd hear him out. Before we knew it, a group of four men sitting at another table leaped up and struck before we could defend ourselves. I was knocked unconscious. When I woke up, I was tied to my horse. When we arrived at the querl, a Black Cloak came out and paid the stranger and the four men. Then they rode off."

"Hired swords."

Brook nodded. "Paid to find us and deliver us to the Ordseer."

"And yet we know now that the Ordseer was a fraud."

"Aye, but a fraud who disappeared into the air."

"There must be someone else behind all this trouble."

"A real sorcerer perhaps," Brook said.

"And the three of us remain where we've always been," Stone said. "In the dark."

Chapter 17 - Aliya's Story

Stone, Brook, and Bennald, along with Aliya, arrived in Sevnpools and went to the Six and One Inn. Stone untied Aliya's hands before they entered, warning her not to make trouble. They paid for three rooms and asked the innkeeper to send food and ale for four to the larger room. Once inside the room, Stone began to retie Aliya's hands behind her back.

"Is that necessary?" Aliya asked, looking again as if she might cry. "How will I eat?"

"Do you promise not to make trouble or kill anyone?" Stone asked.

"I promise."

Stone relented and left her hands free. "Watch her at all times," he said to Brook and Bennald. "Don't let her near any blades. If you have to get close to her, put one hand on the hilt of your dagger and the other on the hilt of your sword. If she makes any sudden moves, run her through."

The food arrived, mutton stew with carrots, onions, and golden mushrooms along with tankards of ale. The four sat at a table in a corner of the room overlooking Seven Street, Sevnpools' main avenue. They allowed Aliya a spoon but no knife. As they ate, Aliya told her tale.

"What I said about being from Banderry was true enough, as far as it went," she began. "From as early as I can remember, I lived just outside the village on a lord's manor with my mother and my younger sister, Jannela. I never knew my father. My mother always told people he died when I was little, before my sister was born, but everyone knew he abandoned us and never married her. I didn't care.

"The lord of the manor hired my mother to cook, and his steward put Jannela and me to work as soon as we were old enough to do anything useful. It was hard work. We watered the hens, collected eggs, gathered kindling, picked stones from fields about to be plowed, and pulled weeds from the garden. We learned to cook and clean and fold the mistress's linens, and we fed the dogs and cats and picked flaws out of wool. Sometimes we helped brush the horses. I liked that best.

"The lord had three sons. When the eldest turned sixteen, the lord sent him to the Red City to study at the Ruby Querl, to prepare him to become a high freykon. The local freykon was getting on in years, and the lord figured his son would take over Banderry's querl whenever the old freykon finally died.

"The eldest son was a haughty sort, and he carried his sharp nose much too high in the air for one so young. He had no merriment in him. He was worse even than his father, who took little joy in much besides his estate and his gold. The middle son was quiet and timid, like his mother, a bit of a nimpling if truth be told, and he even seemed fearful of Jannela and me, lowly servants though we were. His lordship was always comparing him to his elder brother, which only made him all the more shy. The youngest, who was my own age, was grand, bold and fun-loving, always laughing, always planning and plotting some good-natured mischief.

He was our friend, despite the sharpish looks he got from his father and especially from his eldest brother, and he included Jannela and me in his schemes and games and little adventures. We ran races, climbed trees, swam in the creek, played at swords with wooden blades, lost ourselves in the forest, and had knife-throwing contests with real daggers."

"I'll wager you won your share of those knife-throwing contests," Stone said.

"I did," Aliya said. "I had the knack for it."

"Go on," Brook said.

"The youngest son never minded that we were girls, and we never cried when we got skinned knees or knocks on the head. And if any of the little lordlings who visited the manor complained about having to play with girls, he'd threaten to black their eyes or bloody their noses. He made good on those threats once or twice."

Aliya paused for a moment and smiled, as if she were recalling a fond memory. "He taught us to read and write as well, unbeknown to the rest of his family, of course. For that, I'll be forever grateful to him, wherever he is." A tear slipped from her eye, and she let if fall before continuing.

"Things might have gone on as they were, except that our mother took ill and died. I was thirteen years old, Jannela was twelve. Our position altered, in more ways than we expected. The lady of the manor was a fragile sort, thin and pale and stiff. She looked as if she might snap like a twig if you shot her a hard look. She was melancholy and spoke little, although she was fond of our mother. She would talk to her more than to her own husband. She paid Jannela and me little mind, but she never treated us badly. But once our mother was gone, the lady weakened, not only in her body but also in her spirit, such as it was. Soon enough, she was in her grave as well.

"The eldest son, the supposed future freykon of Banderry, took quarters in the Red City near the Ruby Querl, and it was decided that I should serve him there. I was to make his meals, wash his clothes, and clean his quarters. The lord arranged for me to stay in the servants' quarters at the querl, which sits on a large piece of land near the Farro River. Jannela was to remain at the manor and continue serving there.

"My sister and I protested this arrangement, but it did no good. I think his lordship wanted to separate us, for some secret reason of his own, perhaps just to be cruel. His youngest promised he'd look after my sister and told me he'd visit the Red City as often as he could to see me and bring me food and whatever coin he could get his hands on. He began feigning interest in the eldest brother's studies, hoping for invitations to visit. Sometimes he would drive a wagon to town on market days and try to see me in his brother's quarters or in the servants' quarters at the querl. We devised signs and signals so we could meet without arousing suspicion—a ribbon left on a back gate of the querl grounds, a note left in the hollow of a certain tree— and he also carried notes back and forth between my sister and me. It was like another of our games, and we were good at it.

"By this time, I was blooming into my womanhood, and I began noticing the eldest brother giving me odd, sidelong looks. He started keeping me in his quarters later than I was accustomed to, taking his dinner late in the evening or asking me to tidy something that didn't need tidying. I told him that the keeper of the querl's servant quarters locked the doors at a certain hour, but whenever I complained about being late, he shot me one of his superior looks, as if I had no right to complain to a high and mighty lord about anything. One night when I complained over the lateness of the hour, he said it didn't matter and that I could sleep in his quarters, on the floor. When I balked, he said no one needed to know. He was staring at me in a way that made me uneasy, and his voice had gone strange. I bolted and ran back to my own little cell, though, truth be told, I knew more than one way to slip in and out of the Ruby Querl's servant quarters, locked doors or no.

"After that, I left his rooms at the same time every day, even if he had to cook his own supper. He treated me as if I had committed some fault, all haughty and proud. I had a key to get into his rooms, and he started throwing hints that I had been stealing from him. He would make a great show of looking for some book or for a certain candlestick or kitchen knife or goblet and then ask if I knew where it was or what had become of it. I knew what had become of it. He had hidden it somewhere so he could cast his suspicions and prepare his false accusations.

"The next time I saw the youngest son, I told him what had happened. He offered to thrash his brother, but I told him not to. Instead, we planned an escape, mine and Jannela's. He said he would sneak my sister out of the manor in the wagon when the time was right, and she and I would find servant work in the Red City or on another manor. But before we could carry out our plan, the eldest brother tried to carry out a plan of his own.

"It was a month after he tried to keep me in his rooms overnight. He had returned to his quarters earlier than usual, and I could smell wine on his breath. That surprised me. I had never known him to touch a drop of wine or ale, and he had no merry friends, if he had any friends at all. I didn't know what to make of it. He didn't realize that I knew, and he tried to speak without slurring and walk without wambling. It was so funny, I couldn't help but laugh.

"He asked me what I was laughing about. I told him that one of the other girls in the servant quarters had made a jape the night before and something had made me recall it just then. He frowned and demanded to know what it was made me think of it. Just then, I saw a tiny little spider on top of his head, making its way through his hair. I couldn't help myself. I said, 'Perhaps it was that spider on your head reminded me of the lass's jape.'

"His eyes went wide, and he brushed his hand through his hair back and forth like he was trying to put out a fire. I laughed again, may the gods forgive me. He went red in the face, as red as the walls of his precious Ruby Querl. 'What are you laughing at?' he said in a shrill voice.

"Again, I couldn't stop myself. 'You better make sure his little spider family didn't build a nest there,' I said. 'Perhaps you've heard them whispering.'

"His face twisted into an ugly scowl and he came toward me, his face redder than ever. 'Bitch,' he said. 'Worthless, menial bitch.' He grabbed my left arm and pulled me toward him. I thought he was going to strike me, but instead he tried to kiss me. I spun away, but he still had my arm, and he wrenched me toward him again and used his other hand to clutch at the top of my blouse. He pulled on it, trying to rip it off me, but by then I had a blade in my other hand."

"Why am I not surprised?" Stone asked.

"Of course, I had got it from the youngest brother," Aliya said. "It was a fine blade, and he thought I should have it for my own protection in the Red City. Ever since our games in the woods I had been in the habit of always having at least one dagger secreted about my person. Most often nowadays it's more. You'd be surprised at all the places a woman can hide a dagger."

"Nothing about you and daggers would surprise me," Stone said. "Is your sister a blade mistress as well?"

Aliya nodded. "Jannela is almost as skilled as I am."

"But what happened with you and this wretched eldest brother?" Brook asked. "After you produced the blade?"

Aliya looked at Brook and smiled. "I stabbed the future freykon of Banderry in his arm, and he squealed like a wounded pig. He backed off, his anger and amazement glowing in his eyes. I said, 'If you touch me again, I'll cut your throat,' and I would have done it. Then I left."

"Good for you," Brook said.

"Don't encourage her," said Stone.

"Then what happened?" Brook asked.

"I ran to my quarters and gathered my things, put it all in an old leather satchel his lordship had seen fit to give me on the day I left the manor. I left a note for the youngest son in our special tree, and then I headed into the city, wondering what I would do.

"The eldest brother, meanwhile, cleaned up and hied himself back to the manor. He told his father I had been stealing from him and that when he confronted me with my crimes I attacked him with a knife. The youngest didn't believe the tale, fair show to him, but his lordship sent his reeve and some porters to seize me. Our grand plan of escape was in ruins, but the youngest did what he could to right things. He took my sister and a couple of horses and made for the Red City, taking a shortway to get ahead of the reeve's party. But they were found out, and his lordship sent his marshal after them. When the youngest brother spied the marshal in pursuit, he told my sister where she might find a message from me, sent her on her way, and put himself between her and the marshal. He must have delayed the man long enough, because Jannela got to the Red City unhindered and ahead of the reeve.

She found the note I'd left and then found me. We rode the horse south to Covetown, and there we made our way in the world. I was fourteen and Jannela was thirteen. We never saw his lordship or any of his sons again."

The room fell silent for a moment, and then Brook asked, "What happened to deliver Jannela into the Ordseer's clutches?"

"We had been making our way well enough, first serving at other manors, then helping at the market in Covetown, and eventually moving to the Red City, where we made ourselves useful to some farmers by managing their affairs at the big market. And then one day, not long ago, I came home and found that Jannela had signed a pledge."

"A fastle pledge," Stone said.

Aliya nodded. "At the time, I didn't know the pledges were sorcerer's work, but I still couldn't believe it. I was cross with her and said, 'Our only pledges are to one another.' She said, 'But this was a pledge to the king.' 'Damn the king,' I told her. 'What did he ever do for us?'

"I told her we didn't need our names floating around the city. Because of the eldest brother's lies, I was still an outlaw. We both were. But Jannela just smiled and told me she didn't sign her real name. She made something up. She signed it *Merry Rover*. We had a good long laugh about it, but there was something wrong. It wasn't plain at first, but something was amiss with Jannela. And then one of the Black Cloaks came to our door. He said she hadn't signed properly and had to make amends, and he demanded that I sign one as well. We refused. He left but said he'd be back with others. We left the Red City that night and kept going. I thought we were safe, but a troop of Black Cloaks eventually caught us." Aliya looked at Brook. "They took us to that querl, and the Ordseer showed up the next day. We were there when the men they had hired showed up with you and your friend." Aliya looked at Stone. "The Black Cloaks knew there was a third, but the hired swords apparently wanted no more doings with the Black Cloaks or the Ordseer. So the Ordseer told me that if I lured you to the querl, he would fix Jannela and let us go. He lied. I'm sorry. I beg your forgiveness."

"Never mind," Stone said. "I forgive you, may the gods have mercy on me and my soft head."

"You believe me then?" Aliya asked.

"We believe you," Brook said. "And we'll help you rescue your sister." She looked at Stone. "Won't we?"

Stone nodded and stood up. "I need more ale. Let's go down to the common room. Tomorrow we'll head for Greenport."

When they entered the common room, Stone and Brook were surprised and delighted to see Sir Elling and Sir Panwer sitting at a table and taking a meal. As Stone and the others approached them, the two knights looked up and smiled in recognition.

"Just the people we were looking for," Elling said as he stood up to greet the four.

Stone saw Elling glance curiously at Aliya. He was about to introduce her when he saw the knight's eyes go wide and his jaw drop. At the same time, he heard Aliya gasp.

"Aliya?" Elling whispered. "Can it be?"

A great sob escaped from Aliya, and she ran to embrace Sir Elling, who caught her up in his arms and held her like a long-lost love.

Stone, Brook, Bennald, and Sir Panwer watched the scene in silence. Finally, Stone turned to Panwer and said, "Tell me, Sir Panwer, is Sir Elling the youngest son of a lord who owns a manor near Banderry?"

"Indeed, he is," Sir Panwer replied, a look of surprise on his face. "How did you know?"

"A lucky guess," Stone said. "But tell me, where is Sir Kaemon?"

"He and the king's wistlord are also looking for you, in Greenport. I hope you and your friends will come with Elling and me tomorrow to meet up with them."

"We will," Stone said. "We have tidings to report about the infamous Ordseer."

***

In the small hours of the morning, Stone crept out of the room he was sharing with Bennald and went to Brook's room. He knocked softly, then harder, and then he called her in a loud whisper. The door opened an inch. "What do you want?" Brook demanded, glaring at him.

"I need to talk to you."

"You can talk to me tomorrow."

"It's important."

"Go away," she said, and began to close the door.

"I cured a Redmonder thrall. Just after the battle outside Blackpond."

The door opened an inch wider. Behind it, Brook was giving him a hard stare. "You disenthralled a Redmonder?"

Stone nodded. "More than one. And it gave me an idea. I need to talk to you."

The door opened wider and he slipped inside the room and took a chair near the window. Brook closed the door and locked it. She remained standing as Stone described what had happened outside Captain Nollup's tent after the battle. When he was finished she sat down opposite him.

"What's your idea?" she asked.

"I think I can do it again. I'd like to try it on you."

She frowned. "I'm no thrall."

"No, but we must be under some enchantment. If I can enter your mind the way I did with those Redmonders, I may discover your name or something about you."

"I'm not sure I want you traipsing around inside my head."

"All right," he said, standing up. "Perhaps Bennald will be willing." He headed for the door.

"Just a minute," she said. He stopped and looked at her. "Do you really believe you might solve the riddle?"

"I won't lie to you, Brook. I don't know. But surely it's worth the attempt."

She let out a long breath and gave him a nod. "All right. Tell me what to do."

When he came out of his trance, he was gazing at Brook. She seemed to be staring through him, but after a moment, her eyes focused, and she gave him a nod. "Well," she said. "Do you know my name?"

"I don't know your name," he replied.

She looked away for a moment and then back at Stone. "Ah, well," she said with a sad smile. "It was worth a go."

"I don't know your name," he said again. "But I know who you are."

Chapter 18 - The Auction

It took Kaemon and Thig four days to reach Greenport, a medium-sized river town on the west bank of the Larka River. Although Greenport was smaller than Drumkin, it boasted more mills than any other town in Ruxland outside the Red City, and it was as prosperous as any place in the realm. River Street, with its docks and mills and markets, ran the full length of the town and into the surrounding farmland to the north, where it joined the main road. River Street also boasted a number of large stone houses and elegant inns and taverns. At the south end of the street, on the Shillian Inlet of the Larka River, skilled shipwrights plied their trade at the famed Shillian Shipyard.

After entering Greenport from the south, Kaemon and Thig veered left, away from the river, and entered Gaunt Street, which ran north and south. They proceeded north, past the town square, and turned left onto Winter Street. They crossed Green Street, which also ran north and south, and entered the quarter known as Mootle, in the northwest corner of Greenport. When they reached the Smoking Sky Inn, a modest but clean establishment that Kaemon had stayed in once or twice before, they dismounted, tied their horses to a wooden rail in front of the building, and went inside, hoping to find rooms. The savory smells of roasting game birds and rabbit stew filled the common room, and the laughter and chatter of a fair-sized crowd sounded like an invitation to a festival. The two travelers paid for a pair of rooms, arranged for their horses to be stabled, and took a meal before turning in for the night.

They woke early the next morning and went down to breakfast in the Smoking Sky's dining room. The innkeeper, a sandy-haired man with a rosy face named Rodd Tregaskle, served them himself, a feast of boiled eggs, dark barley bread with cubes of hard cheese baked into its top crust, slabs of bacon, and tankards of ale.

"You've arrived just in time for the hanging," Rodd informed them after he set down the plates and tankards.

"Who's being hanged?" Kaemon asked as he peered at the steaming plate in front of him.

"Some brute named Hake."

"What did he do?"

"Stole a horse. Tried to steal the blacksmith's daughter as well."

"Sounds as if Greenport is a lively town these days," Thig said.

Rodd chuckled. "Aye. I heard the girl brained the brute with his own blacksmith hammer as they rode out of town on the stolen horse."

"Good for her," Thig said.

Rodd looked thoughtful for a moment. "Funny thing, that. Such a blow would have killed most men, but not Hake. Some say his head is made of iron."

"I've known a few iron-heads," Kaemon said.

The innkeeper nodded. "I've known a few as well. Still, it was an odd business, taking a blow like that. Some people believe Hake isn't quite human."

237

Kaemon and Thig glanced at one another quickly, and then Kaemon turned back to Rodd. "Is this Hake a local fellow?"

The innkeeper shook his head. "He showed up a couple of months ago. He went to one of the blacksmith shops, Hipnog's it was, and signed on as a 'prentice. Old Hipnog says Hake's as fine a smith as he's ever come across. Course, that was before he tried to steal Hipnog's daughter."

"Where did this Hake fellow come from?" Thig asked.

Rodd shrugged. "Nobody knows, though there's no shortage of rumors. Hake never talked much, and he's such a grim-looking piece of work that not many cared to strike up a chat with him."

"Your Hipnog must have known something about him," Kaemon said.

"No more than anyone else. Hipnog told Hake what to do, and Hake did it. When his work was done for the day, he'd head out of town to who knows where and return the next morning."

"Perhaps Hake lived in a tent," Thig said.

"Or a hole in the ground," said Kaemon.

"Most people think he has a hovel somewhere in the woods, but no one ever laid eyes on it," Rodd said. "Some young fellows tried to follow him one night, but all they got for their trouble were blacked eyes. That put a quick end to trying to find out where Hake lived."

"When's the hanging?" Thig asked.

"Midmorning or so," said Rodd. "First, the constable is going to auction off his hammer and a few other articles of his."

238

"Thanks for the tidings," Kaemon said. "I wonder if you've seen some friends of ours who might be here in Greenport. A man about my height, with darkish hair and beard, a slightly shorter but sturdy man with sandy hair, and a pretty woman with dark hair down to her shoulders."

The innkeeper shook his head. "Haven't seen any such, but there's other inns in town."

"We'll have a look around," Kaemon said.

"Do that," said Rodd. "And don't forget about the hangin'."

Kaemon and Thig paid for their breakfast and then went out to stroll around Greenport and check the other inns for any sign of Stone and Brook and Bennald. A bank of low, dark clouds threatened rain, and a slight breeze stirred, but the cool morning air was not unpleasant. As they approached the town square, which was located at the intersection of Green Street and Spring Street, they saw that a small crowd had gathered there for the auction of the doomed blacksmith's personal effects. Except for a fine blacksmith hammer, the effects were meager. A small table held the hammer, some clothing, a leather apron, a dagger, an axe, and a gold ring with a red stone. The ring was on a long silver chain that was bolted to the table. Kaemon and Thig joined the group huddled around the table to have a look at the articles. A big, barrel-chested man was scrutinizing the hammer, and when he set it down, Kaemon picked it up. As he looked it over, he heard Thig gasp. He turned to look at the wistlord, who was holding the ring and staring at it.

"What is it, Thig?" Kaemon asked.

Thig passed him the ring, still held by the silver chain, and pointed to the insignia on it. Kaemon felt his stomach lurch. It was the four-sided insignia of Jole Arrick. He looked at the hammer in his right hand and saw the same insignia burned into the bottom of the handle.

"What's going on?" Thig whispered.

Kaemon shook his head. "I don't know. The other three never mentioned a fourth."

"Perhaps they don't know about him."

The auctioneer's assistant appeared and shooed the crowd away from the table so the auction could begin. The auctioneer, a thin gray-haired man dressed all in black, stood on a podium that his assistant had placed next to the table and announced that the bidding would begin. His assistant held up the leather apron and someone in the crowd called out a number.

"What'll we do?" Thig asked.

"I'm going to bid on the ring," Kaemon said.

"What about the hammer? If this Hake is another wandreme, it may have magical properties."

Kaemon shook his head. "I don't think so. The other three didn't believe their rings and weapons had such properties, despite the insignia. If they possess any magic, it's in them, not in their belongings."

Kaemon and Thig counted their coins, and Kaemon decided how much he could spend. He was determined to outbid anyone else.

The blacksmith hammer was the next-to-last item to be sold, and it went to the big man who had examined it before Kaemon, a young blacksmith named Jaynum Stant. The ring was the final item. Kaemon and Thig edged their way to the front of the crowd. The dark clouds broke, and sunlight came pouring into the town square.

The auctioneer took the ring from its chain and held it up. The crowd pressed closer for a better view.

"One gold ring, with a nicely sized, excellently cut redstone. Who will make the opening bid?"

A man with sparse white hair and a spindly frame raised his hand and said, "One silver."

Kaemon waited. A short, heavy man with huge jowls and a necklace of fat bulging out above a stiff white shirt collar raised a hand and bid two silvers.

"Haster Mellis'll win this one," a man standing next to Kaemon whispered.

"Which one is Haster Mellis?" Kaemon asked.

"That pudgy fellow," the man replied.

The first bidder bid three silvers, and Haster Mellis bid four.

Kaemon waited. The first bidder upped his offer to five silvers.

"Who's that?" Kaemon asked the man next to him.

"Pellington Scray, a rich landowner."

The bidding continued back and forth between Haster Mellis and Pellington Scray, and Kaemon continued to bide his time. Finally, when it appeared as if Pellington had given up, Kaemon bid one gold coin. The crowd turned to him, murmuring and whispering. Haster Mellis glared at him and upped the bid, adding a silver to Kaemon's gold.

Now the bidding was between Haster and Kaemon, but Kaemon meant to keep bidding until he won.

In the end, Kaemon outbid Haster and took possession of the ring. Haster shot him a baleful look and muttered something about "rich young idlers from the capital coming into the provinces to throw their father's money around."

"It was a fair auction, so mind your tongue," Thig shot back at the man, who stalked off, still muttering.

The auctioneer and his assistant took away the table and podium, but the crowd remained. A group of men came and cleared a space on the square, and then a team of draft horses arrived hauling a wagon with sections of a wooden gallows and a crew of carpenters. The men set up the gallows, much to the delight of the onlookers.

"We have to stop this," Kaemon said.

"How will we do that?" Thig asked.

"We'll tell them about the insignia, about Jole Arrick."

"The people in the outer provinces aren't so familiar with Jole or his emblem."

"We need to find the constable," Kaemon said. "Come on."

Kaemon, in his duties as First Knight of the Realm, had visited all the major towns and most of the minor ones in all four of Ruxland's provinces and had met the Greenport constable on one or two occasions. He knew the constable's quarters were located on Green Street below the square, and he and Thig made their way there and entered. A squire greeted them and then fetched the constable, a broad-shouldered man named Tenney, with a ruddy face, thinning blond hair, and a wispy beard.

"What can I do for you gentlemen?" Constable Tenney said when he stepped into the front room.

"Sir Constable, I am Kaemon Krowe, First Knight of the Kingdom of Ruxland, and this is Thig Grennell, King Harrin's wistlord," Kaemon began. "You and I met briefly a year and a half ago, here in Greenport."

Constable Tenney eyed Kaemon warily. "Yes, maybe so. I might remember you. You're not dressed as a knight."

"You must have heard about the trouble in the Red City," Thig said.

"Aye, that I have. Something to do with a character named the Ordseer."

Kaemon nodded. "We two and some others escaped from the Ordseer's treachery. But he's taken over Redmond and sent agents to the outer provinces to trick people into signing what are called fastle pledges. Signing one turns the signer into a thrall."

The constable raised an eyebrow but gave no indication whether or not he believed Kaemon. "What brings you two to Greenport?" he asked.

"We're looking for some people—two men and a woman—who may hold the key to overcoming the Ordseer's sorcery and treachery. They have a connection to a virrling named Jole Arrick, who's a counselor to King Harrin. Unfortunately, Jole has disappeared."

"What do these three look like?" Tenney asked. When Kaemon described them, the constable shook his head. "Haven't seen 'em."

"There's more," Kaemon said, and he produced the ring he had just bought at auction. "This ring belonged to the man you're about to hang, the blacksmith named Hake." He pointed to the ring's insignia. "This is the symbol of the virrling Jole Arrick. We believe Hake has the same connection to Jole as the three I told you about, the ones we're looking for."

Tenney narrowed his eyes. "And what connection could a horse thief have with your virrling friend or these three others? Except maybe that he stole that ring?"

"I don't know," Kaemon said. "The other three have lost their memories. I suspect Hake has done so as well, but we need to speak with him."

Tenney eyed Kaemon as if he'd just claimed to have flown to Greenport on the back of a dragon. "This is a load of odd particulars you've just laid at my doorstep, Sir Kaemon. Or a load of quagwash, meaning no disrespect."

"I know it's hard to credit," Thig said. "But it's all true, and the future of the realm is at stake."

"Braant Province can get along without the Red City or Redmond Province," Tenney replied.

"The Ordseer means to take control of the entire kingdom," Kaemon said. "No place will be safe, not even Braant."

"I've no desire to get on the wrong side of the First Knight of the Realm, even if the Red City has been conquered by sorcery," the constable said.

"But justice must be served, and the brute must be hanged. There's nothing I can do but hang him."

"At least let me talk to him."

"I'm afraid not. And now I have to ask you to leave, Sir Kaemon, meaning no disrespect. I have to prepare for the execution."

Chapter 19 - Hake

Kaemon and Thig left the constable's quarters and headed back to the town square. Dark clouds were again blotting out the sun and threatening rain, but the crowd had grown even larger in anticipation of the hanging, and people were beginning to fill the street that led to the gallows.

Halfway back to the town square, Kaemon stopped. "I'm going back to the jail."

Thig looked alarmed. "What do you propose to do?"

"Nothing. I just want to get a look at this Hake fellow."

"Very well," Thig said. "But don't do anything rash."

"As First Knight of the Realm, I could order the constable to let me speak to Hake."

"And as a Braanter, he would most likely refuse, meaning no disrespect, of course."

"I'll meet you back at the square," Kaemon said.

He made his way south on Green Street, shouldering his way through the crowd, toward the constable's quarters. Hawkers had set up rolling stands on small carts and were selling pots of ale, mugs of cider, roasted kepples, hard-cooked eggs, small meat pies, and other delicacies. A half dozen young men were capering and pretending to argue among themselves to distract the hawkers so that an equal number of their fellow roisterers could help themselves to ale and meat pies without paying. The young men were raising the boisterousness of the crowd to a level that would have done a shipload of drunken sailors proud.

When Kaemon neared the jail, he saw that a small group of officials had gathered outside. Constable Tenney was there, and Kaemon also recognized Sir Herrick Felkin, the justiciar of Braant Province, a tall man with protruding blue eyes, a hawk nose, and a rounded chest that reminded Kaemon of an orange-breasted barrowbird. The justiciar was wearing the bright red cape and red leggings that denoted his office. The high freykon of Braant, a white-haired man named Lemus Goodlock, was on hand as well.

The front door opened, and two uniformed pikemen came out followed by a powerfully built man of medium height whose hands were bound in front of him. Two more pikemen followed him out, and one of them closed the door and locked it. The prisoner had a black beard and curly black hair that glistened even in the subdued light of the cloudy day. Stable hands arrived with horses, and the officials mounted up. As Kaemon looked on, the slow march to the gallows began.

Sir Herrick, riding a black horse with a red blanket, led the way, keeping a slow but steady pace. He would serve as the official executioner. Lemus Goodlock, the high freykon, came next, on foot and chanting prayers. Hake walked behind the freykon, turning his head right and left to glare at the crowd. Constable Tenney, also on horseback, followed Hake. A plainly dressed gray-bearded man with broad shoulders and thick arms walked behind

Constable Tenney. Kaemon figured the graybeard must be old Hipnog, the blacksmith Hake had wronged. The four pikemen were on hand to keep an eye on the hundreds of spectators who lined the street from the jail to the town square, a distance of nearly a mile.

A drunk in the crowd threw an egg at Hake that hit one of the pikemen. The procession halted, and the pikemen surged into the crowd and caught the miscreant, who was thrashed and thrown to the ground. The pikemen bound his arms behind him, and two of them hauled him off to the jail. That left two pikemen and Constable Tenney to control the crowd.

During the scuffle, the young roisterers made off with an ale cart, and others in the crowd chased them. Kaemon left the chaotic scene to rejoin Thig at the town square.

"Anything?" Thig asked.

Kaemon shook his head. "We have to do something. We need to think."

While they were thinking, the procession arrived. Constable Tenney and the two remaining pikemen cleared the middle of the square, and the pikemen took positions between the crowd and the gallows. The high freykon recited the final prayers, and then the justiciar climbed the steps leading to the platform and took the noose in his hand. Constable Tenney directed the two pikemen to lead Hake up the steps and onto the platform and the waiting noose.

The sound of galloping came from up Spring Street, an avenue that ran east and west and ended at the square. Everyone turned to look. A group of thirteen mounted Black Cloaks entered the west side of the square and halted. The Black Cloak leader pulled a white parchment from his cloak and held it up for all to see. He spurred his horse to a walk and approached the gallows. His men waited not far behind him. Kaemon felt his insides clench. The Black Cloak leader was Sir Borus Renovar.

Sir Herrick Felkin, still on the platform with the noose in his hand, glared down at Sir Borus. "What is the meaning of this?"

"I have a writ from King Harrin," Sir Borus replied in a voice loud enough for everyone in the square to hear. "We're to take the prisoner to the Red City. Alive."

Muttering and grumbling and cries of "No!" rose up from the crowd. The loudest voice was old Hipnog's.

Constable Tenney approached Sir Borus and pointed at the parchment. "Let me see that," Tenney demanded.

Sir Borus, still mounted, handed the parchment down to Tenney. The constable quickly read it before turning to the justiciar. "It has King Harrin's seal and signature."

Kaemon elbowed his way through the crowd and ran to the gallows. He charged up the steps to the platform and faced Sir Herrick, who stared at him. "Now what?" the justiciar shouted. "Who are you?"

Sir Borus pointed at Kaemon and bellowed, "You!"

"Aye, me," Kaemon said to Sir Borus before turning back to Sir Herrick. "I am Sir Kaemon Krowe, First Knight of the Kingdom of Ruxland. You and I have met before, Sir Justiciar."

As another murmur rolled through the crowd, Sir Herrick narrowed his eyes and gazed at Kaemon. "Yes, I think we have. Perhaps you'll explain to me, Sir Kaemon, what in blazes is going on."

"He can't explain anything," Sir Borus shouted. "He's a traitor."

"You and the Ordseer are usurpers," Kaemon shot back before turning to Sir Herrick again. "These black-clad knights owe their allegiance to a sorcerer known as the Ordseer," he told the justiciar. "The Ordseer used dark magic in the form of fastle pledges to make thralls of the Redmonders, including King Harrin. The Ordseer means to take over the entire realm. No province, no town, no village will be safe from his sorcery." Kaemon paused and pointed toward Thig, who was standing near the gallows steps. "Here is Thig Grennell, King Harrin's wistlord. Neither he nor I signed fastle pledges, and we remain free of the Ordseer's thralldom. Some others among the Redmonders also remain free."

"He lies," Sir Borus said. "The Ordseer is King Harrin's most trusted counselor."

"Sir Kaemon speaks the truth," Thig said. "The Ordseer has turned the Red City and most of Redmond Province into a wasteland of dead-eyed thralls."

250

"I would see this document from King Harrin," Sir Herrick said to Constable Tenney. The constable climbed the steps to the platform and handed the parchment to the justiciar.

Sir Herrick read it and turned to Kaemon. "It does, indeed, bear the king's seal."

Kaemon raised an eyebrow. "May I see it, if you please?"

"Very well," said Sir Herrick, and he gave the parchment to Kaemon.

Kaemon took it, read it quickly, and then drew his dagger and drove it through the parchment. As he held it aloft on the blade, the parchment burst into flames, and a loud shriek, like an old metal shield rubbing hard against slate, pierced the air. The crowd in the square roared their shock and disbelief. Seconds later, all that remained of the parchment was a wisp of black smoke that soon dissipated, leaving behind an acrid scent. The crowd went silent but for angry muttering.

"Dark magic from the trickster Ordseer," Kaemon said to Sir Herrick, who was staring openmouthed at Kaemon's smoking dagger.

"Pay no attention to the traitor's parlor tricks," Sir Borus said to Sir Herrick. "I'll take the prisoner now."

The prisoner, Hake, had been watching the proceedings in silence, but now he turned to Sir Borus. "You'll take nothing, you great stinking barrel of pig filth," he shouted from the gallows platform. "I'd rather hang than go with you, you swine-breathed kettle of scum."

251

Everyone turned to look at the prisoner. Hake rewarded them with a great gob of spit aimed at Sir Borus, which hit the Black Cloak leader's arm. Sir Borus drew his sword and raised it over his head. "Dismount," he commanded his men, who were close behind him. "Swords at the ready."

As the twelve Black Cloaks dismounted, Constable Tenney drew his sword and ran down the gallows steps to join his two pikemen. "Pikemen, weapons at charge," the constable called out to his men, who lined up on either side of him.

Kaemon and Sir Herrick descended the gallows steps right behind the constable, and Thig Grennell elbowed through the muttering crowd to stand with them as well. The crowd pulled back, and many headed for home, but Jaynum Stant, the young blacksmith who had purchased Hake's hammer, stepped forward and took a position next to Thig, swinging the hammer like a mace.

"Advance and form up on me," Sir Borus ordered his men.

The Black Cloaks stepped forward, spreading out on either side of Sir Borus, who remained mounted. "We're thirteen to your seven," Sir Borus said as his black-clad knights lowered their helms and formed a line on either side of him. "Yield and live. Resist and die."

Up on the platform, Hake let fly another gob of spit. This one hit Sir Borus square in the eye. Hake roared with laughter as the Black Cloak tried to wipe his eye with a mailed hand. Sir Borus looked up at the platform and glared at Hake, his upper lip twitching in anger. "You'll regret that, villain."

Hake let fly another gob, and Sir Borus had to duck out of the way.

"When I plunge my fist down your throat and rip out your black heart and eat it, you'll regret being born, you useless stain of pig droppings," Hake barked before laughing again.

Sir Borus turned toward the seven men facing his line and pointed his sword at Sir Herrick. "This is your last chance, Sir Justiciar. Hand over the prisoner. Now."

As Hake aimed another gob of spit toward the Black Cloak leader, the sound of approaching horses rose up from the south.

***

Stone, his vision like an eagle's, recognized Sir Borus from the other end of Green Street. He called out to his five companions, and they spurred their horses toward the town square. A boiling crowd of citizens parted to let them through, and they swept into the square, quickly taking positions on the flanks of Kaemon's line, Stone, Brook, and Bennald on the right, Elling, Panwer, and Aliya on the left. The line of Black Cloaks stopped their advance.

"Greetings, Sir Borus," Stone called out cheerfully. "You look as if you've eaten something rotten."

The Black Cloak leader stared at him and snarled, his face flushed with anger. "Petty trickster," he snapped.

"Something wrong, Sir Borus?" Kaemon asked. "Are the odds no longer to your liking?"

A young Black Cloak took a step forward. "To blazes with the odds," he called out. "I challenge any of you misbegotten rogues to single combat. Is anyone brave enough to face me?"

Up on the gallows platform, Hakc roared like a wounded dragon. With the muscles of his arms looking as if they might burst through his skin, he snapped the rope binding his wrists. He launched himself from the platform, executed a perfect forward flip in midair, and landed on his feet next to Jaynum Stant. In a single fluid move, he snatched the hammer out of the blacksmith's hand, spun around once, and smashed the hammer against the young Black Cloak's head, staving it in like an egg hit by a brick. The black-clad knight fell heavily, raising a cloud of dust. The other Black Cloaks drew back.

Hake snarled and brandished his hammer at them. "Single combat," he roared. "Anyone brave enough to face me?"

Stone drew his sword pointed it at Sir Borus. A whirlwind gathered and rose up in front of the Black Cloak leader, and his horse whinnied and reared, nearly throwing him.

"Easy, there, boy," Bennald said to the horse.

The whirlwind began to move down the Black Cloak line, like a spinning top moving down an incline. "What do we do?" one of Black Cloaks called out to Sir Borus.

"Mount up," Sir Borus yelled. "Head back to the castle." Then he wheeled around and spurred his horse to a gallop.

The other Black Cloaks turned and ran, but they stopped short suddenly, shouting and swearing. Their mounts were not where they had left them. The horses were halfway down Spring Street, a young roisterer atop each. The young men made rude gestures as Sir Borus sped past, and then they headed back to the square at a stately trot.

"I'll go after Borus," Panwer said.

"Best not," Stone said. "We'll deal with him later."

"We yield," one of the Black Cloaks called out, desperation in his voice. The whirlwind faded and died away. Stone and the five who had arrived with him dismounted.

"Drop your swords and yourselves and plant your faces on the ground," Stone commanded the Black Cloaks.

Eleven black-clad knights tossed away their swords and flung themselves to the ground.

"Shall I bash in their heads for them?" Hake asked no one in particular.

"No!" Aliya shouted. "They have my sister. I need one of them alive. You can bash the rest."

Hake's deep-throated laughter rolled like thunder. He pointed at Aliya. "I like you."

Constable Tenney ordered the two pikemen to bind the Black Cloaks' hands behind them. The young roisterers entered the square on the Black Cloaks' horses, and the constable directed them to pick up the prisoners' swords and take their daggers.

"Can we keep their swords?" one of the lads asked the constable. "And their knives?"

"Mayhap," Tenney replied. "First you can help my men tie their hands."

The roisterers set about the task with nearly as much enthusiasm as they had shown during the march to the gallows. When they were finished, one of them asked Tenney, "What about their 'orses? Can we keep them, too?"

"Don't press your luck," the constable replied.

"What about the hanging?" Old Hipnog shouted. "I want justice." He pointed at Hake and glared. "That unholy creature stole my horse. And my daughter."

"Stuff a dead rat down your throat, you stale, stinking, wreck of a drunken bloodsucker," Hake snarled. "Your daughter needed a night out."

"She was terrified, you brute," Old Hipnog screamed.

"She was having the time of her life."

"I want this man hanged!"

"Just a moment," Kaemon said.

"I want this man …"

"Silence, old man, or I'll hang *you*!" Sir Herrick roared at Hipnog. "The First Knight of the Realm has something to say."

"Thank the gods," Stone whispered to Brook, who was staring intently at Hake, frowning.

Kaemon nodded at the justiciar and then turned back to Hipnog. "You'll get your justice, Sir Blacksmith. But I ask you, was the horse returned to you unharmed?"

Old Hipnog nodded.

"Was your daughter returned to you … intact?"

"Aye, but terrified she was."

256

Hake snorted and spat. "Time of her life," he muttered under his breath.

"If I were to pledge, say, twenty gold pieces from my own coffers in recompense for your troubles, would that suffice to give you justice?" Kaemon asked.

Old Hipnog considered that for a half second. "Aye, but twenty-five golds would suffice better."

Kaemon turned to Sir Herrick. "Sir Justiciar, bear witness that I pledge this day to give twenty gold pieces to Hipnog the blacksmith. And now, in the performance of my duties as First Knight of the Kingdom of Ruxland, I request in the name of King Harrin that the prisoner Hake be turned over to me."

"By all means, take the prisoner," Sir Herrick said with a quick backhand flick of his wrist. "Take him away. Take him far away."

"Good show," said Hake, nodding at Sir Herrick. "I'll just be running along, then."

"Just a moment," said Kaemon. He fished Hake's ring from a pocket and held it out. "This is yours, is it not?"

"Aye," Hake muttered. "Give it to me."

Kaemon turned and handed the ring to Stone. Stone looked at it for a moment and then passed it to Brook, who eyed it before giving it to Bennald. The three approached Hake.

"Who are you?" Stone asked.

"I'm the king of go hang yourself, you sniveling sack of rancid fish guts."

"You don't know, do you?" Brook said. "You don't know who you are."

Hake stared back at her. "I didn't. Now I do."

"You must come with us," Stone said.

"I know," Hake murmured.

Chapter 20 - The Cave

"What about my sister?" Aliya said.

"This is my friend Aliya," Elling said to Kaemon. "She and her sister Jannela and I were close comrades in our youth, and I vouch for both of them on my life. Jannela was partly ensorcelled by one of the Ordseer's fastle pledges. These Black Cloaks took her from a querl outside Sevnpools."

Hake strode to the nearest Black Cloak, hauled him to his feet, and lifted him from the ground by his neck as if he were picking up a dressed goose. He yanked the knight's helm from his head with a violent tug, flung it away, and then smashed his forehead against the man's nose. The sound of it breaking split the air like a little crack of thunder. "Where's the lass's sister? If you lie, I'll rip out your throat with my teeth. I'll pluck out your eyes and stuff 'em up your nose. I'll dip your beard in pitch and set a flame to it. I'll ..."

"The Red City," the Black Cloak replied. "They took her to the Red City."

Aliya stepped forward and glared at the knight. "Who took her to the Red City?"

"Two of the knights. After we left the querl."

Aliya stepped back and nearly stumbled as a sob escaped from her. Brook put an arm across her shoulders and steadied her.

"Why did they take her to the Red City?" Stone demanded.

"She ... she's different. They want to find out why."

"They? Who are *they*?"

"I ... I don't know. The Ordseer's people, maybe."

"What about the rest of your company?" Stone asked. "Where are they?"

"A castle near here," the Black Cloak replied.

"What castle, you muck-eating son of a worm?" Hake roared in the man's ear.

The man pointed. "That ... that ... that way. Up the ... up the main road. Five miles from here."

"He must mean Castle Vell," Sir Herrick said. "It's been abandoned for more than twenty years, since the War of the Colors and the Great Merging, when the Vell line ended. It's rumored to be haunted by the gasts of Vells killed in the war."

"That ... that ... that's the one," the Black Cloak stammered.

Hake set the Black Cloak back on his feet but kept a hand on his neck.

"How many Black Cloaks are at the castle?" Stone demanded.

"Fifty maybe," the Black Cloak replied. "No more than sixty."

"You're lying," Hake said, and he hoisted the man in the air again.

"I tell it true," the Black Cloak said. "Fifty knights. Give or take. If Sir Borus makes it back, it'll be fifty-one. Give or take."

"What about foot soldiers?" Stone asked.

The Black Cloak shook his head. "No foot, just knights."

"Why are you here in Greenport?" Kaemon asked.

"We brought fastle pledges," the knight replied. "The Ordseer wants people around here to sign them."

"The Ordseer is dead," Stone told him. "The day of the fastle is over." Stone turned to Sir Herrick. "Do you know this Castle Vell?"

The justiciar nodded. "It sits on a fifty-foot-high bluff that overlooks the river. It isn't as large as it appears, but it was well built in its day."

Kaemon was staring at Stone. "The Ordseer is dead?"

Stone nodded.

"How do you know?"

"Brook and Bennald and I were captured and held in the same querl as Jannela. We escaped and took the Ordseer as a hostage. When I questioned him outside the querl, he took a bad fright and stopped breathing. Then he vanished."

"He attempted no sorcery," Brook added. "He was terrified, and he just … disappeared."

Bennald nodded his agreement. "The man was no sorcerer."

"There's more you need to know," Stone said to Kaemon. "I saw a battle outside Blackpond. A company of mounted Black Cloaks led an army of Redmonders against an equal number of Braanters. It was a suicide mission, Sir Kaemon, I'm saddened to say, and the Redmonders, who were no doubt thralls, were destroyed. The Black Cloaks got away unscathed, but they showed up later in Blackpond with their fastle pledges and turned the city into a madhouse. It was just as you described the Red City on the day you fled."

"How many Redmonders at the battle?" Kaemon asked in a quiet voice.

"Maybe ten thousand," Stone replied. "I'm sorry."

There was silence then, finally broken by Aliya. "What about my sister?"

"We'll find her," Stone said. "Once we've dealt with Sir Borus and put an end to these pledges, we'll ride to the Red City."

"We'll need reinforcements to take Castle Vell," said Kaemon. "And siege engines and catapults."

"We'll need volunteers to cut down trees for battering rams," Elling said.

"Just a moment," Stone said. "We don't need reinforcements, and we won't need siege engines or battering rams."

"You heard the Black Cloak," said Kaemon. "At least fifty knights are at the castle. Even a small castle with a handful of defenders can hold out for days or weeks."

"Things have changed," Stone said. "We'll take the castle by nightfall, before Sir Borus has a chance to poison any more Braanters with the Ordseer's fastle pledges. Then we'll head for the Red City and rescue Jannela—among other things."

Kaemon gave Stone a questioning look. "What has changed?"

"All in good time, Sir Kaemon," Stone replied. "For now, you're going to have to trust me." He turned to Sir Herrick and Constable Tenney. "Hold these Black Cloaks in Greenport's jail and see if you can get anything out of them. Muster everyone you can to see to the defense of Braant and let no one sign any pledges."

***

It was early afternoon when Stone, Brook, Bennald, Hake, and Kaemon left Greenport and headed north on the road that would take them to Castle Vell. Stone had insisted that Elling, Panwer, Thig Grennell, and Aliya stay behind and prepare for the journey to the Red City.

When they reached the grounds of the castle, which lay nearly half a mile away on their right, they stopped for a moment to gaze at it before continuing down the road. After two more miles, they entered a densely wooded area on the right. There was no real trail, but Hake led them through a narrow path that wound between trees and around boulders. The pathway led gradually upward before becoming too steep for the horses. They hobbled the beasts in a clearing before proceeding on foot. The final stage was a hard climb up a steep rock face of more than a hundred feet. When they reached the top, they found themselves on a high ridge overlooking a vast forest. A wide, shallow valley lay below them, and in the distance, they caught a glint of sunlight shining off a wide bend of the Larka River.

Hake began walking, and the others followed him toward the high point of a promontory that overlooked the river. When Hake reached the edge, he sat down, his legs dangling over. He inched forward and slid down on his back to a narrow ledge. At the back of the ledge was a narrow slit in the rock wall.

"Come down one at a time," Hake called up. "Brook first."

Brook slid down and joined him. Hake pointed to the fissure in the rock, and she wriggled through the narrow cave entrance.

"Sir Pretty Pants next," Hake called, and Kaemon clambered down to the ledge and crawled into the cave.

Bennald came next, and then Stone. When Stone entered the cave, he found himself in a chamber about the size of an ale cellar and equally cool. His eyes adjusted, and he could just make out the other three standing there. There was plenty of room above their heads and enough space all around for a lord's banquet. Hake entered behind him and walked to the other side of the cavern.

"There's another narrow opening like the one you just came through," Hake told them. "We'll have to crawl through."

"Are you sure you know where you're going?" Kaemon asked.

"Yes, Sir Porridge Brains, I live in one of these caves," Hake replied. "And I know all of them, every room and every tunnel wide enough for a man to walk or crawl through."

They slipped through one at a time and came to another room, one where sunlight couldn't reach. Even Stone's eagle-like vision was rendered useless. An orange flame flared, and everyone turned toward it. It was coming from the fingertips of Hake's left hand, flickering and wavering in the

264

cool air of the cave. Hake bent down, picked up a torch with his right hand, and set the flame to it. The torch flared. Hake clenched his left hand into a fist, and the flames from his fingertips went out.

"There's another opening up ahead, but we can walk through it," Hake said. "It winds around, but it'll take us where we want to go."

They set off, Hake leading the way. Just over an hour later, they rounded a bend and came to another large room. Columns of rock fifty feet high stretched from floor to ceiling. The grayish white columns looked like huge, misshapen candles that had melted inside a whirlwind. The floor of the huge room sloped downward to the left, and at the bottom of the slope, a hundred feet away, was another tunnel entrance.

"Not that way," Hake said.

They continued down the main tunnel, Hake still in the lead. They came to a narrow opening on the left and Hake stopped. "This main tunnel leads to the castle's under dungeon," he said. He pointed to the opening on the left. "We'll go that way."

After ten minutes, the narrow tunnel opened into another huge cavern through which an underground river flowed. Everyone looked at Brook.

"It's a nice day for a swim, I suppose," she said, giving Stone a vague smile, and then she dived into the river and disappeared under the surface.

Chapter 21 - Castle Vell

Stone, Bennald, Hake, and Kaemon sat their horses two hundred yards from Castle Vell, peering at the thirty-foot-high curtain wall and the gatehouse in the center of it. It was three hours past midday, but thick gray clouds obscured the sun and had turned the afternoon gloomy.

There was movement on one of the towers that flanked the gatehouse, and they saw a black-clad man peering over a battlement.

"We're spotted," Stone said. He turned to Kaemon. "Are you ready?"

"I am," Kaemon replied.

"I know you have your doubts about everything we told you, Sir Kaemon," Stone continued. "But you'll see that we spoke truly."

"It's difficult to credit," Kaemon said.

"I know. When we're finished here and on our way to the Red City, perhaps you'll feel more at ease."

"No doubt I will," Kaemon replied. "If I survive."

"Enough talk," Hake growled. "If you want to survive, Sir Pretty Pants, get a move on before I do you in myself."

They spurred their horses forward and stopped a hundred yards from the dry moat that surrounded the castle wall. After more than twenty years of disuse, weeds and brush grew wild inside the empty moat, but it was still as deep as when it had been filled with water from the river. The curtain wall behind it had a tower at each corner, in addition to the two towers of the gatehouse.

Stone saw activity along the wall-walk and inside the towers, as men in black scurried about. Stone looked at Kaemon. "It's your show now, Sir Kaemon."

Kaemon nodded. As a ray of sunlight slanted through a break in the cloud cover, he unfastened his sword belt, held it up over his head for a few moments, and then lowered his arm and dropped the sword belt to the ground. He pulled a large white handkerchief from a pocket and held it aloft before spurring his horse forward another twenty yards down a slight incline. There he stopped and waited. The castle gate opened, and a drawbridge was lowered over the dry moat. Sir Borus Renovar, mounted on his horse, cantered out over the drawbridge. Four Black Cloaks accompanied him, but they remained a discreet distance behind as he approached Kaemon and stopped a few yards away.

"I won't waste words," Kaemon said to Sir Borus as they stared at each other. "In the name of King Harrin of Ruxland, I demand that you and your company of knights surrender yourselves to me now. I name you enemy of the kingdom, to be tried for treachery and war making according to the laws of the realm."

"You must be mad," Sir Borus said. "I have a hundred knights behind me. And, in case you haven't noticed, I've a castle as well. Do you plan to besiege us with those tricksy street performers? Do you think some mummer's farce will breach the walls of this castle and defeat a hundred well-armed knights?"

"I say again, Sir Borus, yield now, and order your men—all fifty of them—to yield with you."

Sir Borus spat. "I owe my allegiance to the Ordseer," he snapped.

"The Ordseer is dead. Yield now and you may avoid the same fate."

Sir Borus glared at Kaemon and then wheeled about and rode back to the gatehouse with his four knights.

Stone, Bennald, and Hake spurred their horses forward and joined Kaemon.

"What do we do now?" Kaemon asked.

"We wait for them to come out and fight," Stone replied.

They didn't have long to wait.

The gate opened again, and thirty knights, led by Sir Borus, crossed the drawbridge and arrayed themselves in a line just beyond the moat. Behind them, another twenty knights manned the castle walls and towers.

Stone, Kaemon, Bennald, and Hake spread out. The Black Cloaks drew swords or raised maces or war hammers. Stone and Kaemon drew swords, Bennald held his staff aloft, and Hake brandished his hammer in one hand and a sword in the other. The Black Cloaks moved forward.

Stone raised his sword, and the air suddenly grew chill as a harsh wind blew in from the west. A few of the Black Cloaks glanced at one another.

"Keep moving," Sir Borus shouted at them.

A hard rain began to fall. The wind blew fiercely, howling and driving the downpour into the faces of the Black Cloaks, but no rain touched Stone and his companions. Hake raised his hammer over his head and twirled it. A fog rose up out of the ground between the four besiegers and the line of black-clad knights. Many of those knights stopped advancing, and when the others noticed, they stopped as well.

"Advance!" Sir Borus shouted, but he, too, had halted.

"Yield," Stone called out.

"Advance!" Sir Borus yelled.

A huge black cloud formed in the sky, and the grounds were plunged into a dim twilight. The rain, still driven by the wind, changed to hail, and the clatter of hailstones pelting armor accompanied the howling wind. The black cloud descended, revealing itself to be a swarm of buzzing black locusts, which fell upon the Black Cloaks. The knights waved their arms frantically to beat the things back, and some dropped their weapons as they flapped their arms.

"Charge, I say!" Sir Borus called out again, and half the knights surged forward.

Bennald raised his staff, and a hundred wolves charged out of a nearby woods and ran toward the Black Cloaks. The Black Cloaks halted, their horses whinnying. The wolves slowed their charge and slunk toward the knights, growling and snapping. A Black Cloak raised a crossbow. Hake struck his hammer with his sword, and the ground below the knight with the crossbow split apart with a loud crack. Bennald shouted, and the knight's horse reared, throwing its rider into the crevice before galloping off. The other horses reared and began throwing their riders, who were shouting and swearing and trying to control their mounts. The ground continued to split, swallowing a dozen black Cloaks as their fellow knights scampered away on foot. A sheet of flame shot up from the crack in the earth, and men screamed. The wolves edged forward toward the remaining Black Cloaks, who backed up until they were inside the dry moat.

The rain and hail stopped. The air changed and seemed to grow heavy. A deep silence fell, which soon gave way to a low roar. The roar grew louder. Behind the castle, the river had become unmoored from its banks and was rising like a ghost from a grave. As Stone and the others looked on, the river rose above the walls of the castle. Brook was there in the middle of it, riding it like a hawk riding a current of air. The boiling river gathered itself like a huge ocean swell, and then broke. Bennald shouted, and the wolves scattered. Stone and his three companions wheeled around and headed for the high ground as tons of water fell on the castle and the moat, swamping the Black Cloaks standing there, knocking down the towers and most of the curtain wall, and flooding the moat and the low ground where Stone and the others had been standing. When it was over, the grounds around the castle had been transformed into a lake.

Brook surfaced and swam across the newly made lake, standing up when the water was shallow enough and walking toward Stone and the other three. She flung droplets from her glistening hair and then looked at Stone with a little smile. "Stop gawping and bring me some dry clothes, if you please."

Chapter 22 - The Rose Castle

They found Sir Borus Renovar among the survivors, battered, bruised, and missing his boots. They marched him and the other surviving Black Cloaks to Greenport, where Constable Tenney and Sir Herrick Felkin took them into custody.

Stone and the others made their plans at breakfast the next morning in the common room of the Smoking Sky Inn. They decided that Sir Kaemon, Sir Panwer, and Thig Grennell would ride to the Redmonders' encampment near Blaewick Province and muster the Redmond knights. Stone and the others would ride to the village of Banderry, which Aliya and Elling knew well, and wait there for Kaemon. From Banderry the combined force would ride to the Red City and attempt to wrest it back from the Ordseer men.

They set out for their separate destinations the following morning. Kaemon, Panwer, and Thig rode west to the Redmond encampment, and Stone and his group—Brook, Bennald, Hake, Sir Elling, and Aliya—headed for Banderry.

Stone and his companions rode first to Sevnpools, where they warned the people there to be on their guard and spread the warning to the towns and farms in the west and northwest areas of Braant province. From Sevnpools they rode south-southeast, bypassing Blackpond and crossing the base of the Horn of Misheroon, not far from Drumkin, making directly for the village of Banderry.

They entered Banderry twelve days after setting out from Greenport, early in the afternoon. Like the other villages they had passed, Banderry was empty of inhabitants and beginning to show signs of decay.

They came to the village square and halted. Sir Elling pointed to a stone building on the east side of the square. "The Horse Head Inn," he announced. "We can post ourselves there while we wait for Kaemon." He looked at Stone. "I'm going to ride to my father's estate and have a look around. It isn't far."

"I'll go with you," said Aliya, and the two set off soon after.

While Bennald and Hake stabled the horses, Stone and Brook entered the Horse Head Inn to look around. There was no one about, but they found bottles of wine, slabs of cured beef, and a wheel of moldy cheese in the cellar. They cut the mold from the cheese and prepared a meal, setting six places at the table. Sir Elling and Aliya returned as the other four were finishing.

"Any news?" Stone asked when the two entered the common room. He poured two more goblets of wine and gestured toward the two empty places at the table.

Elling shook his head. "There was no one about."

"Have some wine and something to eat," Stone said. "When we find your people, one of us will disenthrall them."

"Aye, if we find them alive," Elling murmured.

273

Two days later, shortly after the noon hour, Sir Kaemon, Sir Panwer, Thig Grennell, and two hundred and fifty Redmond knights arrived in Banderry with a train of wagons loaded with crates of food and barrels of ale. The small army had journeyed south through the Horn of Misheroon before turning east toward Redmond, purchasing supplies along the way. They had encountered neither Black Cloaks nor thralls on their journey.

The leaders met that evening in the common room of the Horse Head Inn to make their plans. Thig Grennell, who had spent considerable time in the Red City after the mass ensorcellment, told them what they could expect to find.

"Most of Redmond's farms have been abandoned, but some of the ones close to the city are still functioning. Thralls work the fields and tend to the animals, and certain Black Cloaks serve as their overseers. Whatever they harvest or slaughter goes to the city to feed the Black Cloaks. The thralls get their scraps."

"With the Ordseer dead and Sir Borus captured, who's in charge?" Stone asked.

Thig shook his head. "I don't know. Perhaps no one."

"I plan to send a small force of knights to scout ahead of the main body," Kaemon said.

Stone nodded. "I'd like to ride with them."

"So would I," said Brook.

"I as well," said Hake.

They looked at Bennald, who nodded his agreement.

As dawn broke the next morning, Stone, Brook, Bennald, and Hake rode off with twenty of Kaemon's knights to scout the approach to the Red City. They passed abandoned farms and weed-choked fields and the rotting carcasses of farm animals.

Around midmorning, they came to a wooded area. Sir Slayton Gyll, the Redmonder in charge of the scouting party, told Stone the forest was three miles long but narrow, a ribbon of tall trees that wound like a river between farms. The road was narrower through the woods, and they had to ride single file. Stone insisted on taking the lead, and Sir Slayton didn't argue.

They came to the end of the woods and saw another farm. A two-story stone farmhouse was set fifty feet back from the road, and behind the house a lush green meadow sloped down to a little creek. A wide field, divided into rows of longbeans, cabbage, lettuce, and other vegetables stretched nearly to the woods, the leaves of the crops glowing in the sun in a dozen different shades of green. Beyond the house, the road curved through a large kepple orchard heavily laden with ripening red fruit.

"This is the Eddrie farm," Sir Slayton called out. "It's one of the farms Thig Grennell said is still working."

The road had widened again, and the column formed into twos. In the distance, with his keen eyesight, Stone could just see the top of the rose-tinted wall surrounding the Red City. Something else caught his eye, and he turned to peer at the farmhouse. The door opened, and two people, a man and a woman, stepped out and gazed at him. Stone called a halt. "I'm going to talk to them," he told Sir Slayton.

"They look like thralls," the knight replied.

Stone nodded. "Keep an eye out for Black Cloaks."

Stone dismounted and headed for the farmhouse. Brook dismounted and followed him. They stepped up to the porch of the house and nodded to the two people, who were standing just outside the door, which they had left open. They were thin and pale, and their eyes were dull, like old armor that hadn't been polished in years.

"Good afternoon," Stone said.

The two nodded but said nothing.

"Anyone else about?" Stone asked.

The man, who had curly brown hair and looked to be around forty years of age, shook his head.

"My name is Stone Falconer, and this is Brook," Stone said. "May we know your names?"

"Sir Yosig calls me Robett Eddrie," the man replied. "He calls my wife Jansie."

"Is Sir Yosig a Black Cloak?" Stone asked.

The man and woman nodded.

"Sir Yosig will be back soon," Jansie said softly.

They heard the sound of a horse cantering. The Redmond knights mounted up and drew their swords as a horse and rider came around a bend in the road near where the kepple orchard grew. The rider, a Black Cloak, pulled up sharply when he saw the Redmonders, and then he wheeled about and galloped off, a half dozen Redmond knights in pursuit. The chase was brief. The Black Cloak, apparently having quickly calculated his odds, halted, turned his horse around again, and tossed his sword to the ground.

A pair of Redmond knights hauled the Black Cloak inside the farmhouse and tied him to a chair in the front room so Stone could talk to him. Robett and Jansie paid little heed to this activity. As soon as the commotion died down, they went to the orchard with a ladder and two large baskets and began picking ripe fruit. Sir Slayton ordered one of his knights keep an eye on the two, and then he and a dozen of his men set off down the road again to continue the scouting expedition. Hake and Bennald went with him, and the remaining knights stayed behind with Stone and Brook, who entered the farmhouse and took chairs opposite the Black Cloak. He was nearly as thin as Robett and Jansie.

"Your name?" Stone asked.

The Black Cloak spat on the floor. Stone drew his sword and placed the point against the knight's throat. As he did, a small whirlwind rose up from the floor, spinning dust and bits of chaff into the Black Cloak's face, which turned the color of boiled parchment.

"Your name?" Stone repeated.

"Sir Yosig," the Black Cloak replied.

Stone sheathed his sword. "You've been overseeing farms near the Red City. How many other Black Cloaks have that duty?"

"Maybe twenty."

"That isn't many," Stone said.

Sir Yosig shrugged. "The thralls don't cause any trouble."

"How many Black Cloaks occupy the Red City?"

"Thousands," Sir Yosig said. "Just waiting for the Ordseer to return."

"They'll have a long wait," said Stone.

"What do you mean?"

"The Ordseer is dead. And Sir Borus Renovar is rotting in a jail in Greenport."

"You lie," Sir Yosig snapped.

Stone reached into a pocket and pulled out the Ordseer's medallion, still hanging on its gold chain. He dropped it on the table in front of Sir Yosig, whose eyes went wide.

"How many Black Cloaks occupy the Red City?" Stone asked again. "And don't tell me thousands, because you and I both know that was a lie."

"I ain't sayin' no more," Sir Yosig replied.

"Who's in charge in the Red City?" Stone asked, but the Black Cloak was true to his word and said no more.

Kaemon arrived with the main body of knights, and they made camp in the meadow behind the farmhouse. Soon after, Sir Slayton's scouting party returned with a half dozen Black Cloak overseers they had captured along with a wagon filled with fresh fruits and vegetables, which had been bound for the Red City from one of the neighboring farms. Sir Slayton had learned that wagons traveled at regular intervals from the working farms to the Red

City, their Black Cloak drivers taking them directly to the castle through the postern gate on the castle's north wall.

They locked Sir Yosig and the other Black Cloaks in a small shed near the main barn and prepared for the evening. Although Sir Kaemon had brought plenty of provisions from the encampment near Blaewick, that night they feasted on produce from the wagon Sir Slayton had commandeered, enjoying fresh honeyfruit, roasted potatoes, and boiled turnips and carrots mashed together and seasoned with salt and pepper, washed down with ale that Kaemon had purchased in the Horn.

The two thralls ate by themselves, in the kitchen of their farmhouse, which was separated from the main house. As dusk fell and the knights settled down to sleep or moved into position to stand their watches, Brook entered the kitchen and lit some candles. Robett and Jansie watched but said nothing. Brook sat down at the small oak table across from them and showed them her ring. They peered at it.

"It's pretty," Jansie murmured, staring at the bright green stone surrounded by the four-sided insignia.

"Some people see it when they look into my eyes," Brook said.

Jansie looked into Brook's eyes.

"Do you see it?" Brook asked.

Jansie shook her head.

"Keep looking," Brook said.

Jansie nodded and kept staring into Brook's eyes.

"I'm going to find you, Jansie," Brook whispered.

***

The next morning broke cool and clear, with gauzy ribbons of pink streaking the eastern horizon. Robett and Jansie directed Sir Slayton to a long trestle table stored in the big barn, and he and his men set up the table behind the house and broke their fast before setting out again on another scouting mission. Most of the other knights ate where they had slept, and groups of knights took turns keeping watch on the road.

The knights were stunned when they saw Robett and Jansie scurrying about, milking cows, checking fields and orchards, and smiling and talking amiably to anyone who came near. Seeing the two in their right minds gave the Redmonders hope that their own family members and friends might be disenthralled one day.

After the scouting party left, Stone, Brook, Kaemon, and the others sat down at the trestle table to break their fast and make their plans.

"What do they remember of their ensorcellment?" Kaemon asked Stone and Brook as they ate sliced kepples, chunks of honeyfruit, and egg-topped flauns.

"Not very much," Brook replied.

"Perhaps that's for the best," said Aliya. "Was it … was it very difficult to disenthrall them?"

"No," Brook said. "We'll make your sister well again."

280

"Jannela is different, though," Aliya said. "She didn't sign her real name to the fastle pledge."

"No matter," Stone said. "We can cure her. We just need to get to her without putting her at risk."

"I wish we knew where she was," Elling said.

"Mayhap one of them Black Cloaks festering in that shed knows where she is," said Hake. He finished the flaun he'd been working on, belched loudly, and stood up from the table. "Mayhap I'll go ask them." He picked up his hammer and strode off toward the shed.

"Try not to kill anyone," Stone called after him.

Hake returned before the others had finished their breakfasts. "Jannela is in a room at the top of the castle's gatehouse," he announced. "The king is a prisoner in his own castle, along with his counselors—all but one of them."

***

"This reminds me of driving the Pilot's Wheel's muck wagon to the farms around Drumkin," Stone said to Brook as the wagon he was driving rolled toward the Red City under a clear blue sky. "I have fond memories of those days."

Brook nodded. "So do I. Sometimes I almost …"

Stone glanced at her. "Almost what?"

"Never mind," she said, staring straight ahead. A moment later, she looked at him. A vague smile played on her lips. "You look almost dashing in your Black Cloak attire."

"Nice of you to say so," he replied, keeping an eye on the team of two horses clip-clopping in front of them.

"Don't let it give you a big head."

"What are you two nattering about," Hake called from the back of the wagon, where he was sitting with Bennald, Elling, Aliya, and a pile of half-full sacks of grain.

"Making plans," Stone said. He looked over his shoulder. "You'd better put on your Black Cloak clothing and helms."

"They stink of sorcery," Hake muttered.

"We're nearing the gate," Stone said. "It's time to get ready."

The other three men put on the Black Cloak garb, and then Hake and Brook traded places. Brook, Bennald, Aliya, and Elling hid themselves under the half-full grain sacks.

It was late morning when the Red City's pink-tinged walls came into view, gleaming under a bright sun. Thirty minutes later, the wagon crossed a wooden bridge that spanned a loop of the Little Farro River. Fifteen minutes after that, they arrived at Westgate, which was standing open. Stone waved at the two Black Cloaks in the guard tower without stopping, hoping no one would challenge him. No one did. Farm wagons coming into the city full and leaving empty were a common sight, and the placid state of the Red City had lulled the Black Cloaks into unwariness.

Stone drove through Westgate and continued down Roxx Street, a major avenue that ran the length of the Red City, from Westgate all the way to the Farro River. The city stank of refuse and dead fish and rotting meat and worse. Most of the buildings still seemed in reasonably good repair, but the once-shining city had a dull, shabby look about it.

Stone turned left down Mygie Street and stopped. He and Hake looked around.

"Do you see anyone?" Elling called from under the pile of sacks.

"No one," Stone said.

"Let's go," Hake growled, and he jumped off the wagon and headed up Mygie Street. Elling and Bennald got out of the wagon and caught up with him. A moment later, the three turned left into an alley and disappeared.

Brook and Aliya sat up and looked around. Trash littered the narrow street, and some of the doors fronting the buildings hung open, but there was no one about. A rag that might once have been a yellow silk scarf billowed and fluttered as a light breeze pushed it slowly down the street.

"I've never seen the city look like this," Aliya said.

"Cities can recover," Stone replied.

"Not without people. How long will it take you and your friends to disenthrall a hundred thousand souls? And that's just in the Red City—assuming most of them are still alive."

"A long time," Stone acknowledged. "But we can teach Thig Grennell and other wistlords to do it, once we disenthrall the other wistlords. And we can teach some of the loresmen from Redmond College as well."

"It sounds as if you won't be staying," Aliya said.

"We'll see," Stone replied. "In the meantime, the city will need people who escaped enthrallment—people like you—to manage things."

Aliya shook her head. "Not me. I'm a criminal, don't forget. As soon as you disenthrall Jannela, we're leaving for Misheroon or northern Braant, or maybe we'll take to the sea and find another country."

"And break Sir Elling's heart," Brook said.

To that, Aliya had no reply.

***

Bennald, Hake, and Elling returned less than an hour later.

"Any trouble?" Stone asked.

Hake shook his head. "No. We took the two Black Cloak guards unawares and waited for Sir Slayton and his scouting party to show up, just like we planned. They have control of Westgate."

Stone glanced skyward, shading his eyes from the sun. "Kaemon and his little army won't be far behind. The plan is proceeding nicely."

"A bit too nicely, if you ask my opinion," Hake grumbled.

"If you stop complaining, perhaps I'll let you kill some Black Cloaks once we're inside the castle," Stone said.

Hake nodded, a solemn expression on his face. "Fair enough."

Hake climbed aboard the wagon and sat next to Stone, and the others hid themselves under the sacks again. Stone turned the wagon around and backtracked down Mygie Street. He crossed Roxx Street and continued to Southend Way, where he turned east, heading toward the Rose Castle. The castle soon loomed into view. It sat in the middle of a grassy expanse of land that formed a rough square nearly a half mile on each side. The square was bordered by Wheat Street to the west, Lamp Street to the north, Southend Way to the south, and the Farro River on the east. The castle itself, a perfect square, was nearly two hundred and fifty feet on each side. It was built of massive blocks of rose-colored stone, boasted a double-towered gatehouse in the south wall, round towers at each corner, and two smaller towers on the east wall facing the river. A moat, fed by the river, surrounded the castle walls and widened in front of the gatehouse. Visitors gained entrance to the castle by crossing a drawbridge lowered from a small outbuilding in front of the gatehouse and then passing through the outbuilding and crossing a short causeway that led to another drawbridge, this one lowered from the gatehouse itself.

Properly manned, the castle's defenses were formidable. But, as they now knew, the castle was not properly manned. Nevertheless, the threat of dark sorcery loomed.

Stone continued past the wide lane that led to the gatehouse. Once the wagon was past the castle, he turned north on a narrow lane that wound through the castle's east grounds, which sloped from the curtain wall down to the Farro River. King Hammond, an ancient ancestor of King Harrin, had turned the east grounds into a wide esplanade known as the Purple Commons. The king had opened the esplanade to the citizens of Redmond, and for two centuries they had strolled its grounds and gardens, sat in the shade of its trees, and enjoyed the troubadours, minstrels, lute players, jugglers, dancers, acrobats, and storytellers who entertained there. The paths that wound through the esplanade had been paved with reddish-purple stone, which gave the Purple Commons its name. The paths were still reddish-purple, but the grassy field through which they meandered was brown and dry and grim, overgrown with weeds and littered with trash. The masts of sunken ships stuck up out of the river like forlorn reeds, and a smell like burning peat hung in the air.

Stone turned west on Lamp Street, the northern border of the castle grounds. Their destination, the castle's postern gate, was in the castle's north wall. As they approached the narrow lane that led to the postern, Stone heard the clip-clopping of horses. He looked to his right and saw four Black Cloaks cantering down Branch Street.

"What is it?" he heard Brook whisper from under the pile of grain sacks.

"Four Black Cloaks," Stone whispered back. He saw a deer draped over one of the horses, in front of the rider, and noted that two of the Black Cloaks carried bows. "Must be a hunting party."

Stone turned left into the lane that led to the postern gate and tried to look harmless. The clip-clopping got louder behind him, and a moment later, the four Black Cloaks cantered past. One of them slowed down and kept pace with the wagon. The black-clad knight glanced at Stone and Hake. "Is that Sir Wunno and Sir Kaster?"

"Aye," Stone said without looking at the Black Cloak. He heard Hake make a low growling sound.

"Haven't seen you two for a while."

"Aye," Stone said.

"How goes the farming?"

Stone shrugged, keeping his eyes straight ahead. "Fair."

A guard opened the postern gate, and the three Black Cloaks riding ahead passed through and onto the castle grounds.

"You taking that grain to the brew house?" the Black Cloak asked.

"Aye," Stone said.

"We'll give you a hand unloading it."

Stone nodded. "Thanks."

The Black Cloak spurred his horse and cantered ahead.

"What do we do?" Elling asked from underneath the grain sacks.

"Where's the brew house?" Stone asked, keeping his voice low and his eyes on the postern gate.

"Next to the kitchen," Elling replied. "The kitchen is red brick with an eight-sided chimney that's wide at the bottom and slopes in toward the top. You can't help but see it. The brew house will be just this side of the kitchen as we approach across the courtyard."

"I'll stop in front of it," Stone said. "When I give the signal, be ready to fight."

Stone drove the wagon through the postern, which a guard closed behind him. The four men of the hunting party accompanied the wagon, two on either side, as Stone headed across the wide courtyard. He passed a wagon shed, a smithy with smoke rising from its brick chimney, and a small querl. Off to his right, he spotted the conical chimney of the kitchen, which stood against the west curtain wall not far from where it formed a corner with the south wall. The brew house was next to it, on the near side, and Stone veered toward it.

When he halted the wagon in front of the brew house, the four Black Cloaks dismounted and drew their swords.

"I don't know who you and your ugly friend are," said the Black Cloak leader. "But you can drop both your swords to the ground and then get down slowly, the ugly one first."

"No need to be insulting," Hake muttered as he slowly drew his sword with his right hand. He picked up his hammer with his left hand and flung it backward over his head, striking a Black Cloak in the chest and knocking him to the ground.

Stone parried a sword thrust from the Black Cloak leader as the spooked horses pulled and reared. Grain sacks flew up from the back of the wagon, and Brook, Bennald, Elling, and Aliya jumped down and drew their weapons. Aliya's dagger whistled through the air and struck a Black Cloak in the throat. A moment later, Brook's dagger embedded itself in another Black Cloak's chest. As the man screamed, Bennald launched himself toward one of the rearing draft horses, landing on the beast's back and wrapping his arms around its neck, trying to calm it. Elling was running toward the Black Cloak who had been struck by Hake's hammer, but Hake got there first. He picked up the hammer and bashed in the Black Cloak's head. Stone was engaged in a duel with the Black Cloak leader, but the man was retreating and calling out the alarm. The sound of heavy footsteps rose as black-clad knights ran along the wall-walk and then down the steps that led to the courtyard.

"We need to get to the gatehouse," Aliya yelled, and she began running toward it, Elling right behind her.

"Go with them," Stone called to Hake, who grunted and took off running.

Brook had drawn her sword, and she and Stone turned toward a group of Black Cloaks who had rushed down from the wall-walk. The team of draft horses, Bennald still astride one of them, bolted toward the oncoming knights, who scattered like a swarm of roaches fleeing from a burning torch as the horses and the lurching farm wagon bore down on them.

Stone and Brook ran to the Gatehouse, where Elling and Hake were fighting a trio of Black Cloaks. The Black Cloaks fled when they saw Stone and Brook, and Aliya dashed into the gatehouse, the others just behind her. Bennald sent the draft horses on a final assault, and then he, too, sprinted for the gatehouse.

The uppermost room had been built atop the gatehouse's twin-tower structure, occupying the space between the two crenellated towers and set back from the short front wall that separated them. The six entered the rear entrance of the gatehouse and bolted up the stairs. Hake and Bennald stopped on the second level to raise the drawbridge and lower the inner portcullis, to keep out any Black Cloaks who wanted to enter from outside or inside the castle. The other four continued up the stairs, past sleeping quarters, a solar, and a small kitchen, all unoccupied.

They found Jannela in the top room, sitting on a chair near the front window and gazing out over the moat toward the south grounds of the castle green and beyond. She had long golden hair, as long as Aliya's dark hair, and the same gray eyes as her sister. She turned when she heard the four enter, and her eyes lit up when she saw Aliya, who ran to her. The sisters embraced, and Aliya had to wait until her tears subsided before she could speak.

"Are you all right?" she asked Jannela. "Have they treated you well?"

"Well enough," Jannela replied. "Though I don't seem quite myself." She gave a little laugh, but she looked at Aliya with a puzzled expression.

"It was that parchment you signed," Aliya said. "Do you remember?"

Jannela nodded her head slowly. "I had almost forgotten."

"You didn't sign your real name. Do you remember that?"

"Oh, yes, I remember. I signed it … What did I sign it?"

"You signed it *Merry Rover*," Aliya said.

Jannela rolled her eyes. "Yes, wasn't that wicked of me?" She frowned then. "The Ordseer kept bothering me about it, but I never told him my real name. That was good, wasn't it?"

Aliya smiled. "Yes, that was very good."

"Who are your friends?" Jannela asked.

Aliya introduced Stone and Brook and then gestured toward Elling. "You might recognize this gentleman," she said, and Elling stepped forward.

"Hello, Jannela," Elling said.

Jannela gazed at him. "Do I know you?"

Elling nodded. "We know each other—from a long time ago."

Jannela's eyes went wide. "Elling?"

He nodded and went to her, and they embraced.

"I'm tired," Jannela said after Elling released her. "Perhaps I'll lie down."

"Brook would like to talk to you," said Aliya.

Jannela looked at Brook. "You would?"

"I can help you," Brook said. "When you signed that pledge, even though you didn't use your real name, you became partly ensorcelled. I can remove the spell. Will you let me try?"

Jannela looked at Aliya, who nodded. Jannela nodded to Brook, and Brook turned the chair around so its back was to the window and gestured for Jannela to sit. Jannela sat. Elling fetched another chair and set it across from Jannela. Brook sat down facing her and raised her right hand, showing

Jannela the ring with the green jewel and the four-sided emblem.

"It's pretty," Jannela said.

"Yes," said Brook. She put her hand down. "Now I'd like you to look into my eyes ..."

Chapter 23 - The Sleithryll

Kaemon, Thig, and Panwer rode at the head of a long column of knights and archers and pikemen. They reached the Rose Castle just after noon and began setting up a camp on the south and west green, as if they were planning a long siege. Kaemon rode toward the gatehouse under a flag of truce. When he neared the moat, he turned right and rode a few yards to the right of the outbuilding that stood above the moat so he would have a clear view of the gatehouse. He called out that he wanted a parley.

Inside the gatehouse, Hake and Bennald lowered the drawbridge. Hake crossed it, continued over the short causeway, and entered the outbuilding. He ran up to the second level and lowered its drawbridge, then went back down and crossed it, laughing heartily at the astonished look on Kaemon's face.

"The plan changed, Sir Pretty Pants," Hake said. "We were discovered and had to fight our way to the gatehouse."

"Did you find Jannela?" Kaemon asked.

"Aye, we did, and Brook disenthralled her. She's a fine lass. I trust you'll get your king to pardon her and Aliya, eh?"

Kaemon's face clouded over. "Aye, if we find the king alive."

***

The Black Cloaks inside the castle quickly saw that the Redmond knights making camp outside vastly outnumbered them. When they realized that the trespassers who had seized control of the gatehouse were allies of the Redmonders, they laid down their arms and hoisted a white flag of surrender.

Fifty Redmond knights entered the castle and herded the thirty-odd Black Cloaks into a thatched barn and stable, under guard. A group of knights searched the dungeons and the castle proper for the king and his counselors. Bennald and Hake went looking for the keeper of the treasury, Lord Vadd Marnum.

Stone and Brook were in the king's council room, standing in front of the Marnum Tapestry, when Kaemon and Thig Grennell entered.

"I never thought I'd see this room again," Kaemon murmured, glancing at the long table where he and Thig and Jole Arrick had sat so often with King Harrin and his other advisors.

"You nearly didn't," Stone said. "Lord Marnum unleashed sorcery he thought he could control, but he couldn't." He gestured toward the tapestry hanging on the wall behind him. "That's how it usually goes with a sleithryll."

Kaemon stared at the massive wall hanging. "Sleithryll," he murmured.

"Powerful sorcery," said Stone. "But few if any know how to wield it. Lord Marnum used his family's great wealth to purchase it from a sorcerer across the sea, in Knaffa, but Jole Arrick knew it for what it was."

Kaemon, still staring at the tapestry, heaved a sigh. "Jole. Will we ever see him again?"

"You can see him now," Stone said. "But you have to gaze on the sleithryll."

Kaemon stared at the hanging for a moment, but then he turned away, shaking his head. "No, I … I can't."

Stone gazed at the tapestry. He began to breathe in long, slow breaths, and he let his eyes soften. He imagined he was looking through the tapestry and into the room on the other side of the wall on which it hung. The tapestry began to shift and flow and pulsate. Stone saw a column of mounted knights begin to canter over a green field, a broad-beamed carrack slowly sail up the river, a child picking flowers in a meadow behind a barn. Clouds sailed across a blue sky, a smith hammered a sword on an anvil outside a smithy, and a perfect formation of geese disappeared behind a distant mountain. A farmer plowed his field, a wagoner drove his team down a winding road, and inside a tavern a serving girl set tankards of dark ale on an oak table. In the distance, beyond a high hill, Stone saw Jole Arrick moving inside a small, secret house. Stone peered deeper into the sleithryll and saw a black tree on top of a faraway mountain. The black tree bore leaves that looked like sheets of parchment.

Stone blinked and shook his head and looked away. When he looked once more at the tapestry, it was as it had been before. Stone looked at Kaemon. "Jole is there. In the mirror world."

"Can he come back?" Kaemon asked.

"I don't know, but we're going to try," Stone replied. "But if he does …"

"If he does?" Kaemon urged.

"Let's sit down," Brook said.

Stone and Brook sat next to each other on one side of the council table, and Kaemon and Thig sat across from them.

"Jole realized that the Marnum Tapestry was actually a sleithryll," Stone said. "What Jole didn't know was that Marnum suspected that he knew something. When Jole confronted Marnum—they were standing mere feet in front of the tapestry—Marnum was ready, or so he thought. He tried to use the sleithryll's powers to send Jole into the mirror world, but at the last second Jole used his own powers to divide himself into what you might call his four essences."

"You, Brook, Bennald, and Hake," Thig said.

Stone nodded. "Marnum's spell succeeded in part, and a mirror version of Jole traversed into the other world. At the same time, we four appeared miles from here, but without any memories and lacking knowledge of our own powers."

"To Marnum's eyes, Jole simply vanished," Brook said. "Yet he was still alive in this world, in a sense, only now embodied in the four of us."

Stone pointed at the tapestry. "In there, in the mirror world, Jole is complete."

"But the mirror world isn't real," Kaemon said.

"It's real," Stone replied. "But it's a different sort of world from this one."

"It's all quite astonishing," Thig said.

Kaemon let out a breath. "And now you're saying that if Jole were to reappear in our world, you four would … you would …"

"Yes, we would exist no more," Brook said. "Except as aspects of Jole."

"It would be as if … as if you had died," said Kaemon.

Stone shook his head. "No. If it happens, it's because it was meant to happen, and we four all accept that possibility with no hesitation."

"Quite, quite astonishing," Thig murmured.

The door to the council chamber opened, and King Harrin, Sir Damrick Brunville, and Sir Doville Pery entered, looking drawn and pale but alert and clear-eyed. King Harrin smiled at Kaemon and took his place at the great oak chair at the head of the long table. The other counselors, looking as if they weren't sure what was happening or about to take place, sat at their usual places at the table.

Kaemon gestured toward a counselor with short golden hair and no beard. "Here is Sir Damrick Brunville, the king's justiciar," he said to Stone and Brook. He turned to the other counselor, a man with a sweep of gray hair and a neatly trimmed gray beard. "And Sir Doville Pery, First Lord of the Realm."

As Kaemon was introducing Stone and Brook to King Harrin and the two counselors, Bennald entered the room and nodded at Stone.

King Harrin brightened when he spotted Bennald. "Ah, Sir Bennald. Welcome. Please sit with us."

Bennald bowed his head and took a seat at the far end of the table.

"It appears that I and Sir Damrick and Sir Doville were enthralled by some foul sorcery of that Ordseer villain," King Harrin said to Kaemon. "Sir Bennald was kind enough to disenthrall us."

"Begging your pardon, Your Grace, but it wasn't the Ordseer who enthralled you," Stone said.

"If it wasn't the Ordseer, then who was it?" the king asked, not unkindly. "And who did Kaemon say you were, you and your lovely lady friend?"

"We're friends of Bennald, Your Grace, and very close friends of Jole Arrick," Stone said.

"Ah, Jole, I wish he was here. Do you know where he is?"

"Close by," Stone replied. "As for the Ordseer, he was a mere fraud, in league with the real villain."

"What real villain?" the king asked. "All this riddling is making my head hurt."

The door opened again, and a short, rotund man with a fat, florid face lurched into the room. Hake, who had shoved the man through the doorway, was right behind him, twirling his hammer like a baton.

"Lord Marnum," the king said. "What's going on?"

"This brute has been shoving me about," Marnum said, but then he stopped and stared at the king. "Your Grace, how did you ...?"

"King Harrin is having a meeting of his counselors," Stone said. "You may be interested to know that they've been released from their ensorcellment."

Marnum's mouth opened, and his red face paled. Hake grabbed him and shoved him into a chair.

"Sir, why are you shoving about my Keeper of the Royal Coffers and Master of the Mint?" King Harrin demanded.

"I like him, Your Grace," Hake replied. "I might eat him."

Lord Marnum's eyes went wide, and his lower lip began to quiver. Stone thought the man might cry. But Marnum composed himself again and gave Stone a hard stare.

"Why are you and these other strangers here at a meeting of the king's council?" Marnum demanded.

"To ask you what you meant to do with your sleithryll," Stone replied.

At the word *sleithryll*, Marnum went pale again.

"What's the matter, Lord Treasurer?" Stone said. "You look unwell."

"What is this sleithryll you mention?" King Harrin asked Stone.

Stone gestured toward the tapestry hanging behind the king. "There hangs the sleithryll, Your Grace. It's an object of powerful sorcery that in the wrong hands can wreak the kind of havoc and ruin that your realm has recently suffered. Lord Marnum only pretended to give it to you as a gift. It actually remained in his possession, but he didn't quite know how to use it. The question is, what did he want to use it for?"

"Is this true, Lord Marnum?" the king asked.

"No, of course it isn't true," Marnum replied, and then he heaved himself out of his chair and bolted for the door on his short legs. Hake tackled him and hauled him back to his chair and shoved him into it again. With his hands gripping Marnum's shoulders, Hake crouched down until he was nose to nose with him. "I'm going to twist your head off and scoop out your brains. Then I'll feed them to the crows."

"Take your hands off me," Marnum sputtered, but he sounded more frightened than defiant.

"We know what you've done," Stone said.

"I've done nothing," Marnum shot back.

"You tried to destroy Redmond," Kaemon said. "You turned Redmonders into thralls. Towns and villages are falling apart. The Red City is headed toward ruin."

"That was the Ordseer," Marnum said. "It was the Ordseer's doing."

"The Ordseer was a sham," Stone said. "Just another sort of thrall, from the mirror world. It was you did all this damage and cost so many lives. And we know how you did it. What we don't know is why you did it."

Marnum's face darkened, and his fleshy pink lips twisted into an ugly sneer. "Look around you," he said, gesturing at the other counselors seated at the table. "For years I've been surrounded by ineffectual fools and indifferent blockheads, a collection of knaves who know nothing except how to jump themselves up in front of a pea-brained king who would rather write maudlin poetry or study the fish in the Farro River than lead a country with a strong arm and an iron fist."

The king frowned but made no comment.

"We're beset on every side by enemies," Marnum hissed. "Traitorous farmers in Blaewick who don't pay their taxes and laugh behind my back while they drink ale and feast on venison and wild boar and honey. Arrogant Misherooners who plot against us while feigning loyalty to the king and mass their knights in the Horn, ready to strike at our heart."

"The Misherooners are peaceful people," Kaemon said evenly. "There are no Misheroon knights massed on the border."

Marnum stood up and pointed a quaking finger at Kaemon, a twisted smile frozen on his face. "Your lies only to prove me right. The First Knight of the Realm may pretend not see the enemies on our frontier, the enemies all around us, but I can. I can see clearly. I can see the danger. I can see Redmonders right here in the Red City, even here in the castle, who sympathize with our sworn enemies. These traitors plague our city and province, spying on me, secretly undermining me, stealing from my coffers, plotting to ensnare me in their intrigues, laughing at me when they think I can't see them. But I can see them. I see their disloyalty in their faces, I hear it in their tricksy voices, I can smell the deceit and treachery coming off them like a stink from a hog's carcass."

Marnum was breathing heavily now, his mouth quivering and specks of spittle flecking his lips.

"Lord Marnum, you're quite mad," King Harrin said quietly.

"Mad, am I?" Marnum growled, and then, with a high-pitched shriek that sounded more animal than human, he jumped onto the table and ran on his short legs toward King Harrin. Stone stood up and reached out with both arms and plucked him out of the air as he launched himself at the king. A whistling whirlwind rose up from the floor for a moment but quickly dissipated. Marnum twisted out of Stone's grasp and fell to the floor, shrieking and moaning and beating his face with his fists.

Red Cloak guards had run to defend the king when Marnum jumped onto the table, and King Harrin turned to them now. "Take the Keeper of the Coffers away, good sirs. And put him in chains and lock him in the dungeon, if you please."

***

Stone was standing with Brook, Bennald, and Hake next to a horse-drawn wagon in the middle of the Purple Commons. Small patches of green grass had appeared amid the expanse of dried-out brown lawn, and a few pink and white wildflowers had begun to bloom at various places throughout the esplanade. A warm sun shone in a cloudless blue sky, and the air smelled fresh and clean. Broad-winged gulls glided and hovered in the air above the Farro River, calling to one another, diving for fish, or feasting on clams and mussels.

Stone spotted Kaemon and a group of Redmond knights approaching, and he gave them a wave. The

302

knights were carrying the rolled-up, burlap-covered sleithryll, and when they reached the wagon, they loaded the tapestry into the back, next to crates and sacks of food and other provisions.

"What will you do with it?" Kaemon asked.

"Take it away and study it," Stone said. "See if we can discover more of its secrets. Try to develop our own powers further and perhaps learn how to bring Jole Arrick back from the mirror world."

"I see," Kaemon murmured.

"We'll be off then," Stone said, and he clasped hands with Kaemon. Bennald and Hake also shook hands with Kaemon, and Brook embraced him.

"You may yet see Jole again," Brook said, as she and Stone climbed onto the front bench of the wagon and Bennald and Hake climbed into the back. "Yes, I think you may."

"If I do, that will mean I won't see any of you four again," Kaemon said.

"I believe Sir Pretty Pants is about to cry," said Hake.

Stone looked at Kaemon. "If you see Jole, you'll be seeing us, in a sense. If you don't …" He shrugged and smiled and said no more.

Kaemon nodded and then took a step back, away from the wagon.

Stone turned his gaze ahead and snapped the reins, and the wagon and its cargo began its long journey from the Red City.

THE END

303